GO FOR BROKE

Daisy Knox

www.BOROUGHSPUBLISHINGGROUP.com

GO FOR BROKE
Copyright © 2021 Daisy Knox

ISBN: 978-1-953810-79-3

To my awesome husband who has supported me every step of the way and has helped make my dreams come true

ACKNOWLEDGMENTS

I'm so grateful to everyone who helped me put Cady and Zack's story out into the world. Thank you to my editor, Susan Stones, for her wisdom, insight and infinite patience with all of my rookie mistakes. To Boroughs Publishing Group for giving me this opportunity, for the formatting, cover design, marketing, and all the hard work that goes into production.

This would not have been possible without the support of my family, especially Mr. Knox. He's read this story more times than I can count and been my biggest cheerleader. I'm so thankful for my besties, Charlene Juratovic and Donna Lynch for being the greatest beta readers ever and giving me constant encouragement. Thank you to all of my friends and family for your excitement and support, especially Baby Knox with his constant pep talks even though he's too young to read this book any time soon.

GO FOR BROKE

Chapter 1

Cady

The phone rings and I tense. The prospect of answering fills me with dread, but not knowing who's on the other end is worse. When I pick up, the initial silence gives way to raspy panting.

"You'll pay," barks the now familiar voice. "You'll be sorry when—"

"Leave me the fuck alone," I choke out before disconnecting.

I'm more angry than frightened. The caller must be one of the countless people cheated by my current employer, Allen Brothers Construction. The calls started a few weeks ago, becoming increasingly menacing. They began with breathing and mumbling, and evolved into insults and threats.

Months ago, I was on top of the world with a promising new job and about to buy a home. Everything was new and exciting as spring melted into summer. But by the time the leaves began changing, something felt off. The owners were always reducing payments to subcontractors and vendors, even while billing owners for extra work. At first, I suspected good old-fashioned incompetence and vowed to find a new job after the holidays. The tapestry of my life began unraveling without warning on a bitter gray winter day when I started to suspect the owners were intentionally committing fraud.

Days later, I began receiving angry calls on my personal phone and emails in the office from angry vendors and subs. I figure they managed to get access to our internal phone list and that's how they reach me on my cell. I've complained to Admin they were too lax in leaving them lying around all over the office and even on job sites.

What a way to start the new year—terrified and stressed.

No rational person blames the powerless office drone, but desperate people aren't rational. I'm the face of the company to the people Allen Brothers cheated. I'm the one making excuses for short payments, late payments, and illegal contract modifications. It's more infuriating than alarming, but my anxiety's worse than ever.

These calls are symbolic of my entire life. I was the kid who got bullied for following the rules and being too nice to stand up for myself. Basically, I was the quintessential doormat. Everyone expects to leave all those problems behind as an adult, but no such luck. Now I have to put up with crazy people invading my privacy. A terrifying thought struck me.

Have I got an actual stalker? Maybe this isn't about the company.

I'm watching the news on TV and hear five people were murdered a block away from my house. Holy crap. Those things don't happen to the people in my quiet suburb. Home invasions are rare and usually involve drug dealers, not strangers creeping into homes in the night to slaughter children in their beds.

Pittsburgh's more like a small town than a city, with little violent crime. This is big news. The crime buff in me is captivated by the story when a reporter asks if it's related to a string of unsolved rapes in the city. The detective says they haven't confirmed or ruled out a connection.

That's a hell of an escalation to go from attacking lone women on deserted streets to breaking into a house and murdering a family as they sleep.

My inner sleuth is already on the case, but the next question for the detective stops me cold. *"The victims complained of missing packages and harassing phone calls in the weeks leading up to the murders."*

Reporter: "Were they being harassed or were they targeted?"

"We're looking at everything right now. Nothing is off the table," another detective says.

The edges of my vision darken, the room starts spinning as fear spikes in my chest. A tight band of panic squeezes my heart as the implications hit me. Women walking dogs are being raped, and a murdered family received harassing calls before getting butchered in their home a block from mine.

I spend lots of time walking my dog near the murder scene and get creepy calls. *Nobody's targeting me. Don't be ridiculous.* My mind is racing and I struggle to slow my breathing. *You're a paranoid crime junkie. Don't be crazy. It's a love triangle or something like it. Nobody will murder you. Now open the door and go to work.*

I've always assumed my death will be hilariously humiliating, like driving into a tunnel painted on the side of a mountain, but now I'm scared.

No, scared is too mild.

I'm terrified.

***

Walking into the office feels like a long march along death row to Old Sparky.

"Cady. Thank God you're alive." Abby, our bubbly, blonde receptionist, and one of my best friends, crushes my ribs in a tackle-hug that rivals one by an NFL lineman. She's shorter than me, but feisty. She nearly knocks me off my feet. "I was afraid the murderer made other stops in the neighborhood." Lana, the third in our BFF triad, trudges through the door with a scowl and I understand why moments later when Pete Allen, one of the owners, comes bounding in with all the joy and energy of a puppy.

"Good morning, ladies. Lana, you must've been in a real hurry this morning, almost running me over in the parking lot. Glad you're so eager to be here, but we need more lighting out there."

Lana responds with a sullen "yeah," and I turn away to hide a giggle knowing Lana saw Pete. There are no lighting issues.

The office pool has four-to-one odds she'll run him over before leaving, and Friday's her last day. Things are getting interesting. We chat briefly with Pete, but I can't rush to my desk quick enough to check the news.

Every story has the same recycled facts, but I'm rewarded with a few additional details after an hour of near-constant clicking. The police are looking at all angles and although they're careful not to say it's a "stranger" crime, the facts seem to insinuate it is.

The aficionado in me knows random crimes are tougher to solve, which makes them even more chilling. Even Mom gets in on the act, calling to suggest I break my lease and come home, but I calm her. She isn't thrilled, but accepts my decision. Before she rings off, she asks, as always, whether I have a boyfriend yet. I mumble something non-committal and put down the phone.

In truth? My love life's no better than my career. About six months ago, I imposed a moratorium on dating and it's been a relief. Except now I'm starting to worry I'll never have a real connection with anyone, friend or lover. The no-dating break helped me realize the circus of my love life was incredibly tedious. I miss sex, though. Which led me into the arms of a sexy stranger last fall—my only one-night-stand ever.

I expected to look back on it like *meh*, but it was phenomenal. He gave me more orgasms in one night than I've had in entire relationships. Zack was sex incarnate. Gorgeous and funny, with deep brown eyes that seemed to peer into my soul. He ravished me and made love to me, and everything in between. I had no idea sex could be that good.

There was something familiar about him that put me at ease. He said repeatedly we should see each other again so I was sure I'd hear from him, but he never called and the dick gave me a fake number.

Sometimes it's like he was a figment of my imagination. The only proof he was real is the shirt I took from him.

Sue me. I wanted some memory of the man who'd rocked my world.

***

At work there's non-stop chatter about the murders, and while everyone engages in morbid fascination, I'm panicking, telling myself there's no connection while obsessing over the parallels.

I'm over-reacting, but I email the police for peace of mind. A detective calls to ask questions: Do I frequent a particular yoga studio? Do I have children at a specific school? Have I ever used this plumbing company, and so on, checking for connections between me and the victims. Finding none, he dismisses my problem as work-related. He tells me to change numbers, and if the calls continue, it's someone close and may be a stalking case. If not: problem solved.

He's probably right, yet I can't let it go. I, mean, why would a murderer be after me? I can't think of one reason.

The facts about the murders are slim despite the police press conferences. The most informative reporting comes from *The Pittsburgh Press,* and most of the articles are written by a guy called Daniel Abbott. A quick search shows he's the crime reporter and has a fascinating crime blog. I'm a captive audience, and my morning is consumed. The writing's fantastic and the blog is addictive. I consider calling, but worry he'll think I'm a nut.

Maybe I am.

***

After immersing myself in the blog for a couple of days, it's easy to see how he became a reporter. He's from Spokane and started the blog in college. The area is rife with serial killers, but the bio says he was inspired by a particularly grisly case. He covered countless cases, all with lengthy, detailed posts, then quit five years later. Despite lots of interaction with readers, and teasers about a big story, the blog ends, which is disappointing, but understandable since it's a college blog.

I have to contact him. Who cares if some stranger thinks I'm insane? There's no other way to get more information, and I need to find out what's going on. I don't believe in coincidence, and there are too many similarities between the murders and my life. I compose a short email to Abbott. Maybe his police contacts will take an interest or share details, which might relieve my fears. That's if he responds.

I press "Send."

An hour later the phone rings. Daniel Abbott wastes no time introducing himself and suggests we meet. I recommend a popular bar where I'll feel safe.

Things at the office are scary since I'm positive my job's not exactly legal, but at least there are distractions. When quitting time rolls around, we're forced to run a gauntlet past Pete's office and the various managers to reach the front door.

"Leaving already?" This is Pete's usual "goodbye."

Not to be outdone, his pet is always there to call out, "Done so *soon*? But it's only five o'clock." I'd like to use Dave's big shiny bald head as a paintball target.

"Thanks, Dave. I was checking the time to make sure I'm not late," I call out as I leave.

No matter I'd started early and worked through lunch, my status as a "team player" is always in question.

I often wonder how Pete Allen and his brother Bob sleep at night. But they've got money falling out of their asses when they sneeze and they always seem well-rested. Clearly, they don't struggle with ethics or morals.

The bar's only two blocks away, but the winter night is brutal. There's no other foot traffic, but rush hour's going strong. Headlights bouncing off the wet, frosty pavement are a slight comfort as I climb the hill, moving quickly past each dark alley.

A handsome mid-twenties lad holds open the bar door, flashing a friendly smile as I thank him. The warmth of the dark little pub is salvation. The jukebox is blasting Johnny Cash, and the place feels like home despite the years that've passed. Small booths line the wall to my right and the bar to my left runs the length of the narrow room, stopping short of the entrance to create a small alcove crammed with two small booths and two tiny tables.

Daniel's recognizable from his byline image. He's seated in the alcove far enough from the bar to afford privacy. He's around thirty, but seems older. The guy looks haunted, as though some great trouble robs him of all peace. His most notable feature is dire exhaustion, but he's probably handsome when he smiles. The rumpled shirt and choppy locks of sandy blond hair underscore the tension in his mannerisms and he gives off a nervous buzz. I introduce myself then greet Jeff, a bartender I've known for years. With a Molson Canadian to steel my nerves, I sit and Daniel gets right to the point.

"Why did you contact me?"

"You reported the victims received weird calls and you know more than the cops are releasing. I want details." I pause. "Should I ignore the calls or go into hiding?"

"I understand your concerns and the police weren't helpful, but out of all the reporters, why *me*?" The accusatory tone makes me bristle. My biggest reservation coming here was he could be dangerous, but he's insinuating *I'm* the nut. Which I half expected.

"Your stories were detailed, and a search led me to your blog." Surprise flickers across his face, but he quickly hides it by staring down into his scotch or whiskey. "You care about more than reporting a story and seem to have insight into what the victims' experience."

"I doubt I can help." He sounded and acted different on the phone. Although he wasn't eager or warm, he seemed willing to help and there was no impatience or hostility.

"Well, it's worth a try. I need to decide if the calls I'm receiving are a genuine threat or are from harmless crackpots."

"It's a valid question, but I don't know if there's a connection. My sources aren't talking about the calls, so they may be important."

"The police were dismissive. I hope to change their minds to put mine at ease."

"What do you know about the Tacoma housewife murders?" His voice is sharp and I'm at a loss. That must've been one of the boring cases on the blog because it doesn't sound familiar.

"Never heard of them."

"Don't bullshit me. Who put you up to this?"

Stunned by his ferocity, I'm offended. "Look, I don't know what you're talking about, and I don't appreciate your tone. I need information on this crime, or for you to share my details with investigators if you think I'm in danger. That's it. Sorry to have *bothered* you." He doesn't meet my gaze as I grab my coat. Jeff seems to've noticed my agitation, and he's watching us closely. I wave like everything's fine, although I don't think it is.

"Wait. Please. I'm sorry." Daniel drums his fingers, taking a deep breath before saying, "Don't go." This is getting weird. He has two minutes to make sense or I'm gone. "There were three similar murders in Tacoma in three years. In those cases, the adult female was home alone." His tone is grim.

"A serial killer crossed the country to murder an entire family?" Unease trickles down my spine. "That's a long-distance and a drastically different crime."

"Those cases are closed. A man was sentenced to death, but capital punishment's been outlawed there so it was commuted to three life sentences with no chance of parole."

I'm still confused. "It's a copycat?"

"No, it's the same killer. Tacoma has the wrong guy."

"He was convicted. Why do you think—"

"I know he's innocent because he's my brother."

The silence stretches between us as I absorb his shocking words.

He continues, his jaw tense. "He didn't kill anyone, especially not Grace. My sister-in-law was the third victim." He speaks with quiet finality, signaling these facts aren't up for debate.

Obsession masquerading as love is often the motive in crimes of passion. Now I know how Daniel got into being a crime reporter.

He sighs, and drains his drink in one fast gulp. "Trust me, I'm not crazy. I sound crazy, but I'm not. I'm not drunk either. This is my first drink in eighteen months." The declaration doesn't inspire confidence. "There's a serial killer, I'm sure of it. When I was thirteen, our parents died. My brother Brandon and his wife Grace raised me. Sloppy investigative work and bad luck put him away. I've spent years trying to free him. There were similar murders in other states they can't blame him for. People say I'm obsessed. I lost my job and started drinking. Everyone thinks I'm too loyal to see the truth. But I *know* Brandon's innocent."

I'm not sure what I expected when I arranged to meet Daniel, but it wasn't this. My head's spinning with questions and he's not finished.

"I recognize this killer and when I read your email, I wanted to help because you may be in danger. Look." He shoves a sheet of paper across the table.

Enjoy your meeting at the bar tonight. Are you sure you know who you can trust?

Chapter 2

Cady

Holy crap.

"This email came via Proton mail through TOR, so it's anonymous. After spending an hour with my laptop, the paper's IT guy discovered whoever sent this also hacked me."

"Someone's spying on you and referenced this meeting, and now you're suspicious of me." A frightening thought strikes. "Does he know who I am now?" I'm beginning to get panicked.

Daniel looks grim. "They said he hacked my cloud and could only see the calendar, but it's only your first name on there, nothing else."

"But he knows we're meeting. He could be here right now. Or waiting outside—"

"No." Daniel shakes his head. "No way."

"It could be anyone." I fling a hand out at the crowd.

He's adamant the killer leaves town after the murders since he can taunt Daniel from anywhere, but I'm not convinced. "Were there other suspects? Someone has lots to lose if your brother's exonerated."

"Yeah, the killer. The bastard's been gaslighting me since I started defending Brandon, undermining me at every turn. So many things make sense. Like emails I sent when I was blackout drunk." He shakes his head. "When I moved to Sioux City, murders fitting the profile occurred in Cedar Rapids, the suburbs of Wichita, and Sioux Falls. I reported on every case. It was him."

He seems like a raving madman, but what if he's right and nobody's listening? People will die. "Why target you?"

"Nobody else believes he exists, and I have evidence. He's an apex predator and I'm the only threat in his world." He gives a defeated shrug.

"If you have evidence, why don't the police care?"

"The cases are in various jurisdictions. Most departments investigating one case don't know the others exist. When I 'share' it doesn't go over well. Ever try telling the police they're wrong? They're not receptive."

"Isn't there a task force or federal agency willing to consider the evidence? Can't one of your contacts put you in touch with someone? If they give the evidence a chance, they'll come to the same conclusion, right?"

Daniel sighs. "Three months ago, I had a chance meeting with a retired Pittsburgh homicide captain and he agreed I'm on to something. Not necessarily a multi-state serial killer with a body count in the thirties, but he agreed it begs for closer inspection and got me a meeting with the FBI. None of this counts as evidence coming from me since they deem me "compromised.""

I nod, seeing the quandary. Evidence has to be objective. Daniel showing the facts of similar murders doesn't mean anything. It's compelling, but circumstantial, and not actionable. That makes this more believable. The FBI doesn't have the locals' evidence, Daniel is an interested party, and nobody's going the extra mile to put this together for the brother of a convicted killer.

"There has to be something—" I begin, but he interrupts.

"The plan was to wait for the next murder because there'll be another. He won't quit. I stay alert, find the next case fresh, and he disappers. The retired cop's a respected profiler so I was confident he'd talk his way in and make headway."

"Your cop can begin here. He must know people who will talk to him."

Daniel's shaking his head again. "No. The killer changed MO. No more single women, now it's families. This case is the third."

"But your contact's out there working his magic?"

"Not with a new MO. Nothing links these crimes to the others. We're back to square one."

This is tough to believe, but damn compelling. Who knows what's true and what Daniel believes since it's his brother in prison. He's a talented journalist, and may be good with fiction too. But I don't think so. "How do you make connections if there's no way to link the cases?"

"Don't have to. He rubs my face in it." He taps his phone, calling up a slideshow. I scroll past a bunch of colorful cityscape postcards, blank but for the Press office address. The rest are truck stop trinkets you collect on road trips: shot glasses and magnets. They're innocuous, yet something about the photos makes me uncomfortable. "He sends me a souvenir from every town where he kills." His tone turns bitter. "It's another thing the authorities won't recognize as 'real' evidence since the postcards could've come from anyone."

The pain in his voice shows this is real to him. The guy's suffering, but I have to consider other possibilities. This would be an elaborate lie, but to what end? What does he gain? Sympathy perhaps, but he'd have to be certifiable to go to such lengths.

"Where does that leave me? Am I a target by association?" What if the calls are a coincidence, but I brought myself to a killer's attention by meeting with Daniel? The irony would be typical. If my instincts say take a left, I should know to go right.

"I can't say no, but it's unlikely. That's not how he operates."

"As far as you know, but what if he's got a bunch of other crimes so dissimilar you're not even aware of them? Maybe he stalks people too. He's stalking you."

"No way. The profile says he studies the victims briefly before the crime, then bolts immediately after the murder. It's not likely he harasses victims for weeks with calls before killing. The victims seem to be random."

Okay. But going from individuals to entire families is a drastic change of MO. Sticking around could be a new strategy. If he came here to target Daniel, maybe he's hanging around to watch the fallout.

Daniel's phone sounds. "Excuse me. I have to take this." As he steps out, I decide this discussion calls for caffeine, not alcohol, and meander to the bar to talk to Jeff.

"That guy's a weirdo." Concern lines his ruddy face.

"Nah, he's a good guy going through a rough time." I crosss my fingers hoping it's true. "Two cokes and a pitcher of ice water, please."

"You sure about that?" Jeff asks, meeting my gaze. He's barely older than me but was the bar's guardian for those of us who were young and stupid. It's been years since I've visited, but I guess old habits die hard.

"Busy job. He's got a tough deadline and I'm helping. The next visit here will be for funsies."

"Coming back to the old stomping grounds? Nobody will believe it. I thought you moved

away."

"Only a few miles, but I can walk to some great places. I love the Middle Road Inn.

We watch hockey there, but I miss this place."

"I'm never away long enough to miss it." Jeff sighs mock wistfully, shaking his head.

I put the Cokes on our table and turn back for the water, nearly bumping into the guy who held open the door earlier. He's holding the water pitcher.

"Sorry, tried to save you a trip. Should've warned you." He smiles, offering the pitcher.

"Thanks." *I guess. Ugh, did this guy dose our water?*

"I didn't poison it. Jeff was watching the whole time, right?" Jeff pauses at the cooler looking stern, but gives a curt nod.

"That's precisely what a creep who roofied the pitcher would say, but I trust Jeff."

"Hi, I'm Trevor. I'm not a creep despite how this has played out. I'm about to double down on the creep factor. I couldn't help but overhear the Middle Road Inn. I love the restaurant but never gave the bar a chance. Is it pretty lit?" He talks with a strange affectation, like a wannabe rapper, and it's irritating, but he's kinda cute.

"Hi. I'm Cady. It's a great place to hang out. Excellent beer selection, cool games in the downstairs bar, and karaoke night is always fun."

"Good to know. I'll give it a chance. Can't come here every time we go out."

"Gotta mix it up sometimes."

"Maybe I'll see you there." He glances over my shoulder as the door opens. "Nice meeting you."

"You too." Trevor may be curious about the bar, or perhaps my charm and natural beauty inspired his approach.

Daniel seems slightly less uptight when he returns, almost friendly, so the night's improving. "Sorry I don't have more to share, but I'll talk to my contacts."

We decide he'll give me a list of cases so I can dig through to see if any others received nuisance calls. We run through the basics, then he explains his brother's appeals and I'm enthralled in a voyeuristic way. To me it's academic, but it's life and death for them. Daniel offers to drive me to my car, and while I don't know what to think of him, I doubt he's a killer.

"Cady," his voice stops me before I shut my door. "Be careful. Maybe the calls are something completely different, but if it is the same guy, he's brutal."

"Don't worry, I can take care of myself," I assure him with my signature false bravado.

He waits until I pull away.

***

The front door opens to a hundred pounds of excited good boy slamming into me like an overzealous linebacker. People say don't get a dog when you live alone, but Sonny is one of the best decisions I've ever made. My fuzzy soulmate must have a bit of Clifford the big red dog in him because he's rapidly getting bigger than any other German Shepherd I've ever seen. He was patiently awaiting my arrival at the shelter while the rest of the litter napped and it was love at first sight. Those whiskey-colored eyes were too expressive for his sweet little puppy face, but they told me everything I needed to know.

"You were mine from the first time I laid eyes on you," I whisper into his thick fur as his tail wags furiously as I scratch his neck. Sonny doesn't eat shoes, my biggest passion, but he sometimes eats cushions, pillows, and comfortable furniture. We're working on that.

Adorable dogs are the ideal wingman, but Sonny hates guys near me, and usually requires physical restraint when I have...had male visitors. Perhaps he's using his keen canine instincts to block losers, which I attract in droves.

I've convinced myself that when Mr. Right happens along, Sonny will fall at his feet or at least not scare him away. A sliver of moon shines enough to bounce off the ice patches during our quick drag around the block. These walks are my favorite time of day, but tonight the shiver along my spine isn't from the frigid temps. Relief floods me as the door to the house shuts. Even with an enormous German Shepherd at my side, the dark streets feel threatening.

Daniel emailed me information so I'm quickly engrossed. The profile gives little to go on. White male between twenty-five and forty, fit, well-groomed, average to handsome, well-dressed, blends in and doesn't cause alarm. A frequent traveler, he has money to live and move. The end.

The phone rings as I'm drifting off to sleep and I expect mom is checking up on me, but I freeze at the now-familiar snarl.

"Going to cut you, bitch," he barks, "'til you bleed like a stuck pig. When— "

There's a certain satisfaction when I disconnect, but now I'm wide awake, my heart pounding like a bass drum.

***

Girls night, and Abby and I settle in with a pizza to watch the Penguins crush Boston. I'm worried she's going to make a whole thing out of my stalker situation, so I wait until we've had some bong hits and dissolve into giggles before broaching the subject.

She's appalled. "This guy's threatening to slice you up and the police don't care?"

"It's probably nothing. I mean, there's no way . . . " I trail off because it sounds ridiculous. "I reported it to Shaler in case it's linked to the murders, but technically it's Etna's jurisdiction." My house is on the border of the two suburban communities.

"Call Etna PD. Don't wait. This escalated from hang-ups to violent threats. You have to call them."

"Tomorrow. I swear. I don't want to think about it anymore tonight. It's probably some sleazy contractor who got my number from the job trailer."

When I get up to let Sonny into the yard, I make a startling discovery. I turn to Abby and tell her in a wobbly voice, "The back door's unlocked, and I wouldn't have forgotten to lock it last night before bed. I walked the dog after work today so we weren't in the backyard." Sonny's whining to go out, but I'm freaking out. I lock the doors and windows obsessively, so much I often lock myself out.

Steph, Abby, and my parents have spare keys and I've used each one.

Abby rolls her eyes. "You probably let Sonny out at lunch and forgot to lock it."

"No, he refused to go out."

Abby puts her arm over my shoulders. "You're sleep-deprived, your stress levels are through the roof, and now you're extra on edge with these murders. You forgot to relock it since he didn't go out."

Abby's probably right. My mind's in too many places at once, but it's no less unsettling. "Then it wasn't a creeper and I'm losing my mind. Great," I mutter, folding into myself.

I can't shake the feeling emailing Daniel was a grave error.

***

I wake early Saturday morning and leave a message at the Etna police station before seven am, not expecting a call until Monday, but the phone rings soon after I made the call.

"Cady Blackwell? This is John Gruber from the Etna police department. Is this a good time? I can come over now."

Sonny has to stay in the bedroom because he can't be free to intimidate, or heaven forbid, eat a public servant. John Gruber is Chief Gruber, and it feels good to see someone's taking this seriously. He's an older, barrel-chested guy with a somber countenance. I appreciate his no-nonsense demeanor. Something tells me he always gets his perp.

"You can press a button to reject blocked and private calls. Why haven't you?"

"I'm in the middle of a job search and sometimes I get legitimate calls from private numbers. Plus, I'm scared if he can't call to yell at me, he'll get madder and come find me. I'm afraid of antagonizing him."

"Stop answering the calls. If he's dumb enough to leave messages, it'll help bring more charges against him," he says.

When he leaves, I thank him again, collapsing on to the couch in relief, grateful someone's doing something. Relief floods my body after weeks of constant tension. This will end soon, then I can focus on the work problems. Semi-relaxed for the first time in weeks, I manage a short but satisfying nap. Now it's time for a walk in the bright sunshine.

Despite the cloudless blue sky, it's only fifteen degrees. The chill is a sharp slap in the face. As I step outside, I trip over a small package. Though it has my name and address on it, there's no postmark or label from a shipping company. I pick it up and listen to it for ticking, like that's going to help. I wonder if I should call Chief Gruber, then decide I'm being foolish. Or maybe not. As I'm struggling to decide what to do, Sonny assumes an offensive posture. He's focused on the package, and I don't take that as a good sign. Taking a deep breath, I squat and open the flaps.

A giant dead rat is hanging out of the box. It's throat's been slit and there's a note stuck in the tacky blood that says "YOU."

My hands are shaking when I drop the box and take Sonny inside. After a month of menacing calls, now there's a dead rodent and a hand-delivered threat. It's gotta be the same guy. I want to believe it's the caller, but I'm worried it's someone else maybe connected to Daniel. If so, I have only myself to blame for bringing a new nutjob into my life.

Maybe someone at Allen Brothers thinks I've turned them in or knows I know what they're up to. They wouldn't send a rat with a note. They'd fire me. Pete and Bob are too arrogant to see me as a threat.

I ring Chief Gruber.

"It's nothing but scare tactics," he says in his gruff voice. "If the stalker's violent, he would've made a move by now. Anonymous callers are usually cowards. Put the evidence in a plastic bag and I'll send someone to collect it."

I spend the rest of the day half-trembling while researching the victims on Daniel's list to check for similarities to what's happening to me.

***

I amuse myself by pricing security systems before going out for the evening. The drive to meet my friends is too quiet for a Saturday night. The frigid streets are bleak and deserted, and my heart stutters at every shadow and random noise. When my phone rings, I nearly jump out of my skin. It's Daniel checking in. I recap Chief Gruber's visit, then try to downplay note attached to the rat in the box. I get another round of safety warnings before he hangs up. I continue on to meet Steph, Nina, and a group of women who worked together at my last job and kept in touch even after the company closed.

There are at least twenty of us, and after a few drinks we're belting out tunes, unfortunately for the other patrons. When it's my turn to grab a round, I'm at the bar when I hear my name and turn to see Trevor. He's a pretty boy, and cute. A little taller than I am, thin but muscular. The bar is dark, but his amiable smile and twinkling blue eyes stand out.

I wave at him. "Hey, you made it to karaoke night. You'll have a blast. It's legendary."

"This place came highly recommended." He smiles. "I had to try it. I'd buy you a drink, but you look set."

"Yeah. My turn to buy a round. Are you here to sing?"

"Nobody wants to hear me sing." He laughs. "Well maybe my brother, but he already left."

"Nobody wants to hear any of us sing. That's why we're at karaoke and not trying out for bands."

"Good point."

The guy Steph wants to set me up with didn't come, so Trevor it is. I introduce him to the group and he fits right in. Abby saunters over with a grin the size of the moon. "Well, Miss Cady. Look what you found at the bar. Who's the hottie?"

"We met at Gooski's when I picked up takeout. He overheard me telling Jeff we hang out here and asked about the bar." One little white lie doesn't hurt. I don't need to tell her about meeting Daniel.

"Earth to Cady. He didn't come here for the bar."

"He's not my type."

"Since when is adorable not your type? Give him a chance."

Abby might be right, but I don't think so. I'm willing to hang out and see what happens. Trevor's prettier than my norm, and with his expensive-looking clothes, I can't help but think we're not a match. Between his metrosexual good looks and having Ferragamo-moccasins-for-a-casual-night-at-the-bar-money. Those shoes cost more than I make in a week, unless they're excellent knock-offs.

We sit and chat and I discover he lives in SoCal and often comes here on business. The brothers started a successful investment company for their father's rich friends right out of college. His brother Owen chose Pittsburgh when they started up an Eastern US branch because he's a huge sports fan. He has a loft in the Strip District near my childhood home in Polish Hill.

"Have dinner with me sometime before I head home?" Trevor asks. "This is the most fun I've had in a long time. I'd love to have someone show me around town."

What's the harm? This may be fun and I'll make a new friend. We exchange contacts and he begs off to call it a night. "Call me about dinner?"

"Definitely." I surprise myself by meaning it. Yes, this violates the dating ban, but the guy doesn't really live here and it's one dinner. "Let's talk tomorrow."

After a few more songs and lengthy goodbyes, I head home. There's almost no traffic this late, so the truck behind me is super obvious. I swear the truck followed me from the bar, but the place was packed and another patron could live in my neighborhood. A few minutes pass as I sit in the Jeep waiting until the truck turns onto my road. It's a small residential street, so every vehicle's noticeable, especially at this hour.

Dread sets in as the truck slows. No longer playing it cool, I'm openly staring. The street lights hit the truck revealing a deep red finish, the color of arterial blood. The driver must see me staring because he speeds up, barely slowing for the turn onto the narrow cross street. *Should I bolt to my door or drive to Steph's, a few blocks away?* If I call, her husband Randy will be here in a flash to walk me in, check for monsters and scope out the neighborhood, but it's the middle of the night.

With a sigh, I hop out of the Jeep, and sprint the ten feet to my front door. As I unlock the door and dash in and slam it shut, my phone signals a text. I take a few deep breaths to settle my anxiety then look at the message. It's from Trevor.

How about dinner tomorrow? Sorry for the short notice, but I had fun tonight and want to see you again before I leave.

A little thrill runs through me thinking he can't wait to see me. Maybe Abby's right. I should give him a chance. Plus, dinner with a cute guy is a fantastic distraction from the chaos of my life.

Tomorrow works. Anywhere special you have in mind?

***

Trevor's waiting outside the restaurant as I score a prime parking spot on the street. He jogs over to meet me, looking casual but expensive. Clothes aren't my thing, but I know shoes like nobody's business. Those plain, understated black boots are Balenciaga and cost over a grand on sale. His company must do well, or he comes from money. Perhaps both.

We sit. We talk. Trevor has all the right interests: good music, gangster movies, and animals. Sadly, he's allergic to dogs. Everything is smooth and easy, but there's no spark. After dinner, we stroll along the river. It's balmy for Pittsburgh in January. With evening temperatures in the forties it's practically swimming weather for us natives. This weather must be tough for a SoCal guy, but he gets points for not complaining.

We walk to my Jeep, and he says, "This was fun. I'd like to see you again before I leave."

"Sure, let's talk." We'll never be more than friends but making a grand pronouncement seems insensitive.

He pulls me closer, leaning in for a kiss and I hug him awkwardly. I have a thing about germs and don't swap spit with strangers.

We have no chemistry, so I don't see the point of kissing him.

Chapter 3

Cady

Under strict instructions from Abby, the first thing I do as I drive home is get her on speaker for a full debrief.

"He's lovely but not for me."

"Of course. He's way too normal. Shocker," she huffs.

"Friends maybe, but there's no attraction whatsoever."

"One date isn't sufficient for a final determination."

"My love life isn't a game show, Abs."

"But you deserve a rich cutie who's got himself together. All the losers were fate's way of making sure you were available when Trevor came along." Abby sounds confident she's

solved the mystery of why my love life has sucked for so long. Heavy rain starts falling, and I say bye-bye to focus on the road.

I'm moving along at a good clip, but not fast enough to miss the same red truck I saw the night before a few cars back as I change lanes to hit my exit.

Damn it. It's time to confront this weirdo.

Turning down the street leading to mine, I hammer it, flying up the driveway to a small apartment complex near the end of the street. Cutting the lights, I drive super slow to the exit as I pray nobody drives through the lot in the dark. I'm close enough to see the truck pass, but I hang back as far as possible before following. If it turns into our lot, I can block the exit. Sure, whoever's following me is a creep, but I'm too angry to be scared.

The creep doesn't turn, only slows, probably looking for my vehicle. I'm still half a block away, hidden in the dark, when a horn startles me. Thank heavens for brake lights. Flipping the headlights back on, I drift up the block as the truck turns. Let's see how Red

Truck Creep likes being followed. He doesn't turn toward the highway as expected. Ugh, is he going to lurk around the neighborhood until I get home? How unsettling.

Good luck lurking here, jackass. Everyone gets noticed, but strangers stand out even more.

I'm a full block away, but any further, and I'll lose him. Turning the corner so soon would be too obvious, so I pull over. I'll stay on this street, guess the creep's direction, and try to head creeper off on a cross street. This might not be the best plan, but it's all I've got and I won't let the creeper get away. When the phone rings, I ignore it, and keep focused on the mission. But it immediately rings again, making my heart sink. There's only one person who keeps calling when I don't answer, and after the fourth time, I decide Red Truck Creep isn't the only one getting a piece of my mind tonight. Unless he's also my mystery caller, but that doesn't seem logical.

I'm in no mood for this crap and don't hide it when I answer. "What? What do you want?" There's a weird chanting and it's slowly getting louder.

"Going to cut you to ribbons, bleed you out," he cackles with a crazy laugh. "Die like your neighbors, cunt. You'll be sorry."

His words freeze my insides and my skin breaks out in goosebumps. I disconnect and check the call log. Crap. I forgot to change the settings to reject anonymous calls after Chief Gruber's recommendation. Activating the feature brings a smug satisfaction until I realize Red Truck Creep is probably long gone. Putting on the lights, I pull out and turn toward home.

Oh boy, I'm on Sutter Road, about to pass the murder house. A further wave of nausea hits my stomach, which does a flip-flop. I've avoided the house all week, but Red Truck Creep is parked in front of the house, which can't be a coincidence.

There's a silhouette visible when the headlights fall over the cab, so this won't be a wasted trip after all. What kind of creep comes here to gawk at the scene of a tragedy? I pull up close enough to block his—now I'm sure it's a guy—driver's side doors. Now he's forced to talk to me unless he prefers to scramble out of the passenger side to run away. I didn't get a look at him last night, and tonight I see only a youngish man with dark hair who's tall. Red Truck Guy's working hard to ignore me, but I refuse to leave. The road's wide enough for vehicles to pass. I can sit here all night.

Lowering the passenger window, I call out, "Hey buddy, how ya doing?" I wave like a loon. The creeper's staring at his phone like it's a map to the Holy Grail, but I won't be ignored. He's ignoring me, but I won't let him.

"Are you ever going to come to see your kids again, you freaking deadbeat?"

The darkness makes it tough to see, but I think he flushes. His eyes are still glued to his phone, and wait... There's something vaguely familiar about him.

I shout, "Your babies cry for daddy and I have no money for diapers because you're spending it all on whores."

Still nothing, so I pull out the big guns.

"Janice Rossi in two R is nothing but a whore. He's my husband, get your own goddamn man," I holler in my best Brooklyn accent, which is awful. Red Truck Guy looks like there's something stuck in his throat, probably his dignity. There's fidgeting, and he runs his hands through his hair but doesn't budge until I hit the music, cranking my system up to max. The entire Jeep's vibrating when he finally gives in and opens his window. His lips are moving, but I can only hear music, so I lower the volume.

"What the hell, Cady?" he barks. "Someone's going to call the cops. Stop making a scene."

He knows my name? Who the hell is this guy? My gut lurches but I keep up the bravado. "And you can't have that. Then the cops will have questions about you following me, creep." His voice sounds familiar, but I can't place it. "How do you know my name?"

"You've got this all wrong. You don't understand—"

"Are you here for inspiration? To get your rocks off until you call again?

"What are you on about, woman?" He's annoyed, but seems more confused than guilty, and now I'm confused. When the single beam of light from the neighboring driveway catches his profile, my heart stops.

"Zack?" What the hell's going on? He stares as cold tendrils of panic grip my insides. "Oh my god. Have you been following me, you fucking creep?" Still nothing. "What the hell?"

"Let me explain. Okay. I'm following you, but not in a creepy way. I swear, it's not as bad as it sounds. I guess Daniel didn't call yet—" Zack's rambling, and I'm even more confused.

"Daniel Abbott?"

"Yeah. He's a friend of mine and asked me to watch out for you because he got a threat."

What a coincidence. What are the odds?

At the end of my rope, I swallow a guttural scream of intense frustration. "Tell Daniel I don't trust him either. Ugh, I can't believe this."

"He's worried you're in danger. Not because of the calls. Well maybe, but also because of him. I guess he didn't have time to explain everything. He's working a big story," he trails off, and sighs again. "Can we go somewhere to talk? It's complicated."

"Whoa there, cowboy. I'm not an idiot."

"I'm not a threat." His hands raise in surrender, and I'm momentarily distracted. Memories of those hands on my body, exploring, and driving me to delights surface, but I squash them. Now's not the time to be thinking about the amazing night we shared.

"That's exactly what a killer would say to lull me into a false sense of security, dumbass."

Zack stares for a moment. "Call Daniel and ask him, but let's get out of here before someone calls the cops."

"Meet me at the Venus diner." The place is busy this time of night and should be safe. Sure, I need to hear what he has to say, but it has to be in a public place because *what the hell*?

A few minutes go by and I'm starting to think Zack ditched me again when the red truck arrives.

We head inside without speaking. Although I'm extremely pissed off, it's impossible to ignore that Zack's still the most perfect male specimen I've ever seen. *Stop swooning over this clown. Focus. You're here for answers, not to get laid.* The waitress stammers when she's in front of him, validating my suspicion he affects all women the same way. We order, and he waits until she's gone to speak, but I have a question.

"Why were you lurking around the murder house?"

His jaw sets at the question. "I stopped to regroup, but you blocked me in by the time I realized it."

I'm not sure I'm buying it, but I don't say anything.

"I work for an investigation and security firm. Daniel's a friend and asked me to make sure you were okay for a few days."

I give him nothing so he's forced to continue.

"The hack compromised all his contacts. All your specifics."

"Phone number, address?" A sick feeling washes over me when he nods.

"Everything he had, they have. He only found out yesterday. The IT guys have had no luck tracing the breach so far, but suspect the hacker had access to everything on Daniel's hard drive."

Fantastic. Every time I think things can't get any worse, they plummet to new lows. "Can they get into my stuff because I'm texting and emailing him?" The waitress arrives with our drinks, puts them down, and leaves. I pick up my coffee and slurp.

"Unlikely, but I'm no expert." Zack doesn't seem confident, which is worrying.

"So this is a recent development, and he thought I'd be in danger?"

"There was also a message, something like 'what a shame if your girlfriend gets butchered and you go to prison for murder like your brother.' There's no woman in his life right now, so he's worried about you, and some female lawyer in Tacoma."

"This bastard knew we were meeting the other night," I mutter. "If he can access everything, he knows we're virtual strangers, so why bother with me?"

Zack shrugs. "Even the death of a stranger's a heavy burden if he wants to mess with Daniel's head." His eyes widen at the barrage of invectives I let fly.

This is a lot to take in, but it makes sense. Daniel was hiding something, and I figure it must be his suspicion I'm in danger by association.

"Someone sent me a dead rat earlier, " I announce, all blasé as if getting such a threat was the norm.

Zack's mouth drops open. "Jeez, that's…sick. Did you call the cops?"

I nod and flip through my phone photos so he can see yesterday's special delivery. He asks for more specifics, so I detail everything. I must seem pretty calm because he shakes his head. "Are you taking this seriously? Doesn't seem like it to me."

I purse my lips. "Okay, the thing with the rat's kind of a biggie," I state. "I'll try to take it more seriously. Any tips?"

"Do you have motion sensors on lights in your house?" I don't. "You should change up your schedule."

We sit silently drinking, and I figure I should I apologize for assuming he's some lurky pervert. "Hey. Sorry about the whole blocking you in thing."

He nods, and his fingers bump mine when we both reach for the coffee carafe. I have to clench my entire body so he doesn't see me shiver.

"The deadbeat dad thing was kind of evil genius. Gotta remember that the next time I corner a skip trace." His sexy smile reaches his dark and broody eyes, which light up when he laughs.

I could get lost staring into them while his hard body is pressed against me. Butterflies flit around in my belly and my nipples are hard enough to cut glass. This is what I want to feel during a kiss, but it's never happened from just *looking at* a guy before. Of course, no other man has ever commanded my body so skillfully. He was so good, I'm still dreaming about him months later. I take a deep breath, and try to pull myself together. "What can I say? I demand answers."

"The Karen Hill line was great, too. I love that movie. 'What do you mean funny? Like a clown? Do I amuse you?'"

"What am I, a mirage? No, I thought you said you were all right, Spider." We both chuckle and I hear the unmistakable strains of Boston playing one of their hits.

He's tapping his fingers to the music. "Awesome song." Zack's voice is so sexy, but I'm mesmerized by his hands. They're big and dexterous and I want to feel them all over me again. *Focus.* I forget what I want to say when our gazes meet. He doesn't look away, but I can't read him.

"I love this song, and it's the story of my life right now," I mutter. "All I want is 'Peace of Mind,' you know?" *Stop staring at his hands.* I glance away when our gazes lock again. Dammit, the butterflies started a mosh pit.

He's looking at me with a sexy smirk. "Did you say, 'Whoa there, cowboy'?"

"You heard me, buckaroo," I deadpan. We both laugh, then I remember why we're here.

Zack's serious again. "It's not ideal, but I can hang around keeping an eye cut from a distance, at least until Daniel's IT buddies have answers."

Zack and Daniel are really strangers, though one's more intimately acquainted with me than the other. Considering everything, I'd be an idiot to trust these guys. But what do they gain from tricking me? My hesitation must speak volumes.

Zack chuckles. It's sexy. "Yeah, yeah. I know. That's what a psycho killer would say to throw you off his trail. But you can ask Nina. Trust me, I've known her and Luke since I was five. They can vouch I'm at my parents' house way too often to be a traveling serial killer."

Of course, I'll ask, but I can probably trust him. *Or do I want to trust him because he's so freaking hot?* "Wait, how do you know I know Nina? Were you at the bar last night watching us?"

Another coincidence? Should I be worried?

He nods, looking away and shifting when I throw up my hands in aggravation. "Didn't it occur to you to call me? A conversation would've been more effective and less creepy than a stranger following me."

Zack looks away before answering. "Not, uh, not until you caught me. Daniel didn't want to scare you in case he was overreacting. We hoped you wouldn't notice if I hung back. Most people don't notice."

"Who are these idiots you follow who don't check their mirrors?"

"Not the best and the brightest, for sure." His eyes dance when he laughs again. "Who's the little weenie from the steakhouse?"

"Rude. And so offensive. What if he's my husband?" I try to act aggrieved, but can't pull it off because he's right. Trevor's a weenie and there's no attraction there at all.

"He's not." Zack smirks.

"God, no," I roll my eyes, but I'd love to know why he cares. "Date. Boring as hell. Total weenie. Never expected the most interesting part of my weekend would be getting lurked by a stranger." The way his jaw tenses satisfies the smartass in me.

"We're not exactly strangers."

"Close enough."

His eyes flash and his luscious lips curve into a smug grin. "If that's how you treat strangers, I want to be your friend."

"Too bad you never called. You missed your chance."

"I was going to call, but I lost your number. Hell, you took one of my favorite shirts."

"I'll leave it in the mailbox so you can grab it next time you're skulking around."

He throws me a look, but ignores the comment. "Do you know this other guy well?"

"Like I just fell off of the turnip truck and went off with a totatl stranger while this is happening?" The implication pisses me off, but as soon as the words leave my mouth, I realize that's exactly what I've done. Zack must see the realization in my expression. I'm mad at myself for being so careless and annoyed with him for pointing it out. "Trevor's safe." It doesn't even sound convincing in my head.

"Yeah, I'm sure *Trevor's* great. A real prince." He rolls his eyes, and it pisses me off. "You went out with a stranger? Did anyone know where you were? Even without a stalker, it's common sense."

"Save the lecture. I have a mom to nag me."

"Hey. Trying to help you not get murdered." He leans back, hands up in surrender. His gaze holds mine for a beat too long. "What do you want me to do?"

Me. Let's head to my place right now.

Sure, I'll feel stupid if we hook up and Zack's the killer, but I wouldn't have to live with it for long so another night like that might be worth it. *Wow, it's been way too long since I got laid. September, to be exact.*

Zack's waiting for an answer. "I'd rather not get butchered. I'm thankful you're watching my back," I concede. "This is all so weird. Awkward, too. I don't want to worry my family or have my coworkers gossiping about me."

"There's no reason to follow you, but I'm available if anything happens." I run him through a typical week including my morning routine. He winces a little because as I say it, I realize my weekdays are all the same.

A thought strikes me as we walk out. "When Daniel showed me the email, I thought, 'Huh. Wouldn't it be ironic if this was all coincidence? But being here tonight puts me on a killer's radar.' I told myself it was crazy, but I feel pretty stupid now."

"Let's hope he's messing with Daniel and there's no real threat."

"Fingers crossed." I laugh, but it's not funny and he looks away, shifting his weight. "Sometimes you gotta laugh so you don't cry." The goal tonight was to solve one mystery, and I did, so it was a productive evening. But it's weird seeing Zack again like this.

"A lot of victims see warning signs but blow them off, thinking 'It can't happen to me'. Don't do that. It's unlikely the killer is stalking you, but there's always the possibility he'll hurt you to mess with Daniel. Better safe than sorry, right? Call me if you don't feel safe or if something seems off."

"Sure, but will I reach you if you gave me another fake number?"

A shadow passes over his face. "I'm sorry about everything, Cady. There's really nothing else to say."

"Did you know it was me you're following?"

"After I saw you in person, yeah, but I was waiting for Daniel to break it to you first that you're under surveillance, then I figured we'd meet."

"Ugh, you're such a dick. You better not have any kind of cooties."

"Cooties? How old are you?" He throws a look I want to slap off his face.

"Giving a fake number to a hook-up is beyond rude. You're probably a whore, and I hope you didn't give me a disease."

I'm not going to tell him my anxiety went into hyperdrive after sleeping with a total stranger so I rushed off to the gyno and already know I don't have cooties, but he doesn't know that, and I'm sure as hell not going to tell him.

"No cooties here, don't worry," he murmurs. "I know I have a lot to make up to you, so...I promise to do my best."

He winks.

Chapter 4

Cady

Daniel calls early Monday wanting to apologize and explain, so we meet for coffee during lunch. Nothing of interest has come up in my research and we agree it's unlikely I'm being targeted by the serial killer. I appreciate the guys are trying to protect me, but their methodology isn't the best. My panic attacks are lessening, so I appreciate Daniel sharing the information to put my mind at ease.

The dark circles under his eyes are more prominent in the bright afternoon sun.

"Is something happening with Brandon's case?"

"No. Nothing new." He blushes slightly. It's adorable. "I did find someone special. Someone I didn't think felt the same, but seems she does." Daniel must not have much of a personal life since he's thrown himself into the case. If Zack's his only close friend in Pittsburgh, that's sad.

"Brandon begged me not to let life pass me by. So this lawyer in Tacoma who I'd talked to about the case... I asked her out, and well, we clicked. Her firm doesn't represent Brandon. They only consulted on a specific facet of the defense at one point so there's no conflict of interest."

He's the guy who always plays by the rules, even though life has been so cruel: losing his parents and Grace, then watching Brandon's life get hijacked. He must be really strong, and I'm already protective of him. Miss Lawyer better treat him right.

Zack's warning to be wary of strangers rings in my mind.

"It's great you met someone, but have you considered doing a background check?"

Daniel laughs. "Zack gave you the stranger danger lecture too, huh? He's not wrong though. This is a unique situation, but people run background check dates all the time, and he's running her for me. But she'll check out." *Zack.* An insistent heat forms in my belly hearing his name.

"What's the deal with Zack?" I ask. "The entire encounter was, uh, different."

Daniel apologizes again, then grins. "He seemed happy to make your acquaintance."

Interesting, he didn't tell Daniel we'd met. Okay. We did more than meet. "So," I ask slowly, "Is he single?"

His grin widens. "Yes. And I'm guessing the feeling's mutual?"

I consider before responding. "Definitely. But I'm a mess right now with no idea what I'm doing or what I should do."

"Or who?" Daniel's been so serious until now I'm momentarily stunned, but I laugh because it's a good one. "Sorry, that was wrong, but I couldn't resist. If it matters, Zack's not a relationship guy, but he's a good guy and lots of fun. What else goes on in your life besides being stalked?"

Talking about myself is always uncomfortable, so I share the bare minimum and focus on my fascination with the case.

His eyes light up. "I love to research. Honestly, I'm a huge nerd. Please call if I can ever be of help."

So Zack's not a relationship guy. If it's just sex, there's little chance of rejection. But his perfect body has already ruined me for other men, so my future sex life is doomed.

All afternoon I struggle to focus on contracts, but my mind keeps going to Zack. I should hate this guy for lying and ditching me, but I still want him. An incoming text derails my train of thought.

Trevor: Dinner at my place tonight? I grill a mean steak.

Time to level with Trevor. No way he's getting friend vibes if he wants to make me dinner.

Me: Sorry, busy tonight.

I hope his interest will wane once he leaves. I tell Abby and Lana about Trevor's dinner invitation.

"That's the third date if you count seeing him at the Middle Road. He expects you to put out," Abby declares.

I'm no prude, but there's not a chance in hell since I'm not even attracted to him. Never mind the stranger danger lecture. I'm not particularly social so it's disappointing to meet a guy my friends see as a great catch and have zero interest. I'm an analog girl in a digital world I guess, flirting with guys at the bar when everyone else is on Tinder. With my luck, Tinder will lead to my untimely death so I avoid dating apps like the plague. Besides, sex isn't fun if I don't like the guy. Except for one annoying bastard in college. And Zack. Who I thought I liked, but didn't know at all. Clearly, my judgment is hardly sound.

The office is bustling as everyone rushes to finish a new bid, so today was relatively peaceful. Quitting time always feels phenomenal, but walking alone through icy darkness, it occurs to me I'm in a deserted parking lot in a dead-end alley under a bridge, with a murderer and serial rapist on the loose.

Shivering, I bolt to the Jeep as if there's a pack of wolves on my heels and sit, impatient for the windshield to defrost because I'm not getting out to scrape windows. The phone rings and I tense.

"Hey, girl. Have dinner with me tonight?" Trevor pleads.

"Wish I could but I've got a thing—"

"Not a date, as friends, I'm sorry for coming on so strong. I'm leaving early tomorrow, but I'm bored out of my mind. Have mercy. I have no idea where to get good pizza here," he implores.

Well, if it's platonic, why not? "Lucky for you I'm a pizza connoisseur."

Oh my god, am I so bored and lonely I'll go on a date with a guy I'm trying to avoid?

I head home to change and Sonny enjoys a long leisurely walk while I look behind me for murderers while wondering what the hell is wrong with me. Why didn't I say no to Trevor?

Abby's stern mom voice plays in my head, telling me to give this guy a chance, but I'm confused and starting to hate myself a little.

Nina calls, so I ask about Zack. She's known him forever and says he's a great guy. "Oh my god, Strozzi's the guy you hooked up with at the party? I didn't see him there, and the way you described him, I never would've guessed it was him."

"Yeah, I ran into him again and want to hate him but can't because he's a sexual genius."

"Damn, girl. He's so hot." She sighs. "But he's a pig. Leaves the bar with a different chick every night, and I don't think he ever sees any of them a second time."

"Of course there's lots wrong with him since I've never wanted anyone more."

"Yeah, but if I was single, I'd totally do him. He's gorgeous." Luke pipes up in the background.

"Hey, I'm right here, *wife*," he calls out sarcastically. "Cady, we were all reckless assholes before finding the right woman. It's worth a shot. Strozzi's cool, even if he's a pig. Now, what exactly qualifies one as a sexual genius? Asking for a friend."

"You name it, he's good at it. He's the best kisser and the best at everything," I get a full body flush remembering the night fondly.

"Strozzi? Zack Strozzi?" There's doubt in Luke's voice.

"Yeah, why?"

"Huh. No reason." He's being evasive, but Nina will get intel.

"We'll talk later." Which means she's already on it.

Trevor's cute in an androgynous model way, but I like my men with more muscles. He's easy to talk to though, and we pick up where we left off last time. By the time the food comes, I'm marveling at everything we have in common since he also loves Led Zeppelin and Batman. On paper, he's perfect, but I want something else. *That something else is about six feet tall and unbelievably sexy, with dreamy eyes and the most beautiful face I've ever seen.*

I want to feel a spark when a guy touches me. With Zack, it's more like a fucking supernova.

Trevor and I meander around Little Italy focusing on the culinary delights. The Italian grocery has authentic grandmas handmaking pasta, and Del's restaurant has spumoni so good, I could eat my weight in it.

The bitter winds cut our tour short, and we rush to the Jeep as the frigid gales bash us. Trevor suggests coffee, directing me to the valet, but I hesitate. The most important thing is to not lead him on, but he insists this wasn't a date. What do I do? There's no attraction here, and I don't want to give him the wrong idea. I give him the benefit of the doubt, taking him at face value.

His loft could be right out of a catalogue. Professionally decorated with high-end everything. Overstuffed chairs boast leather soft as butter. The heated patio has a breathtaking, unobstructed view of the Pittsburgh skyline. Conversation flows, and I'm struck by our similarities. On paper, we'd have the perfect connection, yet I feel nothing for this guy. Is he a great catch and I'm blind to it? A door slams and a heavy presence interrupts my musings.

"What the fuck, man? You can't answer my calls?"

Trevor tenses and speaks without turning around, his voice heavy with defeat. "What do you need, Owen? What couldn't wait?"

Owen's taller and stockier, but shares a likeness with his brother. He lacks the gym body with a bit more weight, and his dark blond hair's a shade lighter. Instead of his brother's amiable smile, he has an angry scowl, dark and uncomfortable.

"Dammit, I've been calling for hours. You know I want in on this."

"Sorry about him," Trevor apologizes. "Can you excuse us for a moment? Go on in and be warm."

"No problem," I assure him. I head to the door, but Owen's blocking the way and doesn't move. "Hi." I smile, but may as well be invisible. He doesn't acknowledge me and radiates a barely contained fury.

His eyes are blank and dead, like a shark, and I shudder. Being near him makes the hair on the back of my neck stand up. His presence is revolting. He's irrationally angry his brother didn't answer the phone for a few hours.

"Jesus Christ, Owen, move. What's wrong with you?" Trevor fumes. Owen flings himself away from the door and starts berating his brother. A while later, the door smacks open again and Owen, the human equivalent of a thundercloud, storms through the front door, slamming it with force. Trevor looks sheepish when he steps back inside. "I'm so sorry," he begins, but I interrupt.

"No need to apologize. Little brothers, right?" He drops on the sofa next to me, shaking his head.

"The boy's a handful sometimes," he confides. "Most of the time it's fine, but sometimes, he's too much. I could chalk it up to our childhood, but he's a grown man. He should know better. I love my brother, but I wish he could make my life easier."

"Having family isn't always easy, even if it's worthwhile. He appreciates you even if he's not good at expressing it." I bet Owen isn't one for heartfelt declarations, so Trevor never gets a thank you for being his punching bag. Owen probably ruins lots of good times, and he sure made me not want to return.

"This isn't how I wanted tonight to go, I'm sorry."

"Tonight was great," I insist. "Don't apologize."

"Can we hang out when I come back in a few weeks?"

Hesitant, I agree, sure I'll never see him again.

No connection was enough to end our brief association, but his enraged brother sealed the deal. When it's time to call it a night, we walk to the valet, and he suggests we grab a drink next time. He leans in for a kiss, but I pretend not to notice, fiddling with my seatbelt.

Why bother with Trevor when Zack's the one I want? Something stirs inside of me, remembering how it felt when he pulled my hair and the way those magic hands made my body respond. *Then call him.* No. Zack is bad news or at least guaranteed heartbreak. I don't do one-night stands anymore, and that's all he does.

***

Sonny's barking at the back door when I walk in. There must be animals in the yard. Probably next door's immense cat. I ignore him thinking he'll settle down once he chases them away. I'm not keen on a late walk on deserted streets, so we head into the yard to play ball. He sniffs every inch, but nothing scurries away. Everything's quiet for a few minutes, then he growls, low and mean. I search the darkness for the beady eyes of nighttime animals, spotting something far more sinister.

There's a red chunk of ground beef in the far corner of the yard. Sonny's ten feet from it and the rumble in his throat signals an impending attack. He stares at the fence, haunches low as if to leap, but the fence is higher than even his powerful legs can spring.

There's a thud from the other side of the fence, like someone creeping around the perimeter lost their footing. I call Sonny. Mad as a hornet, he creeps back to me, obedient even against his will.

Ushering him in without turning my back on the yard, I try to act casual, my movements relaxed and unhurried, I lock the door and shut off the lights. If the creep thinks I went to bed, he may still be here when the police arrive. The operator wastes no time once I explain there's a prowler and I have a stalker.

The officers won't use lights or sirens, he explains and stays on the line until an officer knocks. It took less than five minutes but felt like hours. I open the door without thinking, but luckily the officer's a woman. Sonny loves the ladies.

"Miss Blackwell, I'm Sargent Baron. He's gone. We came from two directions, hoping to catch him, but everyone has scanner apps." Sonny barks at the back door. "An officer's bagging the evidence."

"Please excuse me, he's not always friendly to strangers. I should put him upstairs." Sonny follows as I shake myself out of a fog, remembering my manners. "Come in, it's freezing out there. Thanks for getting here so fast."

"The chief filled us in. There's a protocol for stalking cases."

"Do you think he tried to kill Sonny with poisoned meat?" A numbness buzzes through me as the realization hits. Until now, I've been worried someone might vandalize my Jeep or punch me in the face, but nothing more serious. I hadn't considered the possibility of real danger, but this bastard may be a genuine threat. What I'm thinking must show on my face because Sargent Baron steps closer, laying a hand on my arm.

"Please sit down, you look pale. We're going to get this guy soon. They have a name for the cellular account, but the calls are coming from the son's number and mom's uncooperative. Another day or two and we should be able to bring him in for questioning."

At least they have something on this crazy guy. "Is he dangerous? Chief Gruber says these guys are usually cowards who harass women and don't get physical. What if he's wrong?"

"Anything's possible, but that's unlikely. These guys often cause property damage and pick on animals because they're too cowardly to confront you directly. If he was going to hurt you, he wouldn't't've run away." She looks at me in sympathy. "Is there somewhere you can go tonight? I'll wait while you pack a bag and leave."

I won't freak out my family or wake up my friends, and I won't lead the stalker to my loved ones. For now, he's gone, and he probably won't be back tonight.

"No. I'm staying here. I'll be fine."

"We'll have extra patrols tonight," she promises, looking up as Officer Spencer steps in to introduce himself.

"The ground beef has antifreeze on it, but the lab will verify," he says with a note of disgust in his voice. "We'll get this guy soon, Miss Blackwell. We're so close, but the parents won't cooperate."

"Her son's innocent and it must be one of his friends using his phone. He's a good boy getting his life together," the sergeant quips, and Spencer snorts.

"There were footprints in the snow around the perimeter, but none inside the fence. Put a lock on the gate to be safe. The prints went to the next block and ended at tire tracks so he's gone," Spencer adds. "You sure you're going to be all right staying here tonight?" I nod. For the next couple of days, there'll be extra patrols in the area."

"Thank you," I tell them. Then their shoulder radios go off, and they leave to handle their next thing.

The stalker tips the scales. I'm not able to handle this with my usual steadiness. The fear sits on my chest crushing my equilibrium like a boulder. The last time I sobbed was five years ago at Grandpa's funeral. Tonight I cry until I run out of tears. A new job *was* the priority, but now I'm fixated on someone trying to kill my dog, the murders, and all they imply, so my job search is suffering. And I need to leave my job yesterday.

A wave of nausea hits as I miss my boring, comfortable life. I have a raw ache, coupled with a feeling of impending doom. I don't know what's coming, but cold tendrils of fear claw at my heart.

There's no way I'm falling asleep, so armed with a pillow and my favorite comforter, I free Sonny and set up camp on the couch. I shoot an email to Daniel with the latest developments and consider texting Zack, but it's the middle of the night and there's no reason. The police are handling this and have resources in play.

Things have ramped up since I stopped answering every call. Clearly, being ignored is antagonizing him and making him bolder. The police say it's work-related and I should trust them, but I'm worried. What if the dog murderer is not my caller? This doesn't fit with the caller's behavior. Even though the tone of the calls have escalated, this feels different.

Putting yourself in the middle of Daniel's thing brought you to someone's attention. You know it. If you'd left well enough alone, you wouldn't be in this situation, but now you have a real problem you can't even explain to the police. They'll think you're insane, which may indeed be true.

Why did I ever email Daniel? My great ideas always lead to ruin. Pacing relieves a bit of my nervous energy but quickly loses its charm. This helpless feeling is unbearable. Reading takes my mind off of things for a bit and I begin to drift off, only to snap awake at an incoming text.

Daniel: Get in touch with Zack, give him details. It's probably a jackass from work, but there's always a chance it's more.

Of course, he's right. We can't ignore any potential lead. I text Zack.

Call me in the morning.

Ten seconds later the phone rings. It's Zack. "What's up?"

"Daniel said to fill you in on what happened tonight, but tomorrow's fine. Why are you awake?"

"Working. But I'm headed home now. What happened?"

Zack listens without interrupting as I tell him everything, including the update on the suspect.

"I'll be there in ten minutes. Should I sit around the corner or come in?"

"For what?"

"He could come back. When did the police leave?"

"An hour ago, but they followed the footprints to tire tracks and he's long gone. You don't have to—"

"It's probably not Daniel's guy, but we can't rule it out yet."

Zack's right, but I'm not thrilled even as I tell him to come on over. I don't need a stranger camping out here. I don't trust him. He's a liar and he hurt me, but Nina vouched for him, and he's not a murderer. He might be useful.

Zack: I'm here.

It's too frigid out to make him sit in the truck.

Come in.

I usher Sonny into the kitchen, and put up a flimsy baby gate. He can jump right over it or the kitchen island, but he's trained to stay on command. Still, I give him a quick lecture not to eat guests and remind him to stay put.

I let Zack in, and Sonny's barking up a storm. Even the vet's intimidated by Sonny's enormous teeth. Zack looks nervous. "Sorry, he's not great with strangers," I say, but I'm not sorry.

"Damn, he's huge. And not friendly. Animals usually love me. Especially dogs."

Not this dog, pal. He only loves me. "He hates guys near me, but he's obedient." Zack looks skeptical but enters. "Make yourself comfortable," I gesture to the couch. "Want some hot tea?" Cold air radiates from him.

"Tea sounds great, I'm freezing my ass off."

I get us tea, and then collapse onto the couch.

"Someone could've followed you," he mutters.

I shake my head, "I would've noticed the same way I spotted you following me home from my date." He doesn't say anything, but his jaw tenses. "Sorry, but it's true, *detective*." Sonny's quiet, content Zack isn't murdering me at this moment, so I get up and remove the gate. After I'm settled, he jumps up and rests his head in my lap. Zack flinches as Sonny glowers. He asks about my schedule, but I'm half there. There was a killer on the other side of my fence while I stood in the yard.

Mistaking my silence, he snaps, "You've got to trust me."

"You're at the top of my trustworthy list, mister fake number. Even if you weren't a liar, trusting you makes your job easier. It doesn't make me safer."

His eyes flash and the energy in them travels right to my core. Sitting in the half-dark room, he looks dangerous and hot. Even knowing how he "did" me, he turns me on like no man ever has. A bolt of desire dances through me, and I hope he assumes my shiver is from being tired and scared.

"If I was a bad guy, I could've hurt you before you knew I was there. Why is it so hard for you to trust me?" He scowls and rubs the back of his neck.

"I knew you were there the whole time. You're not great at tailing people."

"Daniel said he'd explain. I wasn't trying to hide. You know, I'm trying to help—"

"Why *are* you trying to help?"

"It's my job." The relaxed posture is gone. It's late, and he's probably tired too, but I take perverse pleasure in pissing him off.

"Is this a paying job?"

"Daniel's a good friend. I'll help him any way I can even if it means putting up with you." He sighs. "If you don't trust me, tell Dan. He's the only one who can call me off of this detail."

Okay. I had that coming.

"I'm sorry. I'm sleep-deprived and my nerves are frayed. I need to get on with my life, but every time I think 'oh you're overreacting, nobody's after you,' this fucker does something else." I'm frustrated and he's no longer meeting my gaze. "The calls started over a month ago. Now he's harassing and stalking me, and he tried to—" I cover Sonny's ears before dropping my voice to a whisper, "*kill my dog*." I detect a ghost of a smile at the corners of Zack's mouth. "I'm too stressed out to sleep, but I've been awake for two days and I'm not thinking straight. I'm sorry for being..." I sigh. "None of this is your fault. I'm at the end of my rope here."

"Don't apologize." He runs a hand through his hair and I ache to touch it. "You'd be crazy not to be suspicious. But stop making new friends while we get this sorted. That'll be tough for you, Miss Congeniality, but pretty please, try real hard."

"Oh, fuck off, Strozzi." Patience gone, I chuck a throw pillow at his face but he easily deflects.

"Cady, I *am* sorry about everything."

"Don't." We're not going there. It's quiet but for the music and I shift my body to appear more relaxed. "Do you think I put myself in danger by contacting Daniel? The rat and this stuff tonight wasn't the caller; he's all talk and wouldn't chance being seen. This is Daniel's guy."

"Why do you think so?"

"Everything the police said about the profile of a typical caller. If they're correct, him coming here doesn't fit. The killer's gone to great lengths to follow Daniel around the country, taunting him. What happened tonight is something he'd do. It fits his profile perfectly."

"There's nothing like that in the profile. I've seen it a thousand times."

"No. I mean a real profile. Daniel's is bare-bones and only covers the crimes and how he kills. It doesn't address personality traits or behavior outside of the crime scenes. I'm no criminologist, but I know enough psychology to know the guy tonight is more likely the killer than the caller."

Zack motions with his hand. "Lay it out for me."

"He's dramatic. A show-off. He needs to intimidate Daniel into feeling powerless. This is a game, and the goal is to make Dan watch people suffer and feel responsible. Why else follow him around and send mementos? The killer gets his rocks off trolling me and making Daniel blame himself, no question."

Zack's quiet and I can't read him. "If that's the case, what do we do?"

"How about you make sure I don't get murdered?"

"Duh. Seriously, what do you suggest?"

"Let's find this fucker because nobody else is stopping him."

"How do you propose we catch him?"

"This isn't my thing. I was hoping you'd have ideas, detective."

"Stop calling me that."

"Aren't you a detective?"

His eyes narrow as he fixes his gaze on me "Not much of one according to you," he mutters.

I want to jump on him, despite his snarky attitude, or possibly because of it. Angry sex would be excellent. I don't want to focus on the horror show my life's become. I want to take off my clothes and watch him fall to his knees—again. Brad Arnold's singing "When I'm Gone" and the lyrics are so apt for my life.

'I'm alive, but I'm alone. Part of me is fighting this, but part of me is gone.' I'm drained physically, mentally, and emotionally. Moments ago, I would've done anything to sleep, but now I long to fall into his lap to feel safe in his arms. Even if I'm not. But I can't move.

"I'm not sure what to do, but I have to do something." The defeat in my voice scares me. "I can't go about my business fingers crossed, hoping for the best." My wake-up alarm shatters the silence and I jump, almost falling off of the couch. "My alarm," I explain, rubbing my hands over my face in exhaustion, annoyed at my entire fucking life. "I hit snooze lots, so I set my alarm way early."

"What time do you leave in the morning? Run me through your routine again."

"After I've walked Sonny, had coffee, and grab food, most days, I'm on my way to the gym by five."

"If someone's watching, they're waiting for you to leave soon. Get some sleep," he mutters. "We'll talk with Dan and figure this out. I've got paperwork to do. I'll sit at the corner. From that angle, I can see this place from three sides. If anyone comes the other way, I'm sure your fuzzy alarm here will alert you." He dips his chin at Sonny.

"Stay. It's too cold to sit outside."

"Yeah?" I suspect he wants to say more, but he doesn't. *Come on, Strozzi, make a move since I'm too chicken.* I'm tempted to extend an invitation. *I'll warm you up, Zack. Come upstairs with me.* But I can't. "Make yourself comfortable. There's more tea and snacks. Help yourself." I get up. "Thank you."

"Sure thing, Cady. Sleep."

I love hearing my name on his lips. My entire body flushes with heat and want when he says it. This is crazy. I grab a blanket from the closet, and toss it to him.

Sleep doesn't come quick despite my exhaustion. I can't stop thinking about his body pressed to mine and all the things his sexy mouth excels at, besides his smart-ass comments.

I'm not thinking of murders or stalkers or work or Trevor and I'm no longer fighting sleep. I'm fighting the urge to stroll down there and take off my clothes without saying a word.

Another night with Zack might ease my stress, but there'd be complications.

He's not a threat, but he's not a good idea either.

Chapter 5

Cady

Eventually, I pass out from pure exhaustion and manage almost four hours of sleep. My phone's blowing up by the time I wake.

Dog walker, Cole: I saw the Jeep and figure Sonny doesn't need me today.

Abby: I'm sure you're late because you had a hot night at Trevor's.

Ugh, gross. I've got to set her straight.

Mom: Did you have trouble getting to work in the snow?

I have twenty minutes to get my ass to work, and turn the music loud to help wake me. Thinking of work makes me sick. I've pushed it to the back of my mind with everything else going on, but things are much worse than I realized. I may be committing crimes without even knowing, and the potential repercussions could ruin my life. Allen Brothers will get busted, not if but when. And what then? No doubt, they'll blame me. My priority was to find a new job fast, but I have to protect myself before I go. I'm going to be their fall-guy.

I take the world's fastest shower, then bolt downstairs in nothing but a towel, desperate for caffeine. I can't drink the coffee at work. The office blend is cheap and bland, plus everyone hates Pete and Bob, so poisoning isn't out of the question.

Nothing seems out of the ordinary to my sleep-deprived brain until I step into my kitchen and see Zack drinking coffee. I want to run out, but instead I freeze when his dark eyes do the sweep. His desire is obvious, and it creates a rush of liquid heat through my core as my nipples jump to attention.

"Well, good morning to me." His wicked smile steals my breath, and I feel the throb from across the room.

"Sorry, cowboy. Thought you left. Stop trying to check out my goodies. It's rude." I pull the towel tighter so my nipples don't poke through, but that makes it a few inches shorter. Of course, his eyes wander lower.

"Looking good, baby. So good. I don't eat breakfast, but I'll make an exception for you."

I want to slap his smart mouth, but I want to ride it again even more. Shaking my head, I retreat upstairs to get dressed and still have two buttons left when I hear him on the steps.

"Are you decent?"

"Yeah."

"Too bad. So what do you want to do?" His eyes are on my boobs as I finish the buttons.

"Not you, Strozzi."

"Liar." He grins. "I meant about your problem."

"The only thing to do is catch him." I pinch the bridge of my nose, trying to stave off the massive headache brewing. "Easier said than done, I know, but catching him would solve one problem."

His sexy grin fades and his stare burns into me. "Do you need help?"

Yes. I'm alone, terrified, exhausted, and falling apart. Hold me and make me feel safe.

"No, I'm fine, thanks." I manage a weak smile, turning away from the pity in his expression.

"Nothing about any of this seems fine."

"Things aren't great," I concede, closing my eyes against gathering tears. My lids fly open when his thumb brushes away the tear rolling down my cheek. His gaze locks onto mine.

"Hey," he begins but I'm distracted by his eyes. Flecks of amber and milky green swim in the irises, reminding me of sea glass. The colors catch the light, and I'm dazzled. "Everything will be okay. Don't worry. We'll find him." His voice is soft and soothing. "I'll call Dan to explain." I nod, afraid to speak. "I promise to keep you safe."

Yeah, just like you promised to call. I'm mad at myself for wanting to believe him since I know better. "Hope you're good at this, cowboy. I don't want to end up in a pit in somebody's basement."

He throws an arm around my shoulders. "None of my clients have ended up in a basement pit yet."

***

I'm sitting at my desk at the end of the work day when Chief Gruber calls to say they're going to question my caller and file charges any day, but I'm not as relieved as I expected to be since I don't believe he's the real threat.

My attention needs to be on Allen Brothers and protecting myself so I can leave, except I have to figure out a way to stop a freaking murderer too. How do I do that? Ignoring it and hoping things work out seems like a bad strategy. It's the equivalent to saying "Be right back" and going to check the basement for monsters in a horror movie.

If someone doesn't catch this guy, I'll worry about him forever. Getting involved means less time and effort to solve my work problems, but there's no other choice. I hope the Allen Brothers situation doesn't explode while I'm busy playing detective. With my luck, I'll catch the killer and save my life only to spend the rest of it in prison for Pete and Bob's crimes.

My body tenses when the phone rings then floods with relief when Zack's name flashes across the screen.

"Howdy, cowboy," I answer, trying to sound casual but the butterflies in my stomach are moshing again.

"Everything okay?" Hearing his voice sends a thrill through me.

"Living the dream."

"Dan asked if we can get together tonight or tomorrow at his place."

"Sure, I can be free tonight or tomorrow." *Or anytime for you.*

"Sounds good." I want this man bad, no matter how much it complicates life. "No calls or creepy visitors today?"

"So far, so good. But work sucks and I miss having a bodyguard."

"I'm around if you need me."

Be at my place in twenty minutes. No shirt, please. "I may take you up on that, Strozzi."

***

I waste no time rushing to Daniel's. He and Zack are skeptical of my theory, but I'm determined to convince them. "Based on everything the police say, I think whoever's been to my house is some other creep, not the jerk who's been calling. I need to know why he picked me and stop him. Let me in on this."

"I'm not sure what you can do." Daniel looks doubtful.

"Let me review the evidence. I can research the hell out of anything. There's no way I can go back to my life without seeing this through."

"This may be the crank caller, but what if it's not? And it can't hurt to have fresh eyes on this," Zack suggests. He asks a lot of questions and seems satisfied with my answers. I had no idea how tense I was until he agrees and my whole body relaxes.

"There's so much information: timelines, maps of crime scenes, trial logs, and evidence files. Do you want it in waves or everything at once?"

"Give me everything so I can start at the beginning. Right now. I won't be sleeping anytime soon."

"This case has that effect on people," Daniel mutters. "Check out today's mail." It's a postcard of the Pittsburgh skyline.

"So even if the Shaler murders weren't him, he's watching you," Zack says.

"It's him," Daniel insists.

My phone's blowing up so I silence it, but not quick enough.

"Is that *Trevor*? Your boyfriend from the steakhouse?" Zack pretty much snarls. *Is he jealous?* Too bad he's riled up only because someone else is interested in me.

"Zip it, Strozzi. The guy can't take a hint," I grumble. "Said he wanted someone to show him around town, but he's super clingy and looking for more than a tour guide."

We discuss patterns and look for evidence of anyone following me but strike out. Calls come in during the day, but most are evenings and late at night. The rat was left on my doorstep in broad daylight, but the prowler came late at night so there's no discernible pattern.

Did he try to poison Sonny so he could get to me without impediment? I explain about the back door being unlocked last week, and how I dismissed it at first, but now I'm concerned. Could someone have been in my house without leaving a sign? Panic zaps through me at the thought.

"We have to assume he's following you or will follow you sometimes," Daniel says gently. I'm sure my expression is making how I feel plain.

"You'd spot a vehicle, but maybe not a stranger in a crowd. He may blend in and stay off your radar." We decide mundane things like work and the gym are probably safe, but places with crowds are riskier.

"When you go to the mall or the bar, take him," Daniel nods at Zack and I dip my chin, feeling defeated. "Go through the original cases with Zack. Nobody's ever compared them to one another." He shrugs. "You might see something I missed."

Daniel hasn't been methodical and Zack's spent most of his time digging into potential suspects, so he hasn't poured through each case. It seems like a viable plan except Daniel's wearing a mischievous little smile, and I think Zack kicked him under the table.

Scheming to hook me up could make Dan my hero. Eventually, we call it quits and I walk out with Zack. Another forty-plus-degree January night in Pittsburgh buoys my spirits, but it's the view that takes my breath away. The city lights glimmer on the inky surface of the Allegheny River in an elegant impressionist image.

"What an awesome picture." Framing it with my hands, I try to decide the best angle.

"Take a picture, your phone has a camera," Zack says like I'm slow.

"My pictures suck." He gives me a look before snapping a picture and seconds later I'm getting a text. "Thanks, Strozzi. You're all right."

I give him a high-five as I hop into the Jeep, feeling a tingle where my hand touched his. Thankfully, those texts weren't all from Trevor. Lana wants to go to lunch, and Evan's asking about concert tickets. I'm texting furiously when a sharp rap at my window startles me, and I drop the phone before I see Zack at the window.

"You scared me. What the hell?"

"Do you know how to not get murdered? Don't sit here playing on your phone in a dark parking lot. Get in, lock the doors and drive away. Be more careful."

He's right, but I won't tell him that. "Can we stop with the murder talk? It's super creepy."

There's that look again. "You said you miss having a bodyguard. I figured I'd step up." *Yes, please. Guard my body and worship it.* His eyes are gorgeous pools fringed by thick lashes any girl would kill to have. "Awesome tune, by the way."

Huh. I'm so in my head, I hadn't realized the radio was on. Mazzy Star's *Fade Into You* is playing. "Yeah, I love this song." He looks like he might say more, so I wait, but he doesn't. "Thanks for the picture." *Ask him out. Or at least invite him to follow you home and get naked with you.*

"If Trevor's bothering you, I'll get rid of him."

"Like, knock him off? Pretty extreme."

"Damn, woman. Not like that. Your mind's a scary place."

"I'm a pro at deflecting losers, but it gets old. I might take you up on the offer."

"Anytime. You have my number. See ya later."

Ask him to go get a drink. But, no. I smile and wave, kicking myself as he walks away.

Why can't I talk to this guy? The worst that can happen is he rejects me, which he'd done before and I lived.

So, why does it feel like it would be the end of the world if Zack rejected me again?

***

By Friday night, I've avoided Trevor like a pro. He texts twice, both of which I ignore, then he leaves a voicemail, but I don't call back. Part of me thinks it's cruel to ghost him, but I don't think telling him no would get me anywhere. He's nothing, if not tenacious.

I'm distracted by news of an attempted rape last night. Details are still scarce, but it has to be part of the serial case to be such big news. Investigators still won't say how the murder and the rapes may be related. The secretive nature of this investigation strikes me as odd, and it's frustrating since I know it all ties in with the killer who's tormenting Daniel.

There's some good news. The creep hasn't called. Pete and Bob are going on a big family cruise soon, and I made it to the gym. Chief Gruber calls to tell me they questioned a guy named Gary

Babinski who's a laborer from an excavating subcontractor. Babinski insists he doesn't know who I am and has never heard of Allen Brothers, but he worked on one of our jobs for nine months.

The calls started about six weeks ago, the day after he got fired. He lives nearby, but swears he's never been to my house or this office and insists someone used his phone without his knowledge, over a hundred times at all hours of the day and night. Gary isn't the sharpest tool in the shed, but he's a tool. He was arrested but released on his own recognizance on the condition he stays at least five hundred feet away from me and doesn't contact me. Chief Gruber sends a picture. I've never seen the guy in my life, but I'm thrilled the police are doing their job. Maybe the creep won't ever call again.

Daniel latest piece on the attempted rape is the most thorough account I've seen. He interviewed the victim and a witness. The victim was heading home with her husky mix after a walk in Mellon Park in Pittsburgh's east end. It wasn't dark yet and traffic was heavy on the road, but foot traffic was light due to frigid temps. The attacker said he'd show her a good time, she said "No." Apparently, he didn't notice the dog, but the dog saw him. The rapist tried pulling her into a dark alley, but let go to fight off her dog. The bastard ran off when a car came. The dog, Sadie, and her owner received a complimentary steak dinner from a local restaurant for her heroics. So far, nobody's turned up for medical treatment with a dog bite, but she bit his thigh multiple times. Police have a BOLO out, extending into neighboring states because even with treatment, animal bites often get infected, and the rapist would need medical attention. But if Daniel's correct about his travels, he could be a thousand miles away by now.

The office snitches cut out early for drinks, so I sneak out early too. There will be hell to pay come Monday, but my time is best spent preventing my untimely death. I head home and go straight into research mode.

My minor act of rebellion pays off with a huge find—the rapist bit a victim in Sioux Falls. Forensics didn't get any hits, but there's a cast of the bite pattern. More than a year later, there was a case in Vancouver with bite marks. A comparison has to be done, but I don't know how to make that happen. We'll need help from Daniel's FBI contact, but first I've got to see if any other victims have bite marks.

Two hours of going through autopsies and forensic rape kits find potential matches in Eugene, Oregon, Dickinson, Texas, and one right here in Pittsburgh. This is the most promising new evidence so far.

There's so much information, I'm struggling with how to keep track of what I've done and still need to do. I resurrect my high school biology lab report format and write a succinct report then send it to Daniel and Zack marked "Urgent."

Daniel calls right away and asks if we can meet tomorrow. He knows this is big. Not only can these bite marks connect cases—many of the cases have DNA that's never been tested. If my theory pans out, they can use the bite marks to push for more testing. If they can match bite marks from multiple unrelated cases, we'd establish a connection, which is a tremendous leap in the right direction. Grace's case has DNA evidence, he adds, so connecting it to other cases could be the key to Brandon's freedom. Daniel's brother's life is on the line and helping to right a wrong feels good.

Zack's hanging around in the background while I'm with Nina at her favorite neighborhood bar. If anyone's following me, he'd spot them. I kind of hope he finds someone so we can end this.

I'm having a blast dancing with Nina. The DJs are awesome. I've made countless requests and we talk music. but then one gets flirty. He follows us when we step out to smoke a blunt. We were having a great discussion about why Prince is the better guitarist, even though I love Tom Petty's music more, when this guy asks, "What are you doing tomorrow?"

"We're talking music. Don't make it weird." I light up, hoping my no-sharing
policy drives him away since nothing else has worked. "Sorry, I don't swap spit with strangers," I explain, waving the blunt.

"Good thing *we're* not strangers. Did Dan call you?" The familiar voice behind me sounds irritated and I smile. Nina's eyes go wide when Strozzi's hand snakes over my shoulder, poaching my smoke. The DJ mutters something and disappears.

"No, what's up?"

Zack takes a deep pull and starts choking hard enough to cough up a lung. "Holy shit. That's fucking strong," he sputters as I snatch it back.

"Want me to shotgun you a hit, honey? It would be much easier on your delicate constitution," I offer sweetly, blowing smoke in his face.

A sullen scowl darkens the planes of his handsome face, and he grabs my arm, pulling me across the patio. "Dan didn't call. I rescued you. You're welcome."

"Maybe he's my soulmate and we'll never meet again thanks to you." I roll my eyes, pulling my smoke from his sexy lips.

"That douche is your soulmate?" Zack looks doubtful. "Really?"

"Let's hope not, since you ran him off." That gets a laugh. "Jealous much, cowboy?"

"I don't get jealous."

"Sure," I drawl. "You could just ask me out. Geez."

"Hey, I was trying to help. Next time, I'll mind my own business when some clown's falling all over you."

"Likely story. By the way, I'd probably say yes." His stare is still on me, but I can't read him.

"I get a 'probably'? Way to make a guy feel appreciated. Can't happen anyway since we work together."

"Do we?" He shrugs. "So if I asked you out, you'd turn me down?"

"Yes."

"Wow, the guy offended by a 'probably' gives me a straight-up 'No.' Thanks for the ego boost, dick." My snark vanishes when he crowds me. He leans down until we're nose-to-nose and my heart is beating faster than a hummingbird's wings. "You going to kiss me, cowboy?"

His mouth twitches, but he doesn't back down. "That's a bad idea." His gaze searchs mine as I pop the blunt between his lips, my fingers brushing his face. He smells delicious, all manly with a dash of cinnamon.

Wonder what he'd do if I called his bluff and planted a kiss on him right now?

Our lips are inches apart in the weirdest game of chicken ever when something draws his attention. My gaze follows his and I forget his tantalizing mouth when I see a gaunt stranger wandering alone. I've noticed this guy so many times tonight and something about him makes me uneasy. Why does he stand out every time I scan the crowd? Maybe Zack can help me solve a mystery.

"What's up with him, detective?" I ask, poking him in the ribs for effect.

His head swivels back to me, a sour look plastered on his face. He growls in annoyance and the sound gives me goosebumps. "What about him?"

"He gives off bad vibes and I don't like the way he looks at girls."

"Hadn't noticed, but I'll pay attention."

"Something's off. Maybe he's some poor sap trying to find a missed connection, but what if he's a psycho mentally measuring chicks for his next skinsuit?"

"Sure, that's not crazy at all," he chides, giving me one of *those* looks.

"He gives me a bad feeling."

"You should always listen to those gut feelings."

"Mine aren't worth much," I admit with a shrug. Stubbing the smoke, I turn to the door, but his arms circle my waist, pulling me back. "Dance with me, baby."

A protest dies on my lips when his body meets mine. I submit, pressing my back to his chest and practically riding his leg. "Thought you don't dance, cowboy."

"Maybe with you I can't help myself." A ball of fire dances in my belly when he murmurs in my ear. "And your buddy's waiting by the door, so I'm making a point."

"So this is some selfless act?" Zack feels perfect and I want to melt into him. "Mostly, but not completely." He presses closer, erasing the last inch between us and the heat spreading through my core intensifies.

A breathy little moan escapes me when his body melds to mine. I've never made that sound before in my life. He plants a kiss on the back of my neck and I breathe his name before I can stop myself. He laughs, low and dark. His arrogance is so fucking hot, I think my panties have melted away. He holds me flush against him as his hips move with the music, grinding into me.

I rest my head on his shoulder, my lips brushing his jaw. His hand dips under the hem of my shirt and skates across bare skin along the edge of my jeans. "I like having a bodyguard."

"Good, because you're not getting rid of me," he murmurs.

"Promise?" I shiver against him as the music stops.

"Promise," he growls.

"Want to get out of here?" My voice still has a breathy quality I don't recognize.

"Not tonight, baby. Go play with your friends. I'll see you in the morning. " He kisses the side of my neck before letting go and I can't believe it.

Did he just turn me down? After *that*? Ouch.

I drag Nina into a corner for a conference because what's wrong with me? This jackass lied and blew me off, yet I'm practically humping him in public. When did I get so desperate?

My problem isn't desperation, it's him. My brain shuts down and my body takes over when he's near. I figured it wouldn't hurt to have a little fun. As long as I have no expectations, I can't get hurt. But when I wanted the bare minimum, he shut me down.

"Do yourself a favor and stay away from Zack," she cautions. "You're too nice and it can't end well for you. Other guys might not be as hot, but there are plenty who won't break your heart." Nina's right, but I don't want anyone else.

Any time the relentless deejay gets close, Strozzi materializes to shield me, but he doesn't get too close. I lose sight of him at last call and assume he left since Nina told him we were leaving. But as we make our way to the door, I see a tall redhead in a two-sizes-too-small bodycon dress wrapped around him with her hand conspicuously in his front pocket. Our gazes meet and he calls my name but I keep walking.

Nina's right, he's a bad for me.

I've got enough problems without him teasing me then walking away.

Chapter 6

Zack

Holding Cady last night was phenomenal. Her hair smells like honeysuckle on a hot summer day, and she feels fucking perfect pressed up against me. Nobody's ever turned me on more, but saying yes to her wasn't an option. I need to get her off my mind. Typically, I charm a girl, we smash and everyone's happy. The End.

I keep things superficial with my hook-ups, but I lost control with Cady. I couldn't stop kissing her exquisite mouth or any other part of her luscious body. I wanted to hold her almost as bad as I needed to be inside her. A repeat would be phenomenal, but things with us already went too far.

I don't do relationships, and she doesn't seem like the casual type. I don't want to give her the wrong idea. Finding hot women for dirty fun is easy. I always lay out the ground rules up front: no last names, no phone numbers, no kissing, unless it counts when they wrap their lips around my cock, but I don't reciprocate. I'm good with my hands and my dick so they're never disappointed, and that works for me. Until I met Cady. Then every rule went out the window. Everything about that night was insane. Feeling a connection with a stranger is irrational.

Watching her leave was rough, but I never called, no matter how much I was tempted. I've never told anyone about that night, but have thought about it and her countless times.

Maybe running into her again is fate. I never guessed she'd matter, and by the time I started to feel regret, coming clean would've ruined the night. She was easy to talk to so I planned to tell her the truth in the morning, but she was sneaking out when she thought I was asleep. That would've been an awkward conversation for multiple reasons so I let her go.

Now I want to forget her but she's everywhere. The other day in her room, I wanted to hold her and kiss away her tears, and nothing has ever scared me more. Last night I thought maybe I still have a shot, but Cindy or Sandy or whatever the fuck her name has nuked that chance when she wouldn't stop trying to climb into my pants. She was wasted, and I was trying to politely extricate myself without being a complete dick when Cady saw me.

Today she's dancing around the kitchen making nachos and blaring music at an obscene volume when we arrive. Her smoking hot ass is so perfect, I'd give anything to tap that again, but she's a good girl. They can be fun, but they tend to cling. Girls like Cady want dates and boyfriends, not casual sex with guys who drop fake numbers. They expect a drawer at your place. My hook-ups don't know where I live.

Even if she's willing, I dig her enough to stay away. There's something fragile about her. Maybe 'cause she's so small and I tower over her, or maybe life hasn't been easy. If Cady was music, she'd be the blues. The kind that tears your heart out and stomps all over it, but you play it on a loop anyway because it's soulful and addictive and beautiful. She needs someone who can appreciate her and take care of her. I'm good for only one thing.

Dan's elbow in my ribs snaps me back to the moment. "Stop staring, man. Just ask her out already."

"I don't mix business with pleasure."

"What business? You're both volunteers, dumbass." This hypocrite has a lot of nerve considering he hasn't had a date in years. Daniel spends every minute at work or fighting to free his brother. Lucky for him Cady walks in so I bite back my response.

"Watch your nachos, boys. Sonny steals food," she warns, setting drinks on the table.

Daniel can't wait any longer and nearly shouts, "Sam thinks you hit it big with the bite marks and is getting a lab involved."

Cady's cheeks flush. Her deep green eyes go wide with shock and she blinks a few times before responding. "Seriously? Wow, I expected a brush-off. I can't believe they agree."

Yeah, she's way too wholesome to ride this. Still, I can't help myself. "Outstanding work, Blackwell," I say with a high-five.

Daniel watches with a smug smile. What a dick. "This could be huge. Sam has a green light to test multiple cases, and any match proves it's a serial offender," he continues.

"The anonymous samples are in the system, right? So these could link to other cases," she says.

"Hopefully, but not necessarily. Not every case gets forensic testing," I tell her.

"Most were closed without running DNA, and Brandon's was only at Grace's crime scene, but they convicted him of the others based on circumstantial evidence," Daniel states.

"So DNA from the killer is sitting in storage while Brandon sits in prison? Why doesn't the defense raise hell? That's reasonable doubt." Cady's incredulous.

"Things get missed: hair, fibers, signs of sexual assault. Evidence degrades when bodies are in water and with animal or insect activity. There are countless ways they miss things," Daniel mutters.

Cady looks horrified as I jump in. "Most labs have budget problems plus insane backlogs. If there's a suspect and a solid case without DNA, the DA thinks why bother chasing up a maybe? It's a waste of resources if it's not needed for conviction, and lots of cases end up at Shields for those reasons. It's easily half of my workload."

"That's scary." Cady looks disgusted. "Exculpatory evidence being ignored is beyond disturbing, especially in capital cases." *This is a brutal topic, but one she needs to understand for this work, so here's a quick crash course, cupcake.*

She goes quiet, like we've traumatized her, but these details are crucial. After covering the rest of the potential links, Daniel has to get back to work and I vow to start on the older cases today. New evidence will move things forward by leaps and bounds, plus this assignment means I'll spend time with her. *Yeah, I'm selfish.*

Cady sees him out, then ushers me over to the mountain of folders in her living room. "Daniel worked backward from Brandon's case, but I'm going in chronological order. The first round includes initial crime scene reports, autopsies, eyewitness statements. Set aside theories, investigative trails, suspects, and forensics. Look at the physical evidence, nothing else. Identify any similarities, then determine if they're actual links. For example, bite marks are a link, but stabbing victims maybe not, unless there's evidence it's the same knife. I made this chart to detail each case for quick comparison, but do whatever works for you. Round two, go deeper and look at suspects, witnesses, everything."

Huh. A sophisticated strategy for an amateur. "Have you done investigative or research work before?"

"No, I'm just a nerd," she shrugs.

"You've got a good system. I'll do it your way. The bite marks report worked, so we'll stick with the format."

Cady smiles. "I struggled with how to organize the results and thought back to high school biology." She's more irresistible by the minute: hot, smart, and resourceful. "Ready to dive in, Strozzi?"

I'm ready to dive into you, woman. Fuck, I have no self-control when it comes to her even with our clothes on. I think about sex a lot, but lately, the *only* thing I seem to think about is ravishing her, and nothing's ever turned me on more.

The more time I spend with her, the more I want her, so working together is rough. She has great ideas, asks the right questions, and gets results. Most of the people I train have degrees and years of experience, but aren't half as capable. Daniel's lucky to have her.

We're working, but I can't keep my eyes off of her. She's constantly in motion: legs bouncing, fingers tapping, worrying the little pink heart on her silver necklace. She shifts constantly, smoothing her clothes and tucking her hair behind her ears. It's rough to watch. I've never seen anyone so uncomfortable in their own skin. Is she ever at peace? Does she ever stop moving and relax? What, if anything, stills her? I wonder if I could calm the storm inside of her by worshipping her delicious body the way I do in my fantasies. Could I turn her back into that carefree girl from September: sexy and happy and moaning all night about how much she loves my dick?

Her hair is dark and glossy with sexy waves like she just got fucked. When she pulls it up, I'm tempted to plant a kiss on the back of her neck to see whether she'd punch me or melt in my arms. It could go either way, but I want my lips on her again and she seems to like it. Holding her last night was perfect, but there's no way to satisfy my urges without adding to her problems. So it can't happen.

I need to focus on the work, but tonight, she's all I see.

She's singing along to the music every time I look over and I wonder how anyone can know every song. "Do you know the words to all the songs?"

Her head comes up, her bright eyes wide like she forgot I was here. "Yeah," she admits with a shy smile. "Movie quotes and song lyrics are my superpowers." *Wrong, cupcake. You have another superpower, deep-throating my cock.* I've gotten a lot of blowjobs, but hers gets the trophy for being perfect in every way. It was fucking magical and I think of it often, but I keep that to myself. She might not take it as a compliment.

Our conversation segues to movies, concerts, then to her enormous music collection. The sheer quantity of electronic files is staggering, but she's got a ton of vinyl, too. This girl is an encyclopedia of entertainment, and it's impressive.

"Practical stuff never sticks, so I'm full of useless knowledge. Sometimes I imagine what I'd know if my head wasn't filled with silly things. Would I be a Nobel laureate physicist or curing cancer or something fantastic?" She laughs, but it doesn't reach her eyes and I feel it in my chest. The self-deprecating humor doesn't seem like a joke. I suspect she has no idea she's awesome. Even worse, I don't think she'd believe me if I told her.

She gets up to put out the dog and takes a call that sounds like she's trying to convince someone named Evan to do something, but he's refusing. Evan's a fucking moron. What idiot says no to her? I get a text.

Daniel: You're welcome, don't screw it up being you.
Me: ????
Daniel: I bounced early so you'd have her all to yourself.
Me: Quit playing matchmaker.
Daniel: Ask her out. You'll wake up one day sad your life's a constant parade of random chicks from some bar.
Here's a picture of my middle finger, always handy for such occasions, dick. I'm not taking suggestions on my personal life.

Cady returns with the dog and Sonny glares like I ate his steak. What's his problem anyway? A few cases later, she declares she needs a break, and turns on some game on her phone. "You play?"

Nope. I'm scrolling through my phone when her kissable mouth lets off an explosive string of curse words that'd make a sailor blush, and it gets my attention.

"Come on, Strozzi, play with me. You know you want to," she goads with a cheeky grin.

Keep your mouth shut so she'll think you're a decent human being, jackass. I relent and download the app, which puts a big smile on her face. How hard can it be?

After a few humiliating starts, I improve enough to survive an entire match, somewhat redeeming myself. It takes several tries, but we finish in the top ten despite me having two left thumbs.

She's way less reserved, and her competitive streak is slightly intimidating, but so damn hot. We call it quits, agreeing we've covered enough for today.

She wants a quiet night at home with a movie, and briefly I consider suggesting dinner since she made us lunch, but don't want to give her the wrong idea, so I leave.

***

The bar isn't any fun tonight after teasing Cady on the patio here yesterday. I'm bored and restless, and everything sucks. There are distractions everywhere, but the only one I want isn't here. I should've taken her to dinner, but I can't be what she needs. I wonder what movie Cady's watching and if she's watching it with *Evan.* Is *Evan* the douche from the steakhouse? No, that's Trevor. So who the fuck is Evan?

What the hell's wrong with me? I don't compete for women's attention. When there's another guy, I move on. But Cady's different. The thought alone of another man touching her makes me want to rip the guy limb from limb. Cady's mine.

Who the fuck is Evan?

There's a bunch of excited chatter as the bartender explains someone tried to kidnap a girl in the parking lot last night. I check the news. Holy shit, it's the guy who skeeved out Cady. I should tell her. Some condescending inner voice chides me for using any excuse to talk to her, but I don't care.

"Howdy, cowboy."

"What are you wearing, baby?"

"Nothing but a smile if you're coming over, stud."

"You're killing me, woman. Is that an invitation? Because I'll break land speed records to lay my hands on your fine ass."

"Sure, come watch a movie with me."

"By 'watch a movie,' you mean put my mouth all over your hot body, yeah?" I need to bury my face in her the way I need to breathe fucking air.

"I can't believe you booty-called me, it's not even late. Are you drunk?"

"This isn't a booty call and I'm not drunk."

"Do you not know how those work? Or are you deflecting because you already have a date with the children's clothing model from last night?"

Cady's sassy and I like it. "Jealous much, baby?" I repeat her words.

"I don't get jealous," she tosses back. This woman makes me crazy, like so out of my mind, I want to drive over there right now and own her all night long. That's a bad idea though, so instead I tell her about the guy. "I knew there was something wrong with him," she says with satisfaction.

"See? Follow your instincts. They served you well last night. Thought you should know."

"Thanks, Strozzi. I needed that." Her voice is quiet and there's no doubt she means it. That makes me feel like even more of a dick for turning her down.

"So, uh, about last night—"

"Hey, I was kidding." She wasn't kidding. "We had fun but that was," she pauses and takes a deep breath. *Don't say mistake, woman. Don't you dare say the best night of my life was a mistake.* "It was an anomaly, okay? I'm no one-night stand, Strozzi."

"No, you're not."

You're an obsession that got into every part of me and so much more.

***

Cady

There's always time for Sunday dinner at my parents' house, which we do as often as possible. My sister, Lily, who lives on campus a few hours away, came home this weekend. Evan, my brother, goes to school locally and still lives at home. I'm only ten minutes away. Since I talk to Mom daily and Lily every few days, keeping secrets isn't easy. Sure, it's tough to keep what's going on quiet, but they'd worry too much. I've convinced myself it's for the best to say nothing. Of course, if some dark fate befalls me, they'll be blindsided, but I keep assuring myself I won't get murdered. Daniel's blowing up my phone with a string of excited texts, and then Zack calls and I wonder what he wants. Me, I hope.

"How's it going?"

"Daniel wants to meet tomorrow to compare notes and see what's new."

Odd Dan didn't mention it in one of the five zillion messages, but okay. "Tomorrow works. I've got good stuff to show you guys. Anything exciting on your end?"

"What do you know about stolen liquor?"

"Lots. Guess you're finding more of the same."

"What are you doing tonight?"

"Research, why?"

"Damn, I wanted to hear 'you, Zack.' This is happening, woman."

"Keep telling yourself that, cowboy. Call me back when you're ready for a date."

"You're going to change your mind." Zack's sexy voice shoots lust straight to my core.

"I'll get you on a date before you talk me into cheap sex, Strozzi."

"It won't be cheap, baby. You'll feel like two million bucks before I'm done with you. It'll be the best night of your life, guaranteed."

"First of all, there's no way you're going to settle for one night. Is there some sort of consolation prize if it's not the best night of my life?"

"It will be, trust me."

"What happened to 'we work together so this can't happen?'"

"I know you're a bad idea, but I'm prepared to live with the consequences."

I think my panties spontaneously combust. Again. "Care to set a friendly wager? Let's make this interesting."

"Sure. What do you want to lose when I rock your world, baby?"

"Winner's choice, but nothing weird."

"Define 'weird'."

A sound near the doorway validates my suspicion Lily's lurking. "Can we work this out later? I'm having Sunday dinner with my family."

"Fair enough. Don't ruin dinner sharing your dirty girl thoughts. Save it for when we're alone."

The list of things I want to do to this man keeps growing, and it's getting out of control. Lily pounces the moment I step back into the room. "Who was that?"

"Coworker, setting up a meeting."

"Huh. Zack called to schedule a meeting on Sunday afternoon and it made you giggle. Sounded real professional." She laughs and raises her eyebrows. "Give me details."

"Hmmm. He's tough to describe. He's super-hot and," I struggle to find the words. "Zack is everything," I sigh, knowing my feelings are too complicated to explain to anyone when I can't understand them myself, so I change the subject. "Hey, I got a part-time job. You know I hate Allen Brothers. My friend Daniel's a reporter at The Press working the murder case and serial rapes. There may be others so he's doing this whole investigative journalist thing and I help with research. Zack's a detective, so we work together."

"That's what you do in your free time? What's wrong with you?" Mom's horrified and I foresee a lecture coming, but Lily's fascinated.

"It sounds super creepy. You should go back to delivering pizzas," Lily suggests. Now I've technically shared my secret, even if I'm hiding a whole hell of a lot.

***

There's been a steady exchange of flirty texts with Zack, and nothing could wipe the goofy smile from my face all week. We had fun last weekend so I've never been more excited for Friday night than I was this week. Trevor's still texting, but he's not calling anymore, so that's progress. A go-away text or call to say buzz off seems too cruel, but the guy won't take a hint, so things may come to that. The whole thing is stressful, but my fault for not being able to say "No thanks."

Sam hasn't responded to my proposed profile yet. The waiting is excruciating, I have no doubt he's going to agree. A few weeks ago,

I would've ignored these hunches, but my instincts have been dead-on recently: Trevor wants to be more than friends no matter what he says; Pete and Bob don't hesitate to break the law and plan to blame the employees for everything; the strange guy at the bar was dangerous; Daniel's trustworthy; and Trevor's annoying.

Figuring some things out calms a bit of the chaos swirling in me, although there's still a long way to go. Things could blow up any moment because of my secret life. Nobody knows what's going on, and I don't plan on making the details known until the killer's locked away. Still, things have been improving since I started working on the case. I know I'm doing the right thing. Taking action is therapeutic. And, most importantly, we're making progress for Brandon.

My package is in route to Daniel via registered mail after one quick stop on the way home.

One of the headhunters called to schedule a second interview this morning, so there's an end in sight at Allen Brothers. The job search is slow, but recruiters are calling and scheduling interviews, so it's only a matter of time. A nagging voice chirps in my head, insisting I'll still get in trouble because ignorance is no defense, which may be true, but I'm doing everything possible and have to hope for the best.

We're at the Middle Road Inn tonight to celebrate Nina's new job. Zack's here with friends who also know Nina and Luke, but we've decided it's better if nobody knows we're working together. If someone's watching me, we don't want to do anything to scare him off, like calling attention to my bodyguard. Luke's hot brother, Liam, is here tonight, and I flirt shamelessly. Nothing will come of it because then the game would end and nobody wants that.

Liam and I have been at this for a few years when we're both single, but the handful of drunken kisses we've shared were unimpressive. There's no chemistry, even though we always have fun together. Doing anything with Liam was off the table since I have a soft spot for Strozzi. Thing is, I learned he left the bar with some random piece of ass last Saturday when I invited him over.

Zack can go to hell.

Chapter 7

Zack

Cady flies around like a force of nature, dancing half the time she moves and always when standing still. Every guy here checks her out and that pisses me off. She's wearing an old Misfits tee that hugs all the right places. I'd give anything to peel it off of her with my mouth. I can't stop watching her, but at least I'm subtle.

"Who's Cady, and what'd you do to piss her off?" Dawn asks curiously.

"More importantly," Ryan demands, "why do you care if she's mad?"

So much for subtlety. I explain why Daniel wanted the surveillance and how she didn't appreciate it, which isn't a lie so much as not the whole truth.

Luke's brother arrives and spins her around for a full-body hug that goes on for way too long. I have an overwhelming urge to break Liam's neck. Doing my best to remain calm, I hit the bar to grab a round, giving my friends time to forget about my personal life and focus on other things.

I text Cady while waiting for the drinks but get no response. Everyone's talking about tattoos when I return and Liam asks when the next one's happening, but she insists she's one and done. It must be new because I've kissed every inch of her body and there was no ink anywhere.

"You have a tattoo? Where?" I ask without thinking.

"Wouldn't you love to know, Strozzi?" she answers smartly, walking away.

Ryan laughs, choking on his beer and Liam gives me a hard look. She's glued to his side all night, and I want to punch his stupid fucking face in the worst way.

"He's got it bad," Dawn tells Ryan when we're alone at the table. "I've never seen him like this."

"Holy shit, isn't she the chick you hooked up with at the lake? Guess you kept in touch."

"It's not like that. This is work."

I tell them about the threats Dan received and why he wants me with her, but it doesn't sound convincing even to me.

"Stop acting like it's such a bad thing to have feelings for another person. Seriously, get over yourself." Ryan laughs. "You used to have a heart, which shriveled up and died, but maybe there's hope for you yet."

He's still talking but I can't listen. I'm too focused on Liam who has his arm around Cady and she's smiling up at him.

"Who needs another?" she asks, heading to the bar.

"Hurry back, sweetness." Liam smacks her ass and I'm almost blind with rage.

I jump up before she passes. "Take a walk with me?" She agrees and I steer her through the crowd to the empty dining room upstairs. My heart races as I pull her into the darkened room, boxing her in with my arms. She leans against the wall, completely at ease.

"What's up?"

"What's the deal with Liam?"

"Why do you care?"

"You're hanging all over the fucker right in front of me."

"So? You're not interested, remember? You've made that *very* clear."

"Don't fucking play with me," I growl, leaning closer.

"Oh, I won't. Which is exactly why you're mad. Sorry, cowboy, I don't want you."

"You sure? I don't feel unwanted." It's the truth. Her breath comes a little quicker as I lean in, resting my hand on her hip. "Look me in the eye and tell me I don't turn you on."

She closes her eyes briefly before answering. "I'm not denying it, but we're not doing anything about it. You have plenty of volunteers to keep you busy."

"But I want you."

"I want you too. But I don't want to want you. Is that what you needed to hear?"

"What the hell? You run hot and cold. I don't get it."

"Me? Wow. Let me spell it out for you. You blew me off when we met, you turned me down and went trolling for ass right in front of me at the bar last week. I invited you over the other night, but you weren't interested because you were picking up randos at the bar. This," she waves between us, "is a game for you, but I'm not some toy."

"So you're trying to make me jealous with him?"

"No, I'm living my life and don't consider you at all."

The fuck? What a cheap shot.

A smart man would apologize for hurting her and admit he's crazy about her and ask for another chance, but not me. I'm at a loss for words, and pissed as all hell she'd "live her life" without me. So I kiss her. I half expect to get shoved or slapped, but she kisses me back.

She presses her lush little body into mine and my needy cock jumps to attention. No matter what she thinks, it's been a while since I've touched anyone else because she's the only one I want. Nobody else compares.

I press closer and she sighs, running her hands through my hair. This is where a smart man would admit he needs her and beg for mercy. But not me. The words die on my lips as I pull away, taking in her flushed cheeks and heavy breathing. I'm terrified of what might come out of my mouth so I go into asshole mode for self-protection.

"Good luck not thinking about me now." I turn to walk away but she grabs my shirt.

"Don't you dare leave yet. We're not done here."

My anger boils over. "Make up your mind. What do you want from me?"

"Stop hitting on me if you're not interested. Don't push me away then go all caveman when I talk to other guys. Leave me alone."

"Cady—"

"I'm not some good time to fall back on when you can't find something you like better." She ducks under my arm, disappearing into the darkness, and I'm left trying to figure out what the fuck just happened.

***

Three days Cady's ignored me since our little talk the other night. It hurts to know how little she thinks of me. I want her more than I've ever wanted anything, but I stay away for her sake, not mine. And I don't fuck every chick Luke sees me talk to in public, no matter what anyone thinks. I'm determined to forget about her until an unhappy Daniel forces me to confront this problem head-on.

"What'd you do, man?" No greeting or anything and he sounds exasperated. "Cady left the group text and canceled for tonight, and I know she's not mad at *me*." So much for keeping work separate from my personal life. I explain everything, starting with how we met last summer, and Daniel groans. "A fake number? What's wrong with you?"

No contact is one way to keep it impersonal, which is fucked up but not something I care to dissect. Cady was willing to work with me until I got in her face about Liam. She has every right to be angry, and I promise to fix things.

I call but she doesn't answer. The only acknowledgment to my voicemail is a picture of her middle finger so now I like her even more. She usually goes straight home after work for Sonny, so I'll sit out front where she'll have to acknowledge me.

There's no sweet smile or warm greeting tonight.

"What, Strozzi?" Those mesmerizing green eyes are missing their usual fiery spark and she looks exhausted. She's pale with dark circles under her eyes and I want to wrap myself around her so completely that nothing can touch her.

"I'm here to apologize for being an ass. I was totally out of line and I'm sorry. I brought pizza."

She doesn't respond right away, then says, "Fine."

"That's it?"

"Should I throw you a parade for displaying a bare minimum of self-awareness?" This is tougher than expected. Luckily, a neighbor waves her over before she can lob another attack.

"What's up, Carl?"

"Been waiting for you. Some guy was looking in your windows." Cady slants me a death glare, but Carl clarifies. "Not him. Shorter, kind of pudgy, blondish, was all I could see. Went around back and disappeared. I almost called, but knew you'd be home soon." We ask

Carl a few questions then Cady thanks him. She stops me at the door. "You said there's pizza." I grab it from the truck and she moves aside to let me enter.

Sonny greets her warmly, but he's clearly stressed, wound up, and panting. He must've been going wild while this guy was skulking around. We check the house carefully and nothing's missing or out of place. All doors and windows are secure so it's unlikely anyone was inside, but the whole thing's unsettling. I try to talk Cady into going elsewhere, but she refuses. She reasons, moving around won't deter him, but it could put her loved ones in his crosshairs.

"Come stay with me. I have plenty of room." We're walking to the deck hockey court and she erupts in laughter.

"Terrible idea, Strozzi. We can't even be in the same bar for a few hours."

"Okay. If you won't budge, I'll stay here."

"How's that any better? No."

"This is serious. What happens if he gets to you?" We go back and forth but her mind is made up. She doesn't want to hear it and I'm out of patience. "Jesus Christ, are you going to get raped and murdered out of spite because I pissed you off the other night? Have some sense." As soon as the words leave my mouth, I'm sorry, but it's too late. Cady's eyes cloud over and her expression shuts down.

"Fine."

"Cady, I'm sorry, I didn't mean --"

"Whatever." She calls Sonny and starts home without looking back.

I don't mean to make her life difficult, but apparently I can't help myself.

This is exactly why I never called.

Now we're stuck together and she's given me plenty of chances so I have to make things right.

***

Cady sets her anger aside long enough to get in a few hours of work, but she's jumpy and way too quiet. Sonny never leaves her side. I'm not sure if it's because she's sad, or due to my proximity. Maybe both. Work offers plenty of distraction since the bite marks aren't all she's found. There's a lot more because she's damn good at this.

Multiple cases had hair or fibers taken into evidence but never processed, and there are unidentified footprints at various crime scenes. Grace's case contained an unidentified DNA sample which was dismissed without discussion. The goal is to prove those biologicals aren't Brandon's, then match them to samples from other crimes to free him and catch the actual killer.

"You're going to give me an inferiority complex, Blackwell." She shrugs and I can't shake the guilt. Can we ever be friends? The thought of her not being in my life feels horrible, but friends won't ever be enough.

She's more relaxed after we smoke a blunt and eat some pizza. Cady hides stress well, but maybe smoking's more than fun. Maybe weed's the only thing relieving the tension enough for her to eat, sleep, and not implode from the pressure.

Her mood improves as the night goes on and I make her to laugh a few times until a noise outside grabs my attention. Sonny bolts to the back door and she turns off the light, crowding me at the window as we scare the hell out of two small raccoons scuffling on the patio. Their reaction is comical, but Cady doesn't seem to notice and sags against the wall, her head in her hands.

"You're safe." She nods, but she's shaking and my heart breaks a little. "I'm sorry you got dragged into this, but we're fixing it. And I'm sorry you're stuck with me, but this is temporary." *Well, not if I can help it. Wait, what?* Even in the dark, I can see the tears in her eyes. I'll deal with my own shit later.

"The last few weeks, I've been so afraid, all I do is hide at home. I didn't really mind, but now being here doesn't feel safe."

"This sucks, and it's probably worse since you hate me, but I'll keep you safe."

"What? I don't hate you, I–." She looks away but not fast enough to hide the blush climbing her cheeks. I wonder what it means. She takes a deep breath. "It's clear you don't want me around so I've tried to keep my distance and not be a bother."

"No, I— Why would you think I don't want you around?" Nothing could be further from the truth. I'd drape myself in this woman if I could. *What the fuck is going on in my head?*

"You would've called if... You know what? Whatever. I don't hold it against you. All that matters is I feel safe with you."

"You *are* safe with me."

"I know," she says with a sad smile. "Thank you." She leans close, planting a quick kiss on my cheek. She looks so defeated.

"I promise you're safe." I wrap my arms around her and she moves into me, burying her face in my chest. She feels so right in my arms, I never want to let her go.

Yeah, it makes me a selfish prick but I can't leave her here alone, scared and worried. Everything about this is so fucked up. I feel guilty for enjoying this, but maybe it's possible to redeem myself if I'm honest with her.

"I deleted your number even though I wanted to see you again." She looks up, a question in her eyes. "I'm bound to disappoint you and liked you too much to let that happen." Admitting it wasn't as hard as I expected. "Why did you leave?"

"I have my own problems."

"Like what?"

"Anxiety," she says quietly. "Occasionally it gets the best of me so I hide. I woke up positive I'd be humiliated somehow and couldn't talk myself down, so I ran away."

"I was so disappointed when you left. I was awake, but I didn't try to stop you."

She squeezes me, resting her head on my chest. "We're all kinds of messed up," she says softly and she's not wrong. My hand moves along her back and she relaxes a little. She feels so small and delicate, even though I know she's not.

"Go get some sleep. You'll feel better in the morning."

Those piercing emerald eyes look away. "Come with me?" Her voice is low. She's scared and I can't imagine what it costs to admit it.

"Sure," I say like it's no big deal, but my heart's racing so hard it might burst.

***

The bedroom ceiling's covered in those glow-in-the-dark star stickers we all had as kids, which makes me laugh.

"Don't judge, Strozzi. I like them."

"No judgment here. It gives the place a certain ambiance." She pokes me in the side, but doesn't respond. "What do you do for fun, Blackwell? Not video games and movies, what do you do when you can do anything at all?" I ask, hoping the answer is something I can deliver.

She mulls it over for a moment. "I love driving on back roads. Exploring. Getting lost."

There's too much space between us as I turn to face her. I grab her hand. "Call off tomorrow and let's go for a drive."

"Okay. Where?" She turns and her smile lights up the room even in the dark.

"Anywhere you want."

Her excitement is contagious as we discuss possibilities. She's still holding my hand so I take a chance and pull her close.

"I might be able to sleep tonight," she murmurs so quiet I barely make out the words.

"That's what I'm here for."

"Oh. I said that out loud?"

Planting another kiss on my cheek, she curls into me and I squeeze her tighter.

She shares Daniel and I are the only ones who know what's going on. She hasn't told anyone in her life the whole story, and keeping this secret seems to be wearing her down almost as much as the threats.

After being scared and worried for weeks, maybe months, there's still no end in sight and she's exhausted. Listening to her, it's obvious she feels weak for hiding things and having fears. I want to tell her how strong she is, and that she doesn't have to do this alone, but she's already asleep.

I'll be at her side until someone catches or kills the fucker, and hopefully after too, if I don't screw this up.

I stopped dating when my girlfriend cheated. Everyone assumes I was devastated and afraid to get hurt again, but I'd made no conscious decision to stop dating or avoid relationships. I just never met anyone who seemed worth the effort, and I was fine with it until I met Cady. Then I realized I have no idea what to do. I'm twenty-five years old and haven't been on a date since I needed a fake ID to buy a drink. Saying I'm clueless is an understatement, but erasing her contact was one of the biggest mistakes of my life.

I'm not letting her go again.

***

Cady

"Let's pretend we're making out to give Creepy Carl a thrill. He's always watching."

"Let's not. I don't want him thinking about either of us, especially me." Zack kisses my head and I don't know what to think, but wish he'd do it again. He's been here for over a week and it's so weird.

We're in this undefined place where I fall asleep in his arms and we hold hands while meandering around on long drives. We skipped the bar last weekend to watch movies and there was some serious snuggling, but nothing else. I want more of him, and don't know if that's possible for Zack.

Being with him is relaxing and fun, and exactly what I need but it's also confusing. We've gotten a lot of work done though, so now we're heading to Daniel's to update him. I still haven't told anyone what's going on, so my friends assume I'm caught up working on a new story and sneaking around because I've broken the dating moratorium.

Zack gets a call as we're walking in, and I ask Daniel about his blog while we wait.

"Crime was always an interest. Everyone teased me, but it wasn't creepy; justice is important." Learning this makes his family's story even worse.

"That comes through in your writing," I tell him. "I'm a huge true crime fan too. It started with the Zodiac killer."

"The Graysmith book, right? Good one. It's scary as hell nobody ever caught him."

"Right. Are you addicted to true crime shows? The way they catch killers is fascinating."

"Profiling too. It's voodoo and a miracle."

"The Pacific Northwest has tons of serial killers, so I guess that piqued your interest."

"Definitely, although the Coeur D'Alene case made the biggest impression. Even after studying people like Bundy, Bonin, Kraft, Corll, Duncan's a monster. Pure evil is hard to fathom."

"Everything about the case is disturbing. He should've never been free to hurt anyone. With such heinous priors, who the hell let him out of prison?"

"Exactly." Talk turns to Brandon. "People think I'm crazy and pathetic. Even my friends started believing I was blind to the truth. But I *know* he's innocent."

Daniel needs to hear this. "He's innocent and you'll prove it soon."

"That's why Zack's golden. He's never stopped working to help." The smile on his face radiates sincerity. At his core, he's a cheerful guy, and a different person from the first night we met. The evidence we're finding has done wonders, giving him hope and his color back. Daniel's easy to talk to, and for the first time I think we can be friends.

"I'm still nervous about you living alone," he says. "Promise you'll call Zack if anything happens, no matter how small. Trust me, he won't mind."

"Something weird happened last week, so he's staying with me." Daniel gives me a look. "It's perfectly innocent." But a goofy grin spreads across my face before I can stop it. "I think."

"Last week?" Apparently, Zack never mentioned it so I explain and Daniel laughs. "You two need to get over yourselves and go for it." I'd love to ask him a few questions but Zack returns. He tugs my hair as he passes and Daniel chuckles so I turn to my notes to hide the red creeping into my cheeks.

"Two of the oldest cases on the no biologicals list have unidentified hair." We've separated the cases into those with DNA evidence and those without, but we're moving some from the latter group to the former. Once there's a suspect, they can test his DNA against these samples. "The circumstantial evidence suggests it could be the same guy. There's nothing huge, but lots of little things form a pattern that can't be ignored." They stole alcohol from the wet bar in nine homes, always the cheapest vodka and gin, nothing else. More expensive brands of vodka and top-shelf spirits remained untouched. It seems the killer comes in while the dog is outside, crated, or not home, except for the local case.

"And it fits with the profile. He learns their routines, knows who's home and when."

"Four houses had unidentified footprints, estimated to be a man's size ten. Ten's smaller than average, so it may help identify a suspect."

"Kid's a natural," Zack says to Dan. "Excellent work, Blackwell." His sexy smile lures the butterflies in my stomach to more sensitive areas. He's looking at his phone, but Daniel stifles a laugh at what I can only assume is another stupid grin on my face, so I quickly turn to my notes.

"Here's the million-dollar question: Is this one killer or two? A lot of the cases scream two, especially Shaler." I detail my theory on how to best control the parents and keep the kids quiet.

"Are you a serial killer? How many people have you killed?" Daniel jokes. "A few crime scenes might suggest two, but it's a stretch."

"How are the rapes linked to the local murder?" I ask. "The link must be important."

"Nobody's talking, but rumor is evidence at the murder scene links specifically to one rape. All details are locked down," Daniel says.

"The street attacks were so bold and impulsive, but the home invasion was more calculated and careful," I note. "If they're linked, it's two guys. One guy isn't switching his MO and personality so drastically. This is multiple people."

Daniel looks skeptical. "I don't know. I'm no profiler."

My cheeks flush. "Me neither, but there's a formula, and...well it's hard to explain. Can you run it by your fed? We have to consider this scenario."

"Two guys," Zack muses. "The hothead raping women, the cool, calm one killing people. It makes sense."

Daniel's editor keeps calling, so we stop for tonight, which is for the best since Tim texted me scary news. The company's accountants have quit because the owners are making questionable decisions. The insurance company and bonding agency have both reduced coverage and started investigations as a result, so they won't have to pay if Allen Brothers get busted doing something stupid.

Clients are being contacted by the bonding agency then calling Tim. He's furious to have found out from a customer, but Pete and

Bob insist these are non-issues. The reality is we could be out of work soon if company assets are frozen during the investigation.

Bob assured Tim these "oversights" are misunderstandings because of the revolving door of inexperienced office help. Of course, they'll throw us under the bus.

"What's wrong?" Zack asks.

"Work sucks." I tell him all about the Allen Brothers saga, and he lets out a low whistle as I explain how I've been sending evidence to Daniel at work via certified mail. The arrival's recorded in the Press mailroom, so if Allen Brothers try to blame me, I'll have original documents and a record of concerns pre-dating their allegations to exonerate myself. I hope.

Back at my place, we're enjoying the stars while Sonny romps around the yard. I don't want to think about work, so I bring up any random topic that pops into my head and learn Zack's favorite animals are wolves, he loves gangster movies, used to race cars, and speaks Italian courtesy of his paternal grandparents. He learned I love lions, hate fruit in my baked goods, and fireflies make me happy.

"How'd you start doing detective work?"

"I got bored with construction, and a family friend offered me a chance to apprentice. I loved it, but honestly, sometimes it's pretty boring. It's mostly cheating spouses and sleazy business partners," he says. "What's your grown-up dream job?"

"Oooh, stunt car driver. I'd kill to do that."

"You're a little fucking crazy, and I dig it, baby."

"You haven't seen anything yet. There's a lot you don't know about me. Most of it good. Prepare to be wowed."

"I'm already wowed." He sits and pulls me onto the seat between his legs. "What do you do for fun besides shooting games, movies, and road trips?"

"I enjoy true crime shows, trashy novels, and catastrophic failure videos."

"So nothing normal?"

"Sometimes I go to the bar." I shrug. "You?"

"I hike and fish. I have a camp in Allegheny National Forest." Nature's foreign to me, but whatever.

We stop talking for a while, and it's quiet except for the music until he chuckles. "Are all these songs about stars, or is that my imagination?"

"This is my lying-in-the-hammock-looking-at-the-stars playlist."

His smile touches places deep inside of me. "Do you do everything with music?"

"Yeah, my life has a soundtrack."

"Interesting way to look at it."

"It used to help me not be alone with my thoughts, but I'm not so anxious anymore." *Why do I tell him whatever I'm thinking?* "Now it's always playing because music makes me happy and I love it."

"Both good reasons. Look. Make a wish."

I follow his hand to see a shooting star zip across the sky. It pulses brightly before fading into the inky darkness. Zack grabs my hands, lacing his fingers through mine, and my lips graze his jaw as I lay my head on his shoulder.

"I'll haunt you if I freeze to death, Strozzi," I warn, shivering but not from the chill.

"Don't worry. I won't let you freeze. We need your help with the case." A sarcastic comeback dies on my tongue when he kisses my cheek.

His body engulfs mine, warm and safe, and we discuss celestial bodies as though sitting here entwined is the most natural thing in the world.

Maybe it is.

***

An odd noise wakes me, but I relax when Sonny's tail hits the blinds. Okay, not a murderer. Zack had to work late and I was trying to start a new story, but I couldn't focus and dozed off fantasizing about him. All this togetherness has me incredibly hot and bothered, but I'm scared to make a move. I keep rehashing our kiss – okay, mini make-out session – at the bar, wondering why nothing more has happened.

Last night felt different and I almost kissed him while we looked at stars. Normally, I'd make a move instead of waiting and wondering, but the last few months have been so draining. With Zack here I feel safe enough to relax for the first time in a very long time. I don't want to do anything that could make things weird between us.

A noise in the hall gets my attention seconds before I hear his voice. "Sorry to wake you, I tried to be quiet."

I roll over in the semi-darkness and see him framed in the doorway, wearing only a towel. His body is a work of art. He's all hard lines and perfection. "It sounded like you were having fun." He leans against the doorframe, smirking.

"What?" I stammer, confused.

"Whoa, I was kidding, but you wouldn't be blushing if I was wrong."

"It's dark. You can't see a blush."

"Don't change the subject. You were having a dirty dream about me, weren't you?"

"Like you star in my sex dreams. As if." He totally does, but I'm not going to admit it.

His devilish grin makes my body flush with heat, and I have to get out from under the duvet. I get one foot on the floor before realizing I'm wearing a little tank and panties. The plan was to outline the next story then make dinner, not to fall asleep half-naked. By some miracle of fate, both of my boobs remained inside the cami, but I'm still exposed.

"We both know it's true." Zack's trying to act casual but the way he's rearranging his towel speaks volumes. It's now or never, and I walk over to him to stand way too close.

"If I agree, are you going to do something about it?" I run my fingers along the edge of the towel, watching his pupils dilate.

"Are you putting the moves on me, cupcake?"

"What do you think?"

Zack shakes his head, backing me into the bedroom. "Took you long enough," he mumbles as his lips land on mine. I sigh into his kiss, giddy with anticipation like I've won some sort of sex lotto.

In seconds, we're on the bed, bodies fused, devouring each other, and he feels better than I remember. He pulls back to remove my shirt then his mouth never leaves my body, not even when he tells me all the dirty things he's going to do to me.

His hands are strong and sure and everywhere at once. My whole body lights up when he skims my clit through the thin lace of my panties. He tears them off in a flash but keeps teasing and I can't take it.

"More," I beg and he complies, driving two fingers inside me, making me cry out at the unexpected pleasure.

"Fuck, you're soaked, baby. So hot and wet."

"Only for you," I pant and he groans into my mouth. Nothing has ever felt so good and it's insane; I've never been so hot. My whole body shakes as his thumb circles my clit in time to his fingers pumping.

"Come for me," he commands.

"You're not the boss of me," I stammer.

"Tonight I am," he growls and that's all it takes. I've never come as fast or as loud as I do on his hand, and he's only getting started. He kisses his way down my body and I shudder under his lips, sucking his fingers to taste myself for the first time.

"You're so beautiful, baby. So fucking perfect." His voice is rough, his expression reverent. His eyes flutter closed when he tastes my desire, then fly open again and I can't look away.

Staring into his eyes as he indulges me is hotter than anything I've ever imagined. Every nerve in my body fires as his tongue moves in slow, deliberate strokes. "You're so sweet, baby. So good. I could eat you all night."

Sounds like a plan, except I'd probably die from pleasure overload. His enthusiasm makes me feel irresistible and when I realize he's stroking himself as he feasts on me, it's the hottest fucking thing ever and I tell him. He groans in response, hot and needy, and the vibrations make me see stars.

He works my body like it was engineered for his pleasure. His kisses are playful, soft, and teasing, then his tongue penetrates me with surprising force, kinetic and insistent. I'm losing my mind, but he's still talking. "I love your pussy, baby. I never want to stop."

Every word stokes my desire until I explode, pushing myself into his mouth, pulling his hair, and gasping his name over and over like a mantra. Euphoria crashes through my body in rapturous waves, leaving me breathless and dazed as he feathers soft kisses all over my sensitive pussy.

"You are so fucking hot. I could watch you come all night," he murmurs, nibbling his way back up my body.

"Well, I could probably come all night since you're really good at that." It's so erotic to taste myself on his mouth and I kiss him until I regain control of my limbs. Heat flashes in his eyes as I push him back, stroking him. He's playing with my hair, wrapping it around his fist as I wrap my lips around him. I hear his sharp intake of breath as I explore his delicate skin, soft as velvet. "Fuck." His voice is rough with desire. "Your mouth is heaven."

His words fill me with need all over again and I've never wanted to please a man more. Nothing has ever made me feel as powerful as his hot, dirty words, and the way his body moves reacting to my touch.

His strong arms wrap around me, pulling me on top of him so he can bury his tongue in me from behind. He's insatiable and I've never felt sexier. Having him in my mouth while he eats me is the most amazing feeling, and I come again almost immediately, choking his name around his cock.

I love feeling his hand on my head and the way he roars oaths as he goes wild, but I love the way he kisses me after even more. Hard and commanding, like he can't stop.

He grabs my hands, threading his fingers through mine before kissing my knuckles, and I have a funny feeling in my chest.

This man is going to destroy my heart, but I couldn't stay away if my life depended on it.

***

Dinner never happened so we're sharing a piece of cake while leftovers heat up. I'm on the counter in Zack's shirt while he stands between my legs in nothing but boxer briefs, which are one of humanity's greatest inventions, right up there with fire and the wheel. Maybe even better.

"You thought I hated you," I scoff, rolling my eyes. "If I didn't like you, I'd have inhaled this cake while you were in the shower." He laughs but I'm not kidding. "Cake's important. I don't share it with just anyone."

"Now I feel special." His hands rest on my hips and pull me closer until his mouth is inches from mine.

"Good, you need to feel appreciated so we can do that again."

"Oh, we're certainly doing that again." He grins. "I'm disappointed I have to wait to take this further, but also ecstatic you don't have condoms." The only stores still open nearby are gas stations and I don't trust gas station condoms. Driving any further seems like a waste since we could spend that time trading orgasms in other ways.

"Calm down there, skippy. I usually have some but ran out," I tease.

"Been busy?" He's laughing but something about this moment makes me want to be honest.

"If you must know, they expired. I didn't replace them because there's been an extended dry spell." That's not an admission I could imagine making to anyone else, but the anxious person inside me isn't as self-conscious with him as she is with everyone else.

He's grinning like an idiot. "I ruined you for other men, didn't I?"

Yeah, but I'm not admitting it to your super-sized ego. I lean back with a sigh when his fingers breach my channel once again. "No, I'm just picky, okay? I'm not as…" I stop, losing my train of thought completely when his fingers curl, caressing a happy spot.

"Not as what, baby? Tell me."

"Not as *sociable* as you."

"I needed you tonight. It's been a while since I've been *sociable*."

"I had no idea."

"Yeah. There's this girl I really like and I can't even look at anyone else."

I'm melting at when he leans in for a kiss. It's languid and sensual, not plundering and raw like before, but it's every bit as hot.

Chapter 8

Cady

Too bad calling in sick isn't an option since I called off last week. Waking up to Zack's face buried between my thighs is a fine consolation prize though, and the second round in the shower is even better. The man loves to eat my pussy and he's incredibly good at it, especially considering the rumors.

"They're not rumors," he says, jarring me from my reverie.

Dammit. I have to stop saying what I'm thinking around him, it's bound to lead to humiliation. "I heard there are rules, Strozzi."

His eyes are dark with desire when they meet my gaze. "There are rules, but not here, *mia stellina*." He points between us. "Anything goes with you and me."

He promises to buy condoms and I promise we won't stay out late tonight. It's Randy's birthday, and I already had plans for dinner and drinks, but Zack and I have plans of our own for later.

***

Trevor's still texting and Sam hasn't responded to the proposed profile yet. Work goes from bad to worse. The one bright spot is Tim solving the mystery of why Gary Babinski targeted me.

The day he was fired for catcalling women, I was the only female ABC employee on-site so he assumed I was the complainant. In reality, I had no idea about his behavior or dismissal. If Babinski thought he got fired because of my complaint, that explains the rat. It doesn't feel right though. I'm worried there's a bigger threat. Still, after months of fear, one mystery is solved. These are all important issues, but it's nearly impossible to focus on anything besides Zack.

***

Steph's teasing me about bailing early when Zack leans against my back. "Ready to get out of here?"

"I don't know. What do you want to do?"

"You," he says, and I can't help but laugh. "Those guys at the next table were staring at your ass. Blue shirt still can't tear his eyes away. I should punch him."

"Give him a break, Strozzi. This ass is impossible to resist, and you of all people should know." I smile up at him.

"True, but nobody else can enjoy it." His lips find the spot on the back of my neck that makes me come apart. Nobody else has ever touched me there, but he has some primal instinct leading to magic points on my body. The sensation's almost too much, so it takes a moment to find my voice again.

"Are you calling dibs, cowboy?"

"I have exclusive rights and VIP access," he states as we head out.

Two girls rock up to the door, crowding him as we exit. They're all giggles and thrusting cleavage, especially when the shorter one leans forward so we can all see down her top effortlessly. It's maybe five degrees out, and her outfit would fit a Barbie doll. Brrr.

"Hey, Zack, we've missed you," she titters as he nods, pivoting to steer me around them. The frigid night air is exhilarating after the humid warmth of the bar.

"Well, aren't you popular?"

"She's . . . someone I know."

"It's none of my business."

"Sure it is, and I love I'm not the only one who gets jealous." A smile tugs the corners of his mouth.

"I'm not jealous." I want to claw their eyes and feed them their push-up bras, which is completely normal.

"You're an awful liar."

"Fine. I've never been more jealous in my life. Okay?"

His smile makes my heart flutter. "Wasn't expecting that, but I love it. I can't wait to get you alone."

He crushes me against the truck, his mouth capturing mine, sweet and hot, and cinnamon-y. Gentle at first, the kiss becomes more demanding as his tongue explores until a frantic urgency overtakes us

His eyes close when my hands brush the warm skin above his jeans, but he pushes them away. "Don't get handsy here, we're not doing it in the truck. At least, not tonight."

"You'd be eating those words if it wasn't freezing tonight."

"Words are *not* what I'd be eating if I was getting you naked in the truck." His insinuation sends a thrill through me and a quiet moan escapes my mouth. We share a soft kiss as I play with his hair. Need's a terrible weakness, the enemy of my independence, but I love feeling it for Zack.

He's quiet, smiling down at me while his finger traces my cheek. "I want to take care of you, Cady, and that scares me."

"I want you to take care of me and it scares me, too."

His smile gets even bigger before I'm lost in another kiss.

***

Zack

We're at Cady's naked and devouring each other before the door shuts. I've never been more eager for anything than I am when rolling on the condom. I'm overwhelmed with her sweet scent and how soft she is under my hands: by the way her lips feel on my neck and the heat of her skin against mine. She's so responsive to even the lightest touch, nobody's ever been so good for my ego. I ease in slowly and she gasps. "Is this okay, baby?"

"It's perfect. Now, fuck me like you mean it. I've waited months for you." That's all it takes for me to lose control and get lost in her. It's impossible not to. She's incredible.

"More," she begs against my lips. "Nothing else could be this good," she moans. "Don't ever stop. I need your cock, Zack," she begs.

I feel like a superhero. The whole night is rough and wild, and perfect, like her. Before the night's over, I find the tattoo: a silvery-pink sparkly star about the size of a quarter on her hip that's completely Cady. Last night, I was too preoccupied to notice the damn thing.

"We should hang out more often," she says casually and we laugh until it hurts, then I kiss her until there's nothing else in the world.

"Buona notte, bellisima."

"Did you say good night and call me pretty?"

"Beautiful."

She flushes, burying her face in my chest. "What does *mia stellina* mean?"

"My little star because I think of you whenever I see one."

The night we met, we sat on the beach looking at the constellations for hours before things got physical. I don't remember anything else about that night except her.

"You're sweet." She kisses my cheek and I grin like a fool.

I'm stuck in my head after she falls asleep, my mind in overdrive. What would it be like to watch movies and take drives and fall asleep with her every night? Really fucking awesome. Finding the people making her life miserable and making them sorry would be beyond satisfying. I'd destroy entire cities for her, and that's dangerous. I've been with more women than I've bothered to count, but she's the only one I've ever made love to. The only one who's special. Tonight, I feel like a god with her in my arms, and I want it all.

But this is so fucking intense, it's tough to process. Sex is fun, but it was always just sex. Until now. With Cady, it's practically a religious experience, unlike anything else. Everything about her shatters my expectations about love and relationships, and being alive.

She makes me need things I've never wanted and feel things I don't understand. I never have feelings for anyone, but I have lots for her and they're wild and scary. Despite the fears, everything about this seems right. Before, casual was fine because I never wanted more with anyone else, but I want everything with her. So what now?

I'm trying to wrap my head around all of this when she bolts awake with a muffled shriek, scaring the living shit out of me.

"What's wrong?"

"Nothing," she mumbles. "A bad dream." She falls back, apologizing and embarrassed.

I want to make it better, but don't know what to say so I hold her tighter. She buries her head in the crook of my neck and all the tension in my body evaporates. This is one of few times in my life I've ever truly felt needed, and I love it but don't know how to say that either.

"Are you okay?" Her hair is so soft and thick, I want to wrap it around me.

"Yeah, but it's a shame you have to keep asking. I'm usually way more fun."

"Are you kidding? Tonight was a blast. The dirty parts were my favorite, but the talking's good, too."

Her laugh is my favorite sound. "I like having you around, cowboy."

"And I love being around, *mia stellina*. Relax and fall asleep with me."

***

Cady

Tuesday goes by in a blur until a letter comes from the IRS. Then time stops. Abby is terrified and I go numb. This is when the hammer drops. There's an immense relief when we read that one of the subcontractors needs to catch up on back taxes, so part of every payment we make will go to the IRS. I'm not in any trouble— yet— and can breathe again, returning my focus to helping Daniel catch a killer. Collaboration may be tricky since Zack's got my head spinning. These two weeks together were fun. Friday was perfect. Things were fine Saturday morning, but then he disappeared. He sent a few apologetic texts claiming to be super busy at work. I'm not buying it. Clearly, he's avoiding me.

I know what he's like, yet I still fell hard. Those vibes scare guys away, especially guys like Zack. Nina mined Luke for details about Zack's past, and it's not a pretty picture. His hook-ups are strictly physical, and there's rarely a second encounter. He doesn't date, kiss, eat pussy, or take women home. The fake phone number is an old favorite, so there's not a single shred of intimacy in his life whatsoever.

Now I'm confused because that wasn't my experience with him. He broke every one of his rules, except we didn't go to his place, but he tried to get me there. He even said the rules don't apply, so what game is he playing?

He made me want to take a chance, and I was stupid enough to believe this could be real. He's the least of my problems, though, despite being the most painful.

I have to find a new job, catch a killer, come clean with everybody since the lie I'm living grows every day, then come to terms with being unable to trust my rotten judgment.

There's no room here for a sexy detective who'll destroy my heart.

I'm jumping at every noise and cringing at shadows, sleeping only a couple of hours at a time because any longer, and the stirrings of a panic attack wake me every time.

I've got one foot in a hot bath when Trevor calls. I'm in no mood to coddle him and ignore it. When the phone rings again, I answer, expecting Abby, but it's Trevor. *Should've checked, dummy.*

"Hey, baby girl," he drawls. He apologizes again for Owen's interruption and I assure him once more the evening was fine. He's pitiable because of his brother. Trevor's handsome and wealthy, nobody would ever guess the weight he carries.

"No, Owen totally ruined the plan. I was hoping for at least second base." *Eww, no thanks.* Just friends, he'd insisted. What a shameless, unapologetic liar.

"Daddy can't wait to get his hands on you." No freaking way, creep. "And my mouth." Wow. That sure escalated. "Get naked and touch yourself, pretend it's me." Phone sex seems so awkward, I've never been willing even with guys I like. This is far more revolting since I'm naked, even if he has no idea. This is getting out of hand.

"Yeah, no. We're not doing *any of those things*. We're practically strangers. "

"Maybe I'll surprise you and show up one of these nights."

"No, I'm an old-fashioned girl."

He has the nerve to laugh like I'm kidding. "We'll see," he chuckles.

Oh really, fucker? I'm not playing games, here.

"Daddy will be back soon because I can't help myself where you're concerned."

"Not a good idea. I've got tons of work events and no free time. Hey, I've got to run."

"Promise you'll think about my mouth on your body until I get to taste you?"

The thought makes me retch. *Won't be able to think of much else, but not for the reason you think, creep.*

He doesn't deserve another minute of my time. I disconnect, reflecting on my newfound appreciation for Owen's interruption. Who knows what might've happened? Trevor might be rich and cute, but he's an even bigger loser than the usual idiots. The phone pings again. *Please don't be Trevor.* I look down and heave a sigh of relief and irritation. It's Zack, texting. *About time, asshole.* But I'm not giving in that easy.

Zack: Need to show you pics. Okay to stop by?
Me: NO.
Zack: Five minutes away will be quick.

Time to put on something sexy, but for me, that's music, not clothes. I take too long choosing a playlist and get clothes on in the nick of time. Jumping back into my jeans commando, I skip the bra with my sheer blouse. Let the fucker see what he's missing and *if* he apologizes, I won't accept. He's a bad idea and I'm done being a fool for him.

The bell rings and I take a deep breath before opening the door. The mere sight of him gets me hot. His dark hair's messy like someone's been running their hands through it, and I'm irrationally angry at the thought. The thin shirt hugging his body makes my knees weak.

"Hey." One word is enough to create a simmering heat in my center. He looks like he knows I'm not wearing underwear and I shift under his gaze.

His expression is hungry as his gaze roams my body. No man has ever looked at me with such naked desire, and for the first time I realize he doesn't have all the power here.

His gaze penetrates me like he knows what I'm thinking, but that's impossible. A thrill runs through me as he closes in, backing me up against the wall. *Put your hands and mouth on my body*, I will silently, testing the mind-reading thing.

"Are you alone?"

"Why—" I freeze when the phone rings, relief flooding me when the screen flashes Evan's name. Zack's eyes darken.

He picks up my phone, silencing it and tossing it on the couch. "Fuck Evan. Who's he?"

"You don't get to be jealous after ghosting me *again*."

The flash of temper in his eyes stokes the fire inside me. He presses closer and the pressure around me changes as if the air's being sucked out of the room.

"I've never been more jealous in my life," he admits, his eyes searching mine.

"Good, I hope it drives you crazy. "

"What if I told you to forget him?"

My body hums in anticipation as he inches closer. He doesn't know Evan's my brother, and even though I'm pissed at him, this jealous tantrum is entertaining.

"Forget who?" I peer through my lashes, mustering an innocent gaze.

"Evan, Liam, Trevor, all of them. You've been mine from the first time I saw you. You just didn't know it," he growls, then his lips are on mine.

God, I'd missed him the last few days. His kiss is urgent and demanding and begs for release. I kiss him as if my life depends on it, and heat shimmies through me making every inch of my body react to him. When he pulls his mouth away, all of me is disappointed. He tilts his head back slightly, cupping my face in his hands.

"I know you feel it, too," he says softly, almost to himself. "The night at the diner, I was so pissed you were on a date and it wasn't with me," he admits, as his fist tugs my hair.

"I wanted you to be jealous then," I admit. "But now, it doesn't matter. You can't waltz in and out of my life. We're done." I bite his bottom lip harder than intended, but he laughs.

"No, *mia stellina*, we're just getting started."

"You're not the boss of me." I'm trying to reassure myself since I can't stop kissing him. "I've wondered if you ever thought about me," my voice is too quiet and telling him this pierces my heart. "So many times."

"You're all I think about. Kissing you, touching you, holding you, fucking you." Kissing him is the last thing I should be doing, but I can't pull myself away. "Letting you walk away is my biggest regret. I'm so sorry, Cady."

"Sorry means nothing. You got laid Friday night, then you disappeared, *again*. You're the worst bodyguard ever. Luckily, I'm still alive, no thanks to you."

Those dark eyes are sad and searching. "I didn't want to leave, but I don't talk about my feelings."

"So instead of talking about *anything* else, you run away and hide? Give me a break. I didn't ask to talk about your stupid feelings."

"After the first time, I was trying to do the right thing. To stay away so you wouldn't get hurt. But I need to be near you. It doesn't make sense, but I can explain." He pauses, running his hands through his hair. This is interesting because I've never seen him flustered before.

"This ends now while I still have a tiny shred of dignity left because I'll never forgive myself if I let you hurt me again." His expression becomes sad, but I give him nothing.

"We're good together. This could be something if you let it."

"If *I* let it? *Me*?" *Wrong thing to say, pal.*

"I keep fucking this up," he mumbles, more to himself. "Look, I'm not great with words but I can show you how much I care if you let me."

"Please stop," I shake my head. "Before you wear me down, okay? I don't need this."

"Baby, please –" His phone rings and he scowls, then tosses it on the couch with mine. "Fuck. I don't have long. I need to get to work."

"Wait, what? You're supposed to be protecting me. You come here and do this, then leave. What the hell, Strozzi?"

"Sorry, baby, I'm on call. I have to go back to work. But think how sweet it'll be the next time we see each other."

"Next time you'll probably disappear for good if I'm dumb enough to sleep with you again." Something flashes in his eyes and I'd like to think it's fear. I want to wrap my arms around him and tell him it'll be okay, so what the hell is wrong with me?

His hands frame my face and I feel his touch everywhere. "Don't say no. Even if you won't say yes, don't say no." His gaze is locked on mine and I want to believe him.

It's stupid and pathetic and the dumbest thing I could do, but I want to believe he means every word and is capable of changing. I've never wanted anything more. The phone buzzes again and he runs his hands through his hair. "Fuck. The timing sucks, but you need to hear this. We didn't know you met Trevor the same night you met Daniel. Not until I went to the bar and one of the bartenders tipped me off."

"So?"

"I ran Trevor and things don't add up."

"What are you saying?" The sinking feeling in my gut gets worse as he explains.

"Trevor's company doesn't exist. He doesn't hold any licenses with any regulating bodies. He didn't graduate from Stanford, has no driver's license, and doesn't own the loft or any other property. I found his birth certificate and social security number, but nothing else. No bank account or credit cards. Not a damn thing." Oh. My. God. "Making up a better job to pick up girls is one thing, but showing up where Daniel's meeting you can't be a coincidence," Zack says, frowning.

"Yeah, he hangs out there all the time. We didn't exchange contact information or anything until we met again at the Middle Road Inn." *Crap. Another guy making a fool of me.*

"Only one bartender knew him, mostly because he threw him out Thursday. Said he's been there only two or three times. The first time being the night you were there."

"He's got the wrong guy, then. Trevor went home to SoCal—"

"No, he didn't. Who's the tall blond bartender? Crazy beard, looks like a Viking?"

"Jeff."

"He was a complete dick. What's his deal? How well do you know him?"

"Why do you care about Jeff?"

"Because you're mine and I'm a jealous motherfucker." Zack never breaks eye contact and I want to climb all over this man.

"I'm not yours, Strozzi. You tanked your chances." His face remains impassive, but the pain in his eyes hits me hard, so I throw him a bone. "Jeff's like a big brother. We'd get stupid drunk, and he'd make sure we all got home safe. Drove me himself more than once. He always chased off creeps and guys who tried to get us to leave with them. He's a good guy."

"There are no truly good guys. They all want to get in your pants. Some are less obvious about it."

"Isn't that what you're doing right now? Trying to get into my pants?"

"Don't change the subject."

"Well, that's a 'yes.'"

"He cares an awful lot for a bartender at a place you haven't been to for years."

"We were friends. No. We were friendly. He's someone I know." I throw his words back, enjoying the spark of anger in his eyes. "Why does it matter?"

"Because I don't share." Possessive is normally a turn-off, but coming from Zack it turns me on so freaking much, which makes me angry. I move to shove him away but he grabs my hands, pinning them to the wall over my head. His body presses into mine and I've never been so wet. I love being at his mercy. "I'm jealous, get used to it," he warns, staring into my eyes as if daring me to defy him.

"I don't have to do anything," I scoff.

"You do. You just don't know it yet."

What a dick. I want to kick him out, but I want to impale myself on his impressive cock even more. "I think I fucking hate you."

"You fucking love me, but you're not ready to admit it yet." He has an answer for everything, which pisses me off more, but I'm also scared he's right.

"Zack, we can't–" He shuts me up with a kiss and I want to pull away but can't. I need to consume him like I've been poisoned and his tongue is the antidote. My body melts into his and I can't think straight.

"I need you, Cady. Be mine, baby," he murmurs. "All mine."

My body is a traitor, begging for more as a familiar tingle flushes through me. His body presses against mine, his hot mouth sucking on my neck. *Stop rubbing against him and make him explain himself, dammit. Have some self-respect.* "What do you want from me?"

"Everything, baby. Everything you've got." His words touch something deep inside of me I want to ignore. When his fingers dip inside my shirt and skim my bare back, I fall apart with hot shocks of pleasure wracking my body as I choke his name. "Fuck, yesss," he drawls, kissing me until I'm limp in his arms.

He smiles, resting his forehead on mine. "I knew you missed me too."

Chapter 9

Zack

There was a nervous buzz inside me all the way to Cady's. I resent anyone having this effect on me. Besides getting hard, I've never had a physical reaction to anyone. In sixth grade, I asked Jenny Pawler to the spring fling. That was the first time I asked a girl out and the last time I was nervous about it. Until now. Staying away until I got my shit figured out seemed like the right thing to do, but that hurt her, which was exactly what I tried to avoid. Hiding was stupid, and I wouldn't blame her for slamming the door in my face. Maybe it's what I want since the alternative is a relationship I'll probably fuck up and regret. I have no business complicating her life. But she's an adult so if she wants to ride my dick and hate my guts, who am I to deny her?

She opens the door in some filmy little black top. It's practically transparent, the top buttons open in invitation and her jeans aren't buttoned, either. If she's not alone, I'll drag the fucker out like a caveman before claiming every inch of her body with my mouth until she begs for mercy.

She has the most spectacular breasts I've ever seen, but I'm always drawn to her eyes first. Deep green and shimmery, like emeralds, the spark in them makes me want to do unholy things to her succulent body. My need for her burns inside me, unlike anything I've ever known.

I want her to take a chance on me, but I also love that she has enough self-respect to make me beg. It takes every ounce of my self-control not to slam her against the wall and peel those tight jeans off of her fine ass, but she deserves so much more. I want to be the one who gives it all to her. She's smart and sexy and I want her to love me, not only fuck me.

Everything about this is crazy. Nobody's ever had this kind of power over me. Sure, it's a massive ego boost when she's begging for my cock, but nearly coming in my pants eating her put me in my place. Nothing like that's ever happened before, but she's so damn self-conscious, seeing her uninhibited blows my mind and knowing *I* do that to her is almost too much.

"I can be back by five, six am and we won't get out of bed," I say. "There are so many things I need to do to you."

"What? You can't leave." She looks adorable sulking, but she's not angry. She's trying to get me out of my jeans, but I have to get to work.

"Guaranteeing my starring role in your fantasies."

"You had it before you disappeared. You don't get it back that easily. Not after you left me alone with a murderer chasing me, dick."

"If I thought you were in any danger, I would've sent Kyle or Ryan. If apologizing and being honest doesn't do it, what do I have to do?"

She shrugs. "Get inventive."

"You're fucking ruthless, woman, but this is important, remember Trevor?"

"Fine," she pouts as I pull back to get my phone.

"Your buddy," I begin, "*Jeff* pulled up the security footage and made screenshots. This is steakhouse guy." I see the light bulb go on over her head. "I'm sorry. We know someone hacked Daniel and knew you two were meeting, so it was simple enough to set you up."

She takes a deep breath before saying while staring at the phone, "I worried about that the night I met Daniel. I asked, 'What if he's here tonight, following you?' But Daniel was so sure he leaves town after a kill. How could I miss it?"

"Con men dupe people every day, and it costs them much more than pride. There's no way you could've known. Trevor heard you mention the other bar, casually brought it up, then hung around there waiting. It's a break that will help us find the killer. He's not the caller, so as long as you're safe, it's a good thing," I assure her.

"Feels different from here," she mutters.

"This isn't the worst thing, even if it feels like it. For the first time, we have someone to connect to Daniel's killer. A tangible lead, and we have this only because of you." I'm going to enjoy crushing Trevor's windpipe for putting this defeated look on her face.

"How did he know things about me? We had so much in common."

"These guys know how to charm people, they're actors. He probably followed your lead to find the right things to say." I run my finger down her cheek. "I'm sorry." I'm unsure what else to say, but I want to go back twenty minutes to her angry kisses and soft hands on me when there was a smile on her face.

"Is he the killer?"

"He may be hired help."

"Or the killer."

"Anything's possible," I say. "Daniel knows, but we should get together. Is tomorrow good?"

"Yeah." She rubs her hands over her face, frustrated. "What a fucking creep."

"Are you okay?" Of course, she's not, but I'm floundering here.

"Extremely pissed off, but it's fine. The rage will help me focus."

"That's slightly disturbing and seriously hot." She almost smiles and it's quiet as we look at one another.

"Why didn't you call?"

"I wanted to tell you in person—"

"Not about Trevor."

I twine my fingers through hers, holding both hands, and love how it feels. "Cady, I don't know what's wrong with me, but I'll do better. I swear on my life." I pull her into a tight hug, planning to say more, but my mind goes blank when she lays her head on my chest.

The last thing I want to do is leave, but I'd be the world's biggest asshole if I didn't work for Kyle tonight when his wife is in labor. There's sadness in her eyes when she looks up but it's not because of Trevor. I feel almost guilty for convincing her to give me another chance and that's the moment I realize I'm completely, hopelessly, without a doubt in love with this woman. She's studying me carefully and I'm braced for more questions, but then she surprises me.

"Liam's a friend and Evan's my brother. There's nobody else. There hasn't been anyone else since before we met at the party."

That makes me insanely happy so I pick her up for one more kiss. It'll make me a few minutes late for work, but I don't care.

**

Cady

Zack's gone, but my heart hasn't stopped racing. I'm terrified to open myself up to him any more than I already have, yet I can't stay away. The Trevor news is stunning and I'm struggling to sort this information. He seemed so laid back and I never got a bad vibe. How could I be so stupid? In hindsight, both chance meetings were so utterly contrived and our shared interests so shallow, yet I was oblivious. I'm not sure if I'm more pissed off at Trevor or myself. And irrationally, I'm angry at Zack for witnessing my moment of weakness.

Why me, anyway? To mess with Daniel, sure, but Trevor and I are strangers. *Even the death of a stranger will weigh heavy if a psycho convinces a person they're responsible.* Zack's warning rings in my head.

There are so many details from the first night I've never considered. I first noticed him holding the door, but did he walk up the street, get out of a car, come from a nearby building? There were no open spots by the bar so I'd parked a couple of blocks away. He could've done the same. He didn't catch a Wednesday flight if Jeff threw him out Thursday night, so he's probably still in town. I doubt he'd help Trevor but I don't know him well so I have to speak to him. Jeff's off tonight, so I leave a message with Lenny, the owner. A lot rests on whether there's any connection between those two.

Trevor said he's twenty-seven but could pass for anything from college-aged to early thirties. Our conversations were the basics you discuss when getting to know someone: places you've traveled, hobbies, music, simple things. We talked so much, but were the things he said true? In retrospect, he copied me in every way. We're both huge Tarantino fans, but *Pulp Fiction* is his favorite. I'm a diehard fan of mob movies and his favorite's *The Godfather*. I love 3 Doors Down and surprise, "Kryptonite" is one of his favorite songs.

As a kid, the book that scared me the most was King's "It." Trevor hasn't read the book, but he loves the movie. He mimicked my favorite things, but his choices are generic pop culture picks, similar to mine, but not the same. He used the most popular examples in each case, the things people know even when they haven't seen the movie, don't love the band, or never read the book. He only mentioned things in popular culture.

The humiliation intensifies as I dissect his personality. Trevor Maines, or whoever he is, thought he could get something over on me, but he picked the wrong person. The best part is the irony of choosing to meet me at Gooski's. The set-up seems clever, but he couldn't've known Jeff watches over the girls in his bar. If Jeff seems off, I'll reassess, but right now it's likely Trevor made a huge mistake.

The family stuff had a ring of truth. Owen could be a friend or cousin, but brother feels right. I write down everything I can recall: mannerisms, quotes, details of the loft. Panic spikes in my chest when a thought strikes: Owen could be a killer. The guy's so spooky with his dead eyes and dark energy, but it's so much worse when I recall what he said: *"Dammit, I've been calling, I want in on this."*

At the time, his words didn't register because I was uncomfortable, but maybe Owen wasn't talking about traveling. Was he talking about *me*? The implications are terrifying.

What did he want 'in on' exactly?

I was alone with those psychos and nobody knew where I was. Owen's words ring in my head and a wave of nausea hits me. They could've done anything and I would've simply vanished. I barely make it to the bathroom before my dinner comes up in violent spasms.

What the hell did I get myself into now?

Trevor dragged me into this, and he's going to regret it forever, even if making him pay takes the rest of my life. The bathroom floor is cold and hard, but nothing registers. I need to talk about this, but my shaking hands keep dropping the phone.

Daniel knows the killer best, but Zack's voice is the one I need to hear. He's probably busy and I shouldn't interrupt. A text ping echoes off the tiles, making me jump. My messed up stomach does a flip, and I hug myself, trying to stop the shaking. *Please don't be Trevor.*

Zack: You okay?
Not at all. How close did I come to dying, or worse?

My trembling fingers can't even hit the right keys to respond, but one thought breaks through the din in my brain: Zack texted me at the exact moment I'm falling apart. Is it coincidence or proof of our connection?

Me: Not really
The phone rings instantly. His voice is reassuring as I jump at every noise, no matter how small. I explain everything, stumbling over my words, and Zack is pissed, stringing together the most innovative list of curses ever uttered. He calms my nerves enough for me to climb into bed, but only after stacking glasses in front of the doors and on all windowsills. Nobody's getting in without waking me.

His tone soothes me, and he even makes me laugh before things get serious again.

No, I don't want to go anywhere. I'm staying right here, even if I never sleep again.

No, you can't install an alarm tomorrow, I have to talk to my landlord first.

No, I won't go to your house because it has an alarm.

My answers frustrate him, but they won't change.

"I'm not leaving your side until those fuckers are dead or locked up for good. If you don't want me around, then I'll get someone else from Shields—"

"No, I want you, Strozzi. Nobody else." We both understand what I mean, right?

"Good. I want to be next to you at all times, *mia stellina*. The last few days, nothing
felt right without you."

***

Sleep never happens. I'm dozing, because life is so much scarier than it was yesterday. If Trevor and Owen are the bad guys, they're not going away. The only reason I didn't block him after his fucked-up call is because Zack's text distracted me. It's probably better to know where Trevor is and what he's doing. I doubt he'll forget about me and go on with his life. If I stay in contact, maybe I can gain his trust or learn something useful. Not that I know how to do that, but how hard can it be to text him and maybe talk on the phone occasionally?

The new day comes too fast. It's hard to believe how much has happened in less than two months, but this is my life. The phone buzzes with Trevor's name and my heart races until my brain calms enough to register it's only a message. Sure, it's a text now, but he'll call soon and what will I do then?

Trevor: Hey beautiful, no go on a red-eye this weekend, but I'll be back soon.

Clearly, he doesn't remember what an ass he was last night. Or is he doubling down? Nausea rolls through me at the sight of his name, but I know I have to respond.

Zack and Daniel may not be on board, but me seeing Trevor again is our best shot at finding the killer. They'll figure out how to protect me so it can happen.

It takes hours to summon the courage to respond and when I finally do, I can't hit send. No matter what I say, I worry it will tip him off that I'm on to him. If I'm mad about last night, he might disappear but if I act like nothing happened, that might be suspicious. Eventually I decide that fawning over him is probably what he wants but my hand shakes so bad, I can hardly reply.

ME: bummer for now but can't wait to see you. Miss you :)

Abby calls, and as usual, she's all sunshine and rainbows. "What's new?"

"Zack came by last night."

"It must've been a great night since you called off again. What happened? Tell me everything."

"Mostly, we talked, with some making out."

"Interesting. You think it'll be like argue, hate fuck, repeat."

"No, there's something here, but I don't know what."

Time to come clean. I tell her the real reason for contacting Daniel wasn't to moonlight as a researcher. I explain about the articles, the threats to Dan, my prowler, Zack's role, and everything else, including the latest on Trevor.

"Holy shit, Cady. A serial killer is after you?"

"Not exactly."

"Come stay with me. Trevor might know where you live and you can't blindly trust Daniel. How could you let a stranger in and be alone with him?"

"Daniel's not the killer. Sonny adores him. They're best friends."

"This is how you end up in a pit in someone's basement, girlie. Why are you doing this?"

"Life always happens to me, so I'm taking control for a change, to get what I want." I'm struggling to explain, but not doing a great job judging by the grunt Abby sends my way.

"So you're going to catch a killer in your spare time because you're bored? Normal people take life by the horns with hobbies, vacations, and Tinder hook-ups, not crazy shit like this. Your way sucks."

This is the right thing to do, I insist, detailing the reasons. Abby's not thrilled, but she supports me so long as I promise to be careful and stop sneaking around alone. After agreeing to her countless warnings, she hangs up minutes before Zack arrives.

"Hi." He picks me up for a torrid kiss. "Waited all night to do that," he breathes, then his mouth is on mine again.

"Missed you, Strozzi." I intended to make him work for this, but that plan sucks, and being attached at the lips is way better. Standing here wrapped in his arms, I can feel his smile on my cheek and it's the sweetest moment of my life.

"Does this mean I get another chance?"

"Yeah. I'm a fool for you," I concede with an eye roll. He smiles, but it's time to
be serious. "But no more games, Zack. No more running away."

"Never again. I'll always run to you."

***

Zack

We're at Cady's house when Daniel tells her, "Sam's ready to recruit you. The experts agree the samples match and once they issue reports on the bite marks, he'll get a green light on DNA testing. We have progress."

Cady's happy to hear it but only wants to discuss Trevor, filling us in on the notes she made last night. She struggles to keep calm, but can't hide her fury.

"Trevor's a con man, a good one," Daniel states. "He blends in and charms people without alarming them. Every facet of his persona is crafted to gain trust by deception."

"How's Trevor involved?" she asks. "You know the killer better than anyone."

"I can't decide. In several ways, he fits the profile: handsome, charming, inconspicuous, presents himself as wealthy, and can afford to travel. But, in other ways, he's not too clever. Sticking around and hanging out with you is sloppy. Why risk getting caught?"

"He doesn't see it as a risk," I offer. "Lots of criminals think they're too smart to get caught."

"Possible, but most likely he's a lackey. The killer can change plans on the fly because Trevor watching Cady is his ace in the hole."

Cady explains why she thinks Trevor's involved, then introduces Owen. After hearing what she knows about him, I say, "The guy's too much of a wildcard to be the killer. But he sounds like a willing, if not necessarily compliant, accomplice."

Cady says, "That's important since only some crime scenes show evidence of two. Best guess, he usually goes alone, but sometimes includes Owen to serve whatever purpose."

Daniel's quiet, then adds, "Anything's possible, but there's no proof of two people."

There is. We didn't see it until now, but I let her explain.

"The circumstantial evidence is pretty suggestive. The one committing most of the murders is five-eight to five-ten, right-handed, and stabs on an upward angle, from the hip. The other one's only done a few and is closer to six feet, stabbing leftie with a downward stroke from the shoulder. There are three crime scenes that suggest two killers."

"How'd nobody catch that?" Daniel exclaims.

I say, "You were looking for similarities to Grace's murder while I was looking at travel patterns and potential suspects. It wasn't until Cady and I studied every case individually and compared them we discovered this."

"Nobody's ever compared all of the cases before," she says.

"So Trevor's not a link to the killer, he is one of the killers," I say slowly. "But why are they still here? Why stick around this time?"

"Changing their MO to kill an entire family is a drastic alteration to their pattern. Maybe he's watching Daniel," she suggests.

"Flight delays or cancellations could affect their plans as well," Dan reasons.

Have they stayed here this whole time, or did they leave and return? Daniel has various searches set up and has received no flags, but they can be unreliable so there could be new crimes we don't know about yet. Cady's going to search for potential matches while I check airline records.

"Keep checking your work mail for souvenirs since he likes to screw around. This makes sense. It could be these two." There's energy in the air as we plough through the information. This revelation is a big fucking deal and progress feels damn good. Until Cady drops another bomb.

"I have a date with Trevor when he comes back from his fake trip. This is an opportunity to find out more, and if it goes well, I can snoop around his place, and hopefully steal a toothbrush to get DNA."

Daniel says, "I want to say hell no, but it might work."

"What?" I'm shocked and pissed Daniel isn't too. "Absolutely not. That's crazy. Are you out of your mind?"

"We need to know more," she insists. "He pretends to leave, then delays his fake return despite never leaving town. Why? What's he doing instead?"

"What if it's a set-up. How do you defend yourself?" I demand.

"I'm not sure yet, but we'll meet in a public place so you guys can watch from nearby and step in if needed."

"That's ridiculous," I insist. "He might make us, which puts you in more danger. If he's not already on to us, we'll tip him off and he'll run." She's trying to argue, but I talk over her because the suggestion is fucking nuts. "Plus, you'd be nervous and reacting to us."

"It's too risky," Daniel concedes.

"Then come up with a better idea because this is a great opportunity and has to happen. Tell him, Daniel." Cady doesn't need my blessing, but they'll need my help with surveillance.

I can see, Daniel's torn. "Any plan has to put your safety first. You're not bait."

"There's no safe way," I say. "Without knowing what he knows, there's no way to design a strategy to keep you from getting hurt."

"We'll never find out what he knows by avoiding him," she fumes.

"You're not a con man and don't know how to play this guy. Even if he's not the killer, he's dangerous. He has no background I can find. It means he could be involved in fraud, or something else he needs to hide because we don't know any details on his fake company. "

"I didn't expect you guys to be thrilled, but don't shut this down without an alternative. Even a lackey might lead us to the killer, it's a perfect opportunity—"

"For you to get murdered if he's involved. This is a terrible idea." I want to shake her by the shoulders until she see reason.

Daniel interrupts, giving me a look. "We can't say no without at least considering it." Then he turns to her. "This could be too dangerous, Cady." He excuses himself to take a call.

"You don't understand, I have to do this." She presses her lips together mutinously.

"I do understand, and I'd think the same. But just because you *can* do something doesn't mean you should."

Daniel returns, apologizing. He has to rush to work. "Promise you won't see Trevor until we figure this out."

Grudgingly, she agrees, but is still spitting fire when she says, "Would you insist this is a terrible idea to anyone or only me?"

"Honestly? I don't know. This is dangerous. You have no undercover experience. What self-defense training have you had? Have you ever handled a weapon?" I warm up to my argument. "Assuming both answers are 'none,' that's like throwing a puppy into a lion's den."

She gazes at me in frustration. "If we meet in a public place so he doesn't have a way to get me alone, then I don't need weapons."

"I hate it, but don't have an alternative because I haven't had a chance to think it through. I'm distracted and struggling with the threat assessment. Does this sonofabitch truly worry me, or am I uncomfortable because it's you meeting with him?"

She breaks into a big grin, falling onto my lap. "Ha, you're worried because you like me. *Like* like."

"Yeah, I do, and it's messing with my head." I wave my hand at the files. "Why are you doing this?"

"There's no one big reason. Mostly a bunch of little things. Lots of free time, it's hella interesting, I liked Daniel right away and wanted to help. I'm always bored, so it takes my mind off my problems."

"Are you an adrenaline junkie?"

"Not at all. I'm a total wimp. But I'm aimless and trying to be more impulsive. My new philosophy is 'Fuck it. Go for broke' so admittedly, I'm not using the best judgment."

I raise my eyebrows, grinning.

"Yeah, I know you want to be one of my bad decisions, Strozzi."

"Too late. We already closed the deal, baby."

"If they get away, I'll have to watch for these guys for the rest of my life." She collapses against me with a sigh. I want to stay with her and make her feel safe, but I have to work tonight. "They'll be locked up soon, I promise." I stretch out on the couch, pulling the soft blanket over us.

"I'd love to think so, but nobody's caught them yet. What makes us so special?" She stretches out on top of me with a yawn.

"We've identified them, for one. That's a game-changer and they have no idea."

"You think?" She looks doubtful, but a little of the stiffness eases from her back as my hands knead her shoulders.

"There's no doubt in my mind, this will be over, soon."

It's going to end, even if I have to hunt them to the ends of the earth because I'd do anything to keep her safe so I can keep her for myself.

Chapter 10

Cady

The rest of the week flew by as we dove deep, trying to find out more about the Maines brothers. Zack's surveillance ended early last night, so he came back and we made out until we were both loopy from being awake for too long. We plan to spend the day in bed because what else are weekends for?

But Daniel's hitting us up before breakfast, ruining everything. "There was a double murder a week ago in Charleston, West Virginia, that fits the pattern."

"Charleston has a bunch of hospitals. Did they get the dog bite BOLO?" I ask, but none of us know the answer.

Zack calls in a favor from his friend Dawn, a Pittsburgh Police detective, and she's happy to contact Charleston PD for more details. There's nothing helpful in the Charleston news, but I'm too far down this rabbit hole to focus on other cases.

"If Owen's the rapist, he's in lousy shape from the dog bite. Charleston's far enough away for nobody in the ER to recognize him, but it's not a long drive. Only three or four hours. Am I jumping to conclusions because Trevor pissed me off and his brother's creepy?"

"No, you probably solved the case. The idea of two killers was wild at first, but you've convinced me they're good for it," Zack says.

"If he wasn't so freaking cocky, he wouldn't even be on anyone's radar," Daniel states.

"As much as I hate the idea of you seeing him, I haven't thought of a better plan." He pulls me onto his lap. "This is getting complicated. You're knocking me off my game, woman."

"Get used to it, Strozzi," she says with a kiss.

"Focus, babe. We have to keep you alive. My friends will handle surveillance, and we can make it safe...enough."

"We need to go somewhere with proper drinking glasses to get prints and DNA."

"Absolutely. Prints can identify him and DNA would connect him to the crime scenes. Do you ever carry a weapon, mace, any means of self-defense?"

"Nope. Steph's dad taught us how to shoot in high school, and often took us to the range, but I've never carried a gun." I'll go with Zack to see how it feels.

We discuss classes and alarm systems. I suggest getting Trevor back to Gooski's when Jeff's working to observe their interaction. Zack says it's too small and loud for surveillance. Instead, we'll talk to Jeff and meet Trevor elsewhere. I fire more questions at him: Can we set this up fast? What if they find out we're asking about them? What if he decides not to meet me? What if they disappear?

"I'll kill him myself before letting the fucker get away," Zack says, and he's serious. He won't let them escape because it would seal Brandon's fate, and Daniel would never recover. "You won't have to worry much longer, trust me. Sam's going to start surveillance on the Maines brothers soon."

"What changed their minds?"

"If they don't, Shields will do it and leak to the media that the FBI refused to help. I'll kill him if I have to, but I'd prefer not to if there's an easier way."

Daniel leaves, and we take a nap. After we wake up, there's still no new information. "I can't concentrate on other cases with the Charleston questions hanging out there. Let's go to the museum and the bar while we wait."

"What are we doing at the museum?"

"Looking at art. I need to get out of the house."

"Sure, but I only look at the real art. I don't do the modern shit where someone stuffs a
fucking parking cone into a toilet with a colored light bulb and calls it's art."

"Now I want to go to the modern art museum purely for the colorful commentary."

***

Zack

Cady's been much more upbeat since our outing, and I'll do whatever she wants to take her mind off this clusterfuck to help her relax. Halfway through the museum, she reveals she painted in high school.

"Are you a bowl of fruit girl, or landscapes, or what?"

"Mostly toilets with parking cones." She laughs. "Kidding. Ever read Brautigan?"

"The beatnik poet? Not my thing."

"I love his book *In Watermelon Sugar*. It inspired my first painting for a school project and defines my style. Kind of trippy."

"Let's see it."

"Eventually. It's at my parents' house. I refuse to hang it in a stupid rental so it'll stay there until I have a home." She cycled through various hobbies unsuccessfully, much like college majors, before eventually finding one that stuck. "Life finally started when I quit school. Having free time for a change, I discovered I love to write and started blogging, then self-publishing short stories."

"What kind of stories?"

"Smut's the easiest thing to sell, so there you go. Only Steph, Abby, Lana, and Nina have ever read my stuff, so keep this quiet. And probably Luke too, but he'd never admit it."

"Oh, I want to read it."

"Okay, but you have to understand, I'm writing to market, not my personal tastes."

"It's going to scare me, isn't it? Sick stuff, huh?"

"No, I avoid the weird stuff–bizarre fetishes, incest, tentacle porn, but—"

"That's a thing? Tentacle porn? Like squids? That's fucking disturbing."

"Aliens, mostly, but maybe squids. I don't want to know."

"What're you writing? Don't leave me hanging."

"Mostly voyeur and exhibitionist stuff. Young blue-collar guys with older sugar mamas. Roughnecks, rodeo clowns, gigolos, models—"

"Whoa, whoa, back the fuck up here. Rodeo clown porn?"

Cady's cheeks flush and she looks around, shifting her weight. "Indoor voice, Strozzi," she hisses. "It's not porn, okay? And the rodeo's his day job. The clown thing has no place in the sex scenes."

"This is the most ridiculous conversation ever." She can't stop laughing and a docent shushes us.

Giggling uncontrollably, she buries her face in my chest. Her whole body's shaking and I've never wanted to kiss her more.

She fascinates me. I've never met anyone else who assigns theme songs for the artwork while strolling through the museum, and I love the way her mind works. I know art, so it's an opportunity to impress her and we laugh the entire time.

This isn't how I normally spend my day, but every minute with her is excellent.

When I wrap my arms around her and she leans back into me, I never want to let go.

***

Jeff's happy to see Cady and answers her questions easily after she explains Trevor may be stalking her. He hates Trevor's guts, and unless he's a fantastic actor, I don't see him being involved. We learn Trevor came in the other night and was already falling-down drunk and really out of it. We soon figure out why. A couple of regulars said Trevor insisted on buying them a round at another bar earlier, despite multiple refusals. When he delivered the drinks, one girl switched the glass he gave her with his. I call it poetic justice for the fucker.

Trevor was kicked out again last night because he was with a big angry guy determined to start a fight, which sounds like Owen. Jeff grabs stills from the security cams and promises to put us in touch with the girls, the cab driver Trevor used, and anyone else he can find who might be helpful. We exchange contact information and thank him.

There's a bachelorette party near the front door, replete with light-up plastic dick jewelry and similar charming accessories. Two of the chicks are heading this way, squealing loudly, and I groan internally.

Can I *please* stop running into former hookups while trying to impress the love of my life? Kim keeps inching closer and Kristy's doing her best to touch me, but I keep moving.

They want to buy me a drink, but I explain I'm working. "Let's go."

Cady waves a fresh beer. "Go ahead, have a beer with your friends. I'm having so much fun catching up with Jeff. Let's take a break, partner."

"We've to get to the other place before they close. So let's hurry, *partner*."

"Be careful," Jeff laughs. "She's brutal."

"You're preaching to the choir, brother."

She punches my shoulder weakly as we leave. "Rude."

"I've had paper cuts more painful. Why didn't you help me out?"

"What was I supposed to do, hump your leg? I'm not big on PDA."

"You could've agreed we have to hurry instead of ordering a drink."

"Oh, yeah. Next time," she promises as I shake my head.

"You told Jeff I'm your boyfriend. Pretty presumptuous."

She rolls her eyes. "What else could I say? Talk to this stranger so we can catch a serial killer? I'd sound insane."

"Ha, you like me. *Like* like."

"Well, yeah. Thought that was obvious since I keep putting your dick in my mouth."

"It was, but I wanted to hear it again." I can feel the stupid grin on my face as I lean in for a kiss.

But as soon as I'm driving again, she's back to busting chops and keeps it up all the way home. "Does every lady who comes into contact with you experience a 'Zack attack' at some point or just the really lucky ones?"

"For the love of god, woman, never say that again. Ever."

"It's so catchy, but I didn't coin the phrase, it's something I overheard back there," she waves a hand casually toward the bar.

"We'll never speak of it again."

"Maybe *you* won't," she mutters under her breath.

"What?"

"You're no fun, Strozzi."

"I'm more fun than you can handle, baby."

"You keep telling me, but I'm waiting for you to show me." She can tease, but I won't give in. We haven't had sex again because no way is one of us rushing off to work after. This is my last week working nights, so we'll have the entire weekend together. What's a few more days? Besides, it's not like we're suddenly platonic, we're having plenty of fun.

She's soaked as I tease a fingertip along the edge of her panties, then groaning in frustration seconds later when my hand goes back to the wheel. "Are you trying to make me beg since I didn't help you out?"

"You're going to beg, but not as punishment. Because it's hot."

***

Cady

Zack drags me into a delicious kiss as soon as we're through the door, but of course, the phone interrupts. Crapola and dammit. I'm never getting laid again unless I smash those things.

"Send photos of your suspects, Strozzi," Dawn, on speakerphone says at the speed of light. "Charleston General is a Level I trauma center with a wound care department. A guy walked into the ER last Friday with a severely infected bite on the thigh. He had no ID and said he was returning home to Ohio from a trip to South Carolina. Called himself Sam Somebody or the other. Claims a friend's dog snapped, and he put off treatment hoping it wouldn't be necessary. They thought the infection had reached the bone and were admitting him when he disappeared.

"Bonus. The outpatient surgical ward is on the same floor as the ER and was closed for the night. That's elective surgeries, not part of the twenty-four-seven operation, you know? A few hours after the dog bite guy disappeared, security discovered a breach during a routine check. Antibiotics, IV meds, and saline were stolen, plus a bunch of heavy-duty painkillers. No leads, fake name. Hospital records and police reports aren't here yet, but I'll forward them right away."

No way are these things a coincidence.

Zack takes over my game of tug with Sonny while I make us a quick dinner. Waiting for the Charleston details is torture.

"He's got my whole arm in his mouth, should I be worried?" Peering over the island, I see Sonny grinning wide with Zack's entire forearm trapped in his enormous pearly whites, his ears back.

"No, he won't break the skin. If it hurts, tell him to stop." Zack doesn't look thrilled but keeps playing as Sonny's tail thumps happily. Lily calls and I make the mistake of telling her I'm making dinner for Zack. The squealing's too much, so I shuffle her off the line. Things are super quiet, and I'm praying Sonny didn't eat Zack.

"I like your mom a lot and I think she likes me, too. I love animals so we can get along well. What do you say?" Sonny's lying across his lap, tail happily thumping the floor. Zack's scratching him under the chin and on his ears. It makes my heart swell, but I won't intrude on their moment.

He's wanted a dog for a long time, but his hours are too erratic. I know he wants Sonny to be his pal. We enjoy a quick dinner and as soon as Dawn sends the records, we jump back into work. He opens the hospital report first, but is instantly frustrated.

"This is a foreign language. We'll have to find someone who can translate."

I lean in for a look and he pulls me onto his lap. "Relax, cowboy. I can read this. They gave him vancomycin in the ER. Vanco's the strongest antibiotic and has to be given intravenously. They'd admit him right away and do tests to identify the infectious agent, then tailor treatment once the pathogen's identified."

"Well, hot damn, baby. Pre-med?"

"Couple semesters of nursing school." I smile. "They stole all the right meds, although the painkillers are a bad idea. Pain's a warning signal. The worse it gets, the more trouble you're in. You shouldn't cover it up, until you correct the cause. These guys aren't stupid, they took normal saline."

"What for?"

"The biggest risk from a severe infection is the body can overreact to it, also known as sepsis. It dehydrates you and dilates the arteries, both of which cause blood pressure to drop. Now you don't have enough blood plus there's less force pumping it, so a real double-whammy. IV saline increases blood volume and pressure, which can keep you from going into shock."

"Trevor's not dumb," Zack says. "They went far enough to avoid the BOLOs, robbed a hospital med room without setting off alarms, and probably committed a double murder for kicks, all in a few hours."

"He's too calm and collected. We need to make him nervous, throw him a curveball. He'll start falling apart fast once he's not in charge anymore. He won't know how to react. This guy's never answered to any authority, as far as we know. No school records or jobs, nothing, so he won't be able to handle the loss of control."

"You seem to be on target profiling this guy so if you think it'll work, let's try it." It's good to hear he has faith in my assessment. "How do we rattle him?"

"I don't know yet, but I'll come up with something. Don't worry, Strozzi. If there was an Olympics of fucking with people, I'd be a gold medalist."

"You were at the bar today. I'm not sure if I should worship or fear you."

"A little of both." I grin. "It's genetic and considered a sport in my family."

"You guys must be popular at family reunions."

"That's where we do our best work. Those pricks are a goldmine."

We both laugh hard, and it feels good amidst the ugliness. I try to get up to grab fresh drinks, but Zack holds me on his lap and I hope he never lets go.

***

Zack

I worked last night, but got back to Cady's before dawn to crash. Things got deep, and I almost blurted out something I'm not ready to say, but she steered the conversation in another direction, asking if I've always been strictly casual.

I told her the truth. I was with one girl for a while until I caught her cheating. Initially, that was the reason I stopped dating and only hooked-up, but over time, it became the way I lived. I had fun, but I haven't been with anyone twice.

Given how she's made it clear, if I pull away one more time, she's through, I have to ask, "Does how I've been so...unattached scare you?"

"Well," she draws out the word, "I think you might be more guarded than most guys, but self-protection isn't a bad thing as long as you can reach for happy when you find it." She smiles, and all the knots in my body start to unravel. All these years I figured I'm some heartless asshole, but she sees me in a more positive light.

Waking up with her wrapped around me is the perfect way to start the day and my mind wanders contemplating the many other potential benefits. We haven't had an actual date yet, but things are crazy right now. I plan to spend today worshiping her body, but the phone rings, ruining everything. Again.

Cady jolts awake, listening intently as Daniel shares details on the Charleston cases. Security footage suggests it's the Maines brothers, but they were careful and the cameras never get more than a profile. Since they've traveled across state lines to commit crimes, the FBI will get involved, but we have to give them evidence to make that happen. Everything is still circumstantial.

"This is so frustrating. Every step forward is two steps back," she fumes. "Now the FBI can get involved, but they need more hard evidence, which is bullshit. Why are we doing their job?"

I can't disagree, but the best way forward is to do a DNA test against the blood samples from the hospital. Trevor better pray someone arrests him before I find the fucker because I'll make sure there's no way he can ever get near her again. There are lots of details to lay out so we get to work, incorporating the new cases into the timeline.

"As weird as the work is, I like it," she says. "Does enjoying this make me creepy?"

"Most definitely, baby." I smile. It's been a long day and we've hit a wall, and now I don't know what to do. Since the cops found her tormenter, she's made it clear she doesn't need me to be her body guard, though I disagree, strongly. I don't want to leave, but she hasn't invited me to stay. "Any plans for tonight?" I try to sound casual, hoping she says no.

"Staying in, watching a movie. The usual."

"I wanted to watch a movie tonight too. We can do it together." That sounded so fucking dorky in my head, but she kisses me anyway, leading to a scorching make-out session until Trevor starts blowing up her phone.

She has to respond. Their communication's been limited to texting, but now she'll start calling since we found a good recording app. I warn here it isn't really legal.

"Who cares," she scoffs. "If he incriminates himself, the FBI can find a way to make it admissible in court, or we can."

"How?"

"Gun to his head. Cattle prod to his balls. We'll think of something that'll persuade him to repeat it willingly."

My baby's a badass and it's so fucking hot.

***

Cady's regaling me with awful date stories while we make dinner. "What about you, cowboy? You must've had an excellent system for reeling in the ladies without wining and dining them. I've heard things."

"What've you heard?" I ask, pulling her close.

"Most of it's been proven false, so I don't believe everything I hear."

"Bet I know which rumor worried you most." I can't stop laughing when her cheeks flush. "Don't be embarrassed, that'd be a deal-breaker for lots of people."

She smiles and it hits me. She doesn't know. "They're not rumors, it's all true. But you're the exception to all the rules. You're special."

Cady flushes. Even the smallest compliment makes her uncomfortable, although I plan to change that. I tell her the truth because there's something important here she needs to know. "There were things I wouldn't do with a hook-up, but I always set clear boundaries up front so nobody was disappointed. Sure, it may seem like I didn't respect women, but the fact I never got involved proves I do. I knew my limits and never promised anything more.

"At first it was fun being single, and the attention pumped my ego. Then one day I realized I was doing it to see if I'd ever feel something for anyone, but I never did, until you."

"Contrary to popular opinion, you're sweet. And super-hot. A great combo."

"I'll admit, when it comes to this," I motion my hand between us, "I don't know what I'm doing a lot of the time. You'll cut me some slack, right?"

"This doesn't have to be complicated unless we make it complicated."

"So if I'm doing stuff wrong, you'll tell me?"

"Do I seem like the type to suffer in silence to coddle your ego?" Her head tilt with a cutting look assures me that's not the case. "We hang out, have fun, and see what happens."

"Sounds easy enough."

"How much slack are we talking? Like, you had a bad day at work so we're not going to dinner tonight or surprise, you have a wife, two kids, and a couple of other girlfriends?"

"So we're tossing the word girlfriend around?" I ask seriously and her eyes widen in surprise, then she punches my arm. "Damn. I've had mosquito bites more painful, we've got to toughen you up."

"Stop, funny guy. This is a serious conversation and it's important. Promise me there are no troubling revelations in the future, particularly of a sexual nature. Swear to me you don't have a Smurfs kink or think you're a werewolf, or any other unique interests."

"First clown porn now Smurfs? Really?"

"Happened to my friend Christina in college. It's one of the few stories where the weirdo was dating someone who wasn't me."

"Have you dated a werewolf?"

"No, but I had a date with a guy who wanted to be one."

"How'd he bring *that* up?"

"Announced over dessert he expected to get lucky tonight and was hoping I was on my period so he could go down on me and pretend he was a werewolf."

"What the actual fuck? That's insane."

"That's been my life so you better be super freaking normal, Strozzi. I'm done with weirdos. You seem okay, and if we're going to really do this, I have some conditions." I make a rolling motion with my hand. "No other girls, no other guys, for either of us."

"Seriously?"

"What's the problem? You need a man in your life?"

"Not funny, woman."

"No fetishes, no costumes, *nobody's peeing on anybody*. If I have to Google anything to find out what it is, we'll probably never going to do it. If you ever call yourself Daddy, I'll stab you."

"If I can't pee on you, I'm out," I state, but can't keep a straight face. "No issues with your list, but you have to promise you'll give me a chance to get it right."

"Of course. I'm selfish. I want you to succeed. Now stop worrying. We'll figure this out together."

Figuring it out together sounds perfect.

Chapter 11

Cady

"Don't move." Zack kisses a line across my body from hip to hip before tossing a blanket over my naked body. "This mental picture will get me through the night." One more long kiss then he's gone, and my heart's still racing long after the door shuts. I've never been happier, and it's scary because this seems too good to be true. This must be *love*. For once, I'm not tense and stressed to the point of breaking when I bend.

No joke, I'm so uptight, once I tore a muscle in my neck simply turning my head on a cold morning. I'm a wreck at the thought of meeting Trevor, and I focus on Zack instead. I'm consumed by how much I enjoy his body and fixated on the glorious things he does to mine. There's a chance for quality sleep if I hop into bed, still loose from multiple orgasms and feeling the imprint of those skillful hands. Might as well tease him with some pics. The phone rings seconds later.

"Enjoying the view, cowboy?" I tease.

"Cady?"

It's a gut punch to hear Trevor's voice when I'm expecting my lover, but a quick recovery is critical and I rush to engage the recorder.

"Hey, cutie. Been missing you." Nearly choking on the words, I struggle to sound happy.

"Damn, it's been a while, baby girl. Have you been avoiding me?"

"Of course not, Trev. Things are crazy at work right now."

If my sudden fondness surprises Trevor, he doesn't let on, but he may be playing me. I doesn't matter: it's crucial to keep up the charade.

"I'm sorry we keep missing each other, but schmoozing new clients is time-consuming," he tells me, and I want to hurl. "I can't wait to get back to town and get my hands on you."

Torn by dual urges to gag at the sound of his voice and run for my life, it takes everything in me to sound flirty and interested. He tells me more lies, like he'll be on a red-eye landing early Monday morning and can't wait to perform a specific sex act he describes in horrifying detail.

It's tough to maintain, but I draw the conversation around to his job under the guise of seeking a new career. Construction's boring, so I'm considering going back to school for accounting or business. "Typing and filing are easy, but what else happens in an office? I mean, as a successful man, do you think I could handle such an important job? How do financial services and investments work?"

Any interaction with Trevor is torture of the highest order, but playing dumb is easy enough because who cares what he thinks?

Determined to blow off the questions, he repeatedly changes the subject, but I keep circling back, pushing until he's out of patience, then I stroke his ego to keep him talking.

He attempts phone sex again, but I shut him down with flirty giggles, stoking his temper. After twenty minutes on the phone, I'm ready to sign off, but he needs to be in control.

Thankfully, he's annoyed enough to end the call. Short term good thing, long term, I'm thinking not so much.

***

The day's flying by and it feels like the company's imploding. Cutting two checks each week, one for the subcontractor and another for the IRS, is easy, but Pete's making up a bunch of bogus back-charges against the subcontractor to deduct from the payments. As a result, both the IRS and the sub will receive less money than agreed. The sub pays less and pays longer, Pete insists, but I don't think it works that way. Taking a stand is scary, but now I have insurance, so let them fire me. If Allen Brothers tries to frame me it may be entertaining since it'll backfire spectacularly.

"Why should the IRS get the money? They don't deserve it," Pete preaches, as his yes men agree.

"The IRS should get the money because the law requires us to honor the agreement," Tim argues, but Pete doesn't care.

Keeping everyone—especially the IRS—happy is in Allen Brothers' best interests. Any breach of the payment schedule allows the IRS to seize the subcontractor's assets.

"If the sub stops workimg, six of our projects grind to a halt," Tim insists.

Work gets delayed while we bring in a new concrete contractor, and other companies will charge a premium since they declare income and pay taxes, unlike the current vendor.

"Why do you think his prices are so freaking low?" Tim thunders, but Pete smiles serenely, waving a dismissive hand. Tim's one of the best project managers in the business with decades of experience, making him a fantastic asset and why everyone should defer to him, but Pete isn't smart.

Thanks to Pete, the morning flies by before I can gather any evidence, so instead of mailing another package to Daniel during lunch, I'm pouting while Sonny romps in the backyard when the phone rings. Trevor again who gets a response crafted to look like an auto-reply saying I'm in a meeting.

The afternoon is the morning 2.0. Zack calls to make plans, but I beg off, determined to finish some work. He's disappointed, but understands.

"Oh Trevor, I miss you so much," he cries in an annoying falsetto. "Please use your penis to explain math. I'm only a girl."

"Hilarious, Strozzi. I'm winging this, you know. Besides, I don't see you batting your eyelashes at him for information."

"It can't be easy to be nice or play dumb, but you keep him interested."

"It's easy enough, but I don't know if I'm doing it right."

"You are, don't worry. He wants to hear he's smart and you're so into him. I hope I meet Trevor. Beating his scrawny ass will be so fulfilling."

Zack's jealous streak is a spectacular turn-on, like everything else about him. Being alone here is a risk, but I promise to call my friends at the body shop next door to walk me to the Jeep. Zack insists he should come over, but it would be counterproductive.

"No. You'll be late again and I won't finish."

"You always finish and quite spectacularly, I might add."

"Miss you, Strozzi."

"Miss you too, baby. Call if you need me."

"I always need you."

I leave Trevor a message pretending I'm excited to see him soon.

Abby stopped at the house to let Sonny out and snuggle him for me so I don't have to rush home. It takes hours but I find everything I need, get back to my house and assemble the final packet. It's an immense relief. Now that the task is complete, I decide to tease Zack with more pictures but get no response. He must be busy.

Exhausted, I fall into a fitful sleep, hoping for major changes and soon, specifically a new job and two killers getting arrested.

Then I'll have loads of free time to spend with my hot boyfriend.

If only life worked that way.

***

Monday's angry meeting set the tone for the week. Yesterday was nasty because Pete grilled me about staying in the office so late. There's a massive backlog, easily enough work for three people, but nothing I said seemed to pacify him. The thought of them having cameras in the office is no surprise since they're paranoid, but they're so cheap, I never imagined they'd spring for something fancy enough to hide.

Things steadily improved on the law enforcement side after I sent the last package. Chief Gruber called to tell me all the charges are filed and the hearing will be scheduled soon. I can't thank him enough. The streak continued with a call from Daniel.

"Sam's impressed with the latest report. It's extremely thorough and shows tons of connections."

"Zack helped. I can't take all the credit."

"You're both golden in Sam's eyes. He's ready to recruit you two. Things are happening, but they move slowly." There's good news on multiple fronts, but nothing's actionable and the waiting is draining.

Abby said Pete and Bob were behind closed doors the whole afternoon yesterday, which doesn't bode well, but better fired than convicted.

Today, there's a weird vibe in the office, and I expect to get fired any minute. The anticipation is awful. Daniel confirms he's gotten every package and the last one should arrive today or tomorrow. I've done everything possible to protect myself.

In typical Pete fashion, he's too much of a wiener to do the dirty work, and makes Tim fire me. Tim refused to reschedule his meetings, hoping Pete would get over his snit, but to no avail, so whatever. Bob and Pete are noticeably absent before and during Tim's extremely apologetic call, but I assure him it's fine, which is true. It's not like I haven't been expecting it, and when the hammer falls, it's a relief.

I head to the gym to burn off nervous energy and get in a swim.

I text Zack so as not to wake him, then call my parents. Dad assures me these things usually work out for the best, and Mom asks if I'm still making dinners for Zack. Lily's so busted for blabbing my stuff all over town.

True, I'm head-over-heels for the guy, but I'm not ready to share details. I talk to Steph, Evan, Abby, Lana, and Lily, and it's not even lunchtime. Zack shows up with my favorite Mexican takeout and the director's cut of *Cruel Intentions* to cheer me up. He hit it out of the ballpark. I'm mad at myself because I should've been running a pizza shop. I picked this stupid job instead and it turned my life completely upside down in six months.

"Are you looking for construction work again or any office job?"

"I can't be picky since I don't have much savings, but construction's interesting so I'd prefer to stick with building or design work."

"You'd make a brilliant researcher. Shields is always hiring. If you enjoy the work, there are opportunities down the road to go into IT or become an investigator. Wasn't that your lifelong dream?"

"Years ago, but I have no qualifications."

"You have no formal training, but you have excellent qualifications. They're not the same. The research you've done for Daniel was a game-changer, and you're great with Trevor. We have a suspect only because of you. It's a big deal."

"Not because of anything I've done. He picked me."

"What matters is you stepped up and rocked it because you're good at this. I know you're enjoying it, even though it can be tough."

"It's fascinating, even if it's scary sometimes."

"Then you'd probably love Shields. What you're doing here is the research job, the only difference is they won't all be murder cases, and there are all kinds of resources available so it's easier. Plus, they'd pay you and you'd never have to go on a date with a possible serial killer."

"It's an attractive offer, but you're biased."

"No, recruiting's part of the job, and I know what I'm doing. It's an option, but there's no pressure."

***

Zack

Cady's had a rough week, between getting fired and preparing to meet Trevor, plus she has to talk to him and act excited to see him. She appears damn relaxed, but she's quieter and tense so I'm trying to make it easier. My cop friends will handle surveillance since they have training and experience. Today, we're meeting to finalize the plan and Cady's coming over.

Opening the door to her is stepping into another world.. Unchartered territory. The entry hall's full of photos, mostly color, a few black and whites. The majority are landscapes and nature shots. She focuses on them as soon as she enters.

"These are excellent. Are they all yours?"

"Yeah, I always grab a camera for hikes." There's something about nature that gets to me. Especially the sheer beauty of unspoiled landscapes.

"You've got a great eye. Is there somewhere specific you go?"

"I do a lot of hiking in Allegheny National Forest and Cook's Forest. The Clarion River's something else."

"Sounds cool. I've never been there."

"Which one?"

"Neither. Pretty sure I've never been in *any* forest."

"What?" I laugh before realizing she's serious. "Any forest?"

She shrugs like it's no big deal. "So do I get the tour or what?"

There's not much to see, so the tour's quick. The kitchen's separated from the large living room by a small dining room. Upstairs we glance at the office-guest room combo and guest bath.

"And this is where the magic happens," I say, pulling her into my room.

"Eh, I'm concerned there's been lots of magic worked here before me."

"I've never had another woman in my bed," I swear, pulling her on top of me and it's the absolute truth. I've graced many beds, but nobody has been in mine, until Cady.

"What happened to going out for breakfast?"

"Food doesn't matter. You're too enthralled by my powers of seduction." I grin, and go in for a kiss.

Her phone rings and we ignore it, but then my phone rings and I'm pissed. "Why are those here?" I mutter, expecting the intrusion to stop, but both keep ringing. I retrieve my phone to see Daniel's name, but he can wait. I find Cady's next and it's Trevor. What a fucking moment-killer. I show her the phone then the familiar chime sounds signaling a voicemail.

"Ugh, play it."

Hey, sweet female. Daddy's hopping on a plane soon, can't wait to see you.

"What a fucking douche," I mutter, then her phone rings again. "What's up, Dan? What's so urgent it can't wait?" I ask through gritted teeth.

"Good, you both need to hear this. Sam's experts have matched the bite marks, so there's a green light for DNA testing. The FBI's officially requesting involvement in those cases, using the missed hairs and the Charleston case as evidence."

This forces our hand. "A DNA sample's more important than ever."

"Precisely. Any word from our boy?"

"He'll be 'back' in town Monday. Zack's cop friends will do surveillance and evidence collection."

"Set up a date with the fucker, and I'll go collect his body fluids," I suggest, wrapping my arms around her.

"The evidence wouldn't be admissible in court." Daniel sighs. "I'm not impartial, and don't want to pit you guys against each other. Let me know what you decide to do." He knows I don't want Cady to do this, but I can't stop her.

She curls into me, taking my hands. "I'm going."

"I hate this so much. I fucking hate it."

Cady promises to get Daniel details soon, then disconnects. "This sucks, but I have to, so let's focus on getting through the meeting."

"Are you sure? Absolutely, positively sure, because if not—"

"Zack, don't," she pleads. "This is the quickest way to end this. If we're lucky, Trevor will give someone a reason and we can end him, too."

Show time's getting closer and shit's getting real. An hour later, Cady's too quiet and I'm not sure how to help. I'm sitting on the bed, making calls. She lies with her head in my lap, probably pondering her mortality.

How the fuck did I let this happen? There had to be a way to prevent this, but things have gone too far to stop it now, so I have to make sure she's safe. Ryan will outfit her with a microphone. Dawn and Lucas will shadow Cady and scoop up Trevor's glass to deliver to Sam, assuring the chain of custody.

Daniel and I will be outside listening with Ryan and Sam.

There's a hollow ache in my gut which must be fear, but I can't let it show. Cady's already a mess. Stretching out, I pull her close. Ryan's coming here to go over the details. The only loose end is to ensure Trevor's on board. She texts again, hoping for a reply during his fake layover.

"Everything will be okay. I promise."

"Why did I insist on doing this? I can't defend myself and have no idea what to do."

"Then we call this off. Nobody will blame you."

"Who's going to stop him?" she snaps. "They'll keep raping and murdering people and I'll never forgive myself."

"Protecting people is the FBI's job, not yours."

"But if the FBI can't catch them, this will never end. I'll have to look over my shoulder forever if we don't end this. Those bastards get away, and I'm never safe again. Tell me I'm wrong."

Of course I can't because she's right. Instead, I explain our security measures, stressing the safety protocols and how Sam will be present along with two police officers.

The tension's suffocating. "Once this wraps up, we're going to the forest. You'll love it there. Cold nights are the best to sit around a big fire. The sky's incredible up there. On a clear night, the Milky Way's visible, sometimes the aurora borealis. It's amazing."

"I love looking at the stars. You know, I've—"

"Taken a bunch of astronomy classes," I guess, and she nods. "Of course you have." I chuckle.

"So camp is a building, right? Because sleeping in a tent or outside is inviting freaks to make a skinsuit out of you."

"Yeah, it's a house. Maybe you need to lay off the true crime."

"Hey, if I didn't worry about serial killers, you and I would still be strangers. Meeting Daniel's what brought us together."

"No. I would've found you again. We're too good together for the universe to keep us apart," I insist, tracing her cheekbone as she burrows closer. "Talk to me," I plead. "What are you thinking?"

"What if he blows me off, or he's on to us?"

"He won't, and you're safe. We'll be right there."

"How can you be so sure? When I first floated this idea, you were positive I'd get murdered."

"I swear on my life, nothing will happen to you. I'll kill Trevor with my bare hands if he tries to touch you."

"I don't doubt that for a second, but we're missing something. He's making this too easy. Hopefully it's arrogance and we'll have the upper hand, but he doesn't care about me, so why's he still calling? Why is he meeting me?" She's right, but I won't consider the possible answers. They're fucking terrifying and Cady might never forgive me if I stop this meeting.

Ryan arrives and goes straight to work. With a male and female tail, they can follow anywhere, even into the restrooms, if needed.

"Couples are best for surveillance, right? Nobody pays much attention to a couple if they're casual.

"True," Ryan says. "See. You're a natural. Why are you slumming with him?" he asks with a wink, making her laugh. "You could do worse though. He's okay."

"Thanks for the glowing recommendation, asshole." I've known this jagoff since we were three years old. He's practically my brother.

"Remember to steer him to one of three spots chosen for ease of surveillance," Ryan reiterates. "If pushing for those locations raises Trevor's suspicions, we'll regroup."

On cue, her phone sounds and Trevor's finally responding to this morning's texts. It's damn coincidental, but there's no other explanation. He's in Chicago and will land at PIT overnight Sunday or early Monday morning, then crash at his place. He asks if she can she come around six or seven.

"Say you have a work thing," Ryan advises. "Meeting a client, an event, whatever at Emiliano's so let's meet there for drinks."

The no-go and suggestion gets an instant and unhappy response.

Trevor: No romantic night at my place? Came a long way to be alone with you.

Cady shudders. I'm consumed by the burning desire to choke him when she tenses up but don't say a word. Ryan's watching us closely.

Cady: Disappointed too but must be there. Hoping it wraps up early.

"No," Ryan barks, but it's too late. "Don't give him the idea you two can leave, we need to keep him there. But it's okay, we'll work with this."

Cady: Most of the clients are impressive names. Could be an opportunity for you too.

"And your fake freaking investment firm," she says, rolling her eyes.

"Good save, baby." I kiss her head. Her focus never leaves the phone so she doesn't notice, but Ryan pretends to die of shock and fall off the couch. Fucking drama queen.

Trevor: Maybe for the best we'll see. Gotta get moving TTYS.

We run through the details again and again until everyone's sure they know every scenario.

Sargent Baron calls Cady to say Gary Babinski has admitted to everything, but adamantly denies ever going to her house. There's no physical evidence Gary left the dead rat or poisoned meat, so he's smart to deny it to avoid additional charges. We know it was Trevor and Owen, but the police have no idea.

I won't leave Cady alone for a minute until they're locked up tight. These guys have too much luck and have gotten away too many times to take any chances.

I beg her to stay at my place tonight since I'll be working, but she declines. My deepest fear is he plans to get to her before Monday, but she refuses to stay here alone and went home when I left for work. If we can get through tonight, everything will be okay because she'll be with me come morning and I'm not leaving her side.

***

Today is ours. No work, no Trevor, no stress; just a quiet day alone. Sonny gallops in, making himself right at home as soon as I open the door. It's cold out, but Cady's wearing a dress and the sight of her smoking hot legs is enough to get me hard. She tosses her phone next to mine, already shut off. "It's great to see you," I tell her, scooping her up. She leans in for a kiss and it takes way too long to get up one flight of steps. She's laughing as I toss her onto the bed, pulling me on top of her.

"I've never wanted anything in my life the way I want you, woman," I admit in between kisses. Her clothes quickly disappear and I'm exploring her body with my mouth. She gets my jeans off, but that's for later, I'm running this show.

Kissing my way down her body in greedy bites, I can hardly contain myself. We have so much chemistry, it's unbelievable.

"You dig this, baby?"

"I do, so much." She sighs and I can't help but laugh.

"Tell me how much you love it when I call you baby, *mia dea*," I order, biting her thigh.

"You're a filthy tease, Strozzi."

She once refused a second date because the guy called her "baby," but she says it's different when I say it. That's perfect because I want to make her happy. Her skin smells like coconut and it's soft as silk under my lips.

"Say it," I order, my words muffled because I refuse to take my mouth off of her.

"I love it when you call me baby." She smiles and plays with my hair. "I love hearing it in your sexy voice and knowing it's only for me."

"That's right. Only you, baby."

I tease her with my tongue and never want to stop. She's sweet and wet and so fucking good. I love the noises she makes and the way her body moves against me, and how she pulls my hair. I'll never get enough of any of it because I love this woman and she makes me feel like a sex god, especially when she screams my name. Usually, she calls me Strozzi or cowboy, but when she's coming apart, it's always Zack and it drives me crazy. Time stops when we kiss and there's so much blood rushing to my dick, passing out is a valid concern. But I can't move. It's physically impossible to stop kissing her.

"Wow," she says, laughing against my lips.

"The way you say my name when you come is the hottest thing ever. I need to hear it every damn day."

"So you'll make me come every day, cowboy? Promise?" she asks sweetly, biting my shoulder.

"There's nothing I'd rather do."

"You're so good at it, but right now you're going to scream my name." She pushes me back, and I relax, giving up control, which I've never done with anyone else. I always call the shots, but not anymore. I've got it so bad for her and nothing's ever been so good.

"I love visiting you, cowboy. This is fun," she breathes, batting her lashes with a smile.

"You haven't seen fun yet. I'm going to do things to you, dirty things you won't believe."

"Can't wait. I still can't decide if I love your big cock or your filthy mouth better."

Like a fucking god. "Woman, you're the best thing that's ever happened to me."

"I've been waiting for this, but now I'm nervous," she frets, biting her lip.

"Yeah, it's been built up an awful lot, huh? There's no way it can live up to the anticipation."

"Strozzi, the only way you could disappoint me is if you're wearing a diaper or horse tail or something equally freaking weird."

"Hold on then, gotta change," I deadpan, rolling over on top of her.

We've already had the talk, and she's on birth control so we don't need condoms anymore. Her skin is warm and soft against mine as I fill her and damn, it's heaven. Slipping into her is a powerful high. Nothing else in my life compares to this moment.

"Cady, baby."

Feeling her this way rips the air from my lungs. I've never gone bare before and had no idea it would be so intense, so indulgent, so fucking amazing, and I haven't even moved yet. We stare at each other and I'm awed by this moment. Once we start moving, it doesn't take long for her to come, and that's some kind of personal record for me.

"Oh yeah, cowboy. That's how you do it." She laughs and I'm so in love. I absorb every detail: how her back arches, the way she wraps around me, the flush in her cheeks, and her soft hands on my face. Nothing can ever beat this feeling. "You're so beautiful, Cady."

"Nothing has ever felt as good as you." She smiles and it's too much, I've never had a connection like this with anyone.

"*Sei tutto ciò che voglio*," I whisper in her ear as she moans softly in mine. You're everything I want. "*Sono cosi innamorato di te*." I'm so in love with you.

Chapter 12

Cady

Zack nuzzles his face in my neck and I've never felt so close to anyone. After all the waiting and interruptions, this is so different from what I envisioned. There's no urgency, no rush, it's slow and intimate, and perfect. Watching his body excites me. The way his arm moves when his hand tangles in my hair, tugging to expose my throat to his hungry mouth. It's intoxicating to watch his taut muscles flex, knowing they're working to feel my body and give me pleasure. I'm overcome by his irresistible scent and the salty taste of his skin. I love having my fingers in his hair and his mouth on mine. His rhythm drives me wild and hearing his sexy voice in my ear while he's inside me is one of the great pleasures of my life.

"*Ti senti troppo bene, mia stellina,*" he breathes, and it's hot even though I have no idea what he's saying. When he moves against me and inside me it's perfect in every way. I'm so overwhelmed by my feelings for him, I don't notice the tears on my face until he kisses them away. A thrill runs through me every time he says my name and the world is black yet full of color as the pleasure shakes me to my core. I'm still coming when he collapses on top of me, spent and breathless. It's quiet for a moment while we catch our breath, then he's laughing.

"That's right, woman. Told ya I'd rock your world," he pants.

"Wow, you're smug. Who gloats after sex?"

"Baby, you passed out cold for a minute. So, I'm damn proud of a job well done." He leans in for another kiss.

"Whatever. I have no comeback because you're freaking magnificent at sex, Strozzi."

"You're pretty talented too, woman. It was too good right at the beginning there, so good it was almost over before we started."

"Never hold back on my account. I'm already impressed or we wouldn't be here."

"I can't take my eyes off of you." He smiles, brushing the hair out of my eyes.

"You're so sweet, cowboy. I have to admit, you were right."

"About what?"

"This is the best night of my life. Or day. Whatever."

"Mine, too."

"You know how to show a girl a good time, Strozzi."

"It's easy when she's hot as hell and drives me crazy." His sexy smile makes my heart skip.

"Whenever I think I can't want you more, you make me want more of you."

"You were right, too. There's no way I'd settle for one night. We're doing this again."

"Hell, yeah we are, lots more."

"Like all the time." He laughs as he pulls me on top of him. "I can't get enough of you, woman."

We spend the next several hours lost in one another, and it's so far beyond anything in my experience. Sex with Zack is addictive and magical. Looking into those bottomless eyes, everything else goes away. Every bit of fear, tension, and worry dissolves.

This was supposed to be one night but now it's the rest of my life. This man is my future, I've never been so sure of anything.

So this is how it feels to be in love.

***

I'm not sure of the day or time or even my name when my eyes open to him with his mouth on my body. The only thing I know for sure is there's no such thing as enough. "Waking up with you naked in my bed, I thought I was dreaming," he murmurs.

"This is the greatest way to wake up ever, cowboy." The sky's dark and we've spent the entire day in bed. Lying in his arms, I'm totally in the moment and not self-conscious, which is a miracle. "Why did it take us so long to do that again, anyway?"

"The night we went to the diner, I was sure you hated me for various reasons."

"No, I still wanted you. I was fixated on your hands, dying to have them on me again."

"And here they are." His hands move all over. "How do they feel?"

"Perfect, like the rest of you," I sigh, holding his hands to my body. "Like they were made to touch me."

"You know how to make a guy feel appreciated," he murmurs with another kiss. "And you haven't even seen my best moves. I want more of you. I need all of you, Cady."

"I was yours since our first kiss on the beach, Strozzi."

"The plan was to ruin you for all other men." He stares into my soul.

"You did, completely and irrevocably," I admit, lost in his eyes, so dark and expressive.

"Damn right. You're all mine." His hands skim my body as he turns me, dragging his lips to the spot on the back of my neck which drives me crazy. How does he know my body better than I do? *Ti amo cosi tanto*," he murmurs, and his mouth crushes mine before I can ask for a translation. I decide kissing Zack is the best thing ever, but then he enters me from behind and I reconsider. This is some secret level of sex I never knew existed.

"Tell me you're mine," he commands, holding me tight against him and I do because it's the truth. Here in his arms, his hot body against mine, this is everything, *Zack* is everything. But we're not making love this time, he's fucking me, hard and rough, and insanely good. And as I decide this can't possibly get any better, he pulls my hair so my head falls back onto his shoulder. Looking into his eyes while he rails me is fucking epic. "You're mine. All mine. And I'm yours in every way."

These are the most amazing minutes of my entire life and I want him so completely it's terrifying, yet it's still the greatest feeling ever.

***

Waking up with those powerful arms wrapped around me, I wondered if I was dreaming but the delicious ache throughout my body tells me this is real.

"Good morning, Miss Blackwell. Can I interest you in some hot Italian sausage for breakfast?"

"There's something wrong with you, Strozzi."

"True, but you didn't say no."

The day started out phenomenal, but the later it gets, the tougher it becomes to relax. Despite our best efforts, it's impossible to concentrate. Zack's uncharacteristically restless as the meeting with Trevor draws closer. It's getting late and we need rest, but he won't cooperate.

"I can't sleep; no way," he mutters.

"You'll sleep, I promise." He looks doubtful, but lets me lead him to the couch. "Relax."

"You relax, too," he commands, pulling me down on top of him.

"This'll get uncomfortable for you fast," I warn, but he only holds me tighter.

"No, this is perfect," he says with a soft kiss. "*Bouna notte, amore mio*," he murmurs, kissing my head.

Once he falls asleep, I slide next to him so he'll be more comfortable, but he turns onto his side, pulling me back. *Fine, have it your way.* I snuggle into him, following his lead, happy to give him whatever he needs and grateful he needs me.

For probably the first time in my adult life, I'm truly content. I wonder if he has any idea how happy he makes me and that he's everything I've ever wanted. My feelings are humbling and intimidating, but I adore this man.

I whisper "I love you" in his ear, suspecting he feels the same but is afraid to say it.

***

Zack

Opening my eyes to Cady in my arms is how every day needs to start. Monday mornings aren't a favorite, but nothing can ruin my mood right now. I don't even get up for coffee because I can't let her go, so I just lay here watching her sleep until she stirs.

"Good morning," she murmurs and her sleepy eyes make my heart beat faster.

Good morning. I love you. Marry me. I want to tell her I'm hopelessly in love, but she doesn't need any distractions right now. After tonight, everything will be simpler.

She shrugs. "The whole thing's terrifying, but this will be over soon."

"If you have any doubts, don't go. You don't have to do this."

"I'm going. But in case I get flattened by an anvil or die trying to drive into a tunnel painted on a mountain, just know this weekend was everything I hoped for and more."

"It was special for me, too," I promise, kissing her head. "We're good together, baby."

"So good, like the best."

"Yeah, we are," I laugh, kissing her neck because we're perfect together and nothing's ever made me happier. My phone sounds and I'm hoping for a message saying the meeting is off, but it's not. "Daniel says nobody knows where Owen is right now."

"Hopefully dead in the gutter somewhere from a severely infected dog bite," she says quietly, snuggling closer.

After that, the phone doesn't stop. Jeff calls to say Trevor was at Gooski's last night, then the Uber driver sent a list of every destination he'd taken them to, which includes one of Cady's neighbors. Surely Trevor had no legitimate business with the elderly couple across the street, which means he could've snuck into Cady's. We've operated under the assumption the feds will scoop these guys up, but I'm starting to worry the brothers will bolt before they're caught. I sure as hell don't want Cady to have to look over her shoulder forever.

"Trevor was in my house," she says what I thought.

My rage is close to boiling over, but I keep reminding myself I don't matter here. "Run through everything about the day." Trevor had to come in the only time Sonny was out. No stranger alone in Sonny's house would leave in one piece.

"Sonny acted strange when we got home, and Carl's cat was under the Jeep. Abby arrived two minutes after we got home. He hates that cat and adores Abby so it made sense for him to be all wound up, but there was probably a lot more to it." While Cady walked Sonny, Trevor was in her house, doing god knows what, and I was cruising around the neighborhood being fucking useless.

"We have to assume he planted a camera or listening device, installed spyware. If Sam won't do a sweep, Shields will, but the findings may not be admissible in court."

"Nothing looked out of place, but I had no reason to check." The haunted look in her eyes stokes my fury. I'm going to break Trevor's neck with my bare hands so he'd better pray the feds get him first.

Cady leaves a message for Sam and I call Daniel.

She's too quiet, and I'm not sure what to do, so I turn on some soft music and lie down to hold her.

***

There are so many ways this could go wrong, but I won't try to stop her. It's a chance to end a killing spree and save Daniel's brother. More than that, it may be her only chance to be free of the threat since I have no confidence the feds would catch them if we weren't orchestrating things. The Jeep rumbles to life, and the music roars to an obnoxious volume, so it takes two calls before she answers.

"A little metal to get pumped up, huh? Excellent choice but lower the volume because every noise comes through the surveillance audio."

"Oh. I forgot. Tell them I'm sorry."

"They can hear everything, remember?"

"Right." She blows out a long breath.

"Don't be nervous. We'll be laughing at this fucker soon. You know what to do and you've got great instincts. Follow them no matter what."

"Yeah, so great you might end up visiting me at SCI Forest on the way to the camp." There's a big state prison near my place in the forest.

"No, baby, Forest is a men's prison. I'll have to go out of my way to visit you in the clink or buy another camp somewhere else."

"Real funny, dick. First thing I'm doing tonight—"

"People are listening," I rush to interrupt, talking too loud.

"Don't flatter yourself, pal. I was going to say pounding a couple fingers of whiskey or five to settle my nerves. Now, do we need a safe word? Abby and I use Copernicus. We could use that."

This is completely out of left field. "No. Hold on a minute. Ryan says no safe word is needed. If things are weird, Dawn will ask if you need help. Why do you and Abby have one?"

"In case a kidnapper uses my phone to tell people I'm on a spontaneous vacation to prevent them from reporting me missing."

"Sure, because that's not crazy at all. Wow. Copernicus, huh? Let me make a mental note in case you need one later tonight." I laugh.

"Rude. Besides, I don't need one unless you're a big weirdo and you promised—"

"Everybody's listening," I yell, far too loud.

Ryan and Dan are enjoying this way too much, laughing so hard I can barely hear, but Sam looks like he'd prefer a root canal.

"Shit, I'm here."

***

Cady

"Are you okay?"

I'm so focused on trying to release the seatbelt, I can't answer, so he tries again.

"What am I, a mirage?"

"No, I thought you said that you were all right, Spider," I mutter on autopilot and he laughs.

"There's my girl."

"Go for broke, right?"

"Right. You're safe. He can't hurt you. We're right outside. Dawn and Lucas are in there," Zack reminds me.

"See you soon, west coast."

Forcing myself out of the Jeep, I float inside and everything's fuzzy, like a dream sequence. The restaurant's busy, but not packed, and perfect seats are open at the bar, visible through the large windows and in the sightline of both entrances. Nobody looks familiar, and there's no sign of Trevor. If he arrived first, I'd say we had dinner around the corner at Savoy, but the client was annoying, so I left as early as possible.

Five fingers of whiskey is my max, so this beer is a prop. It's only been a few minutes but seems like forever. I become conscious of a weird humming noise and struggle to identify the source before realizing I'm the source. The people monitoring the audio probably can't wait for this detail to wrap. Between Allen Brothers and Trevor, I haven't had time to share many details of living out my Zack fantasy, so pass the time texting Abby. The exuberant all-caps response is nearly instant, but I sense his approach, so there's no time to respond. Time to cue fake symptoms, using sniffles and a dry cough to make sure he won't get too close.

"Hey, sweet thing." I try my best but can't help flinching at his touch. Trevor feels the tension and keeps an arm around my shoulders as he sits. His hand skims my back, as though feeling for a wire. *Am I paranoid or is he fucking with me?* I'm pretty sure this mild-mannered dork charms women so he can cut their throats and murders children execution-style in their bedrooms. The realization Trevor's a killer makes me freeze and he notices, staring hard while ordering a vodka tonic.

"You're awful quiet tonight," he says without emotion, studying my face carefully.

"Sorry, I'm a mess today," I sigh. "Sick as a dog, but still had to entertain clients hopped up on cough medicine. What a long day." I'm careful to muffle the fake coughing so it's not phony. There's no Oscar in my future, but it's believable enough.

"What the hell, I came back to see you." Trevor's eyes narrow into snake eyes.

"And I couldn't wait to see you." I try to placate him, striving to sound sincere. Fighting a shudder, I put a hand on his, but he pulls away.

"So much for a fun night at my place."

"I can't exactly control this," I whine, gesturing before fake blowing my nose with a cocktail napkin. "We can still hang out and have a nice time."

"Really, we can have a nice time?" he mocks. *What the hell? Clearly it's important to get me alone. To kill me, or was he so sure he was going to get laid? One or both Maines brothers are rapists, which explains the abundant confidence.*

"I'm not stupid, Cadence," he snarls and his voice is different, cold. "You give it up to everyone else, but insist on leading me on."

What the fuck? "What's your problem? You don't know me, and I don't owe you a thing."

The once warm blue eyes are unrecognizable now, dim and hard in anger. "Yeah, I know everything. For starters, ask me what I have on Daniel Abbott and Zack Strozzi. It's no secret you're fucking them."

This is stunning, but I refuse to let my astonishment show. Sure, I figured Trevor's suspicious but never expected he's on to us. "Yeah, no," I scoff. "You're not half as smart as you think." He's working hard to look casual, but the façade is cracking. Time to drop the pretense and lay my cards on the table. The best way to get something useful is to rattle him so much he'll let something slip.

"Did you enjoy the present Owen left on your doorstep? He does have a flair for the dramatic."

"Is that what you call it? I call it being a pussy, leaving anonymous packages and empty threats" It takes everything in me to act casual.

"Empty? You wish. Tell Abbott to check on his girlfriend in Tacoma or go home to the dog, then we'll see how tough you are," he snarls.

Forcing a laugh at this moment is one of the biggest challenges of my life. "How tough I am? How rich coming from you. You're all talk and small dick complex. Wrong bluff, asshole. Try again." Every muscle in my body works to keep my hand steady as the bottle meets my lips.

"Why are we here, Cadence? So your little fuck buddies can tail me afterward?"

"Don't give yourself so much credit," I chuckle, taking another swig from the bottle and enjoying the way his jaw clenches. "My team chases little cocksuckers like you for fun in between real cases. This is nothing but sport, pure entertainment." I work to muster the biggest smile, praying my voice is half as loud and steady as it sounds in my head.

His mask falters, revealing the explosion bubbling beneath the surface. "You have nothing on me and never will," he hisses.

"Wrong."

"Listen, bitch—"

"Oh, Trevor, learn how to talk to women."

He chuckles, signaling the bartender for another. "I have no problem talking to women. I just don't listen to them."

"Is that why you cut their throats? So they can't talk back? So they can't say no and tell you what a sloppy little pussy you are?" I smile and he freezes.

The rage is taking over, and he's losing the practiced composure. He had no idea we had this much and scaring him is a major victory.

"There's no reason to listen because most of the women I meet have little to say," he laughs. "Owen's going to have so much fun with you. Are you a screamer, Cadence? He enjoys it so much more when they scream and fight back." His voice sounds different: crisp, and detached. The sound makes my stomach flip.

I swallow bile. "Weird how it always comes back to Owen. You two have such an *interesting* relationship," I say, watching his eyes snap at the implication. "Enjoy the time now because you two will never be together again. You'll be someone else's bitch soon." I smile.

"How will Zack react watching Owen rape you before I cut your throat? He's going to weep and beg for his life—"

"Nah, next time you see me I'll be waving from the press gallery at your trial."

Trevor's eyes darken as his pupil dilates, turning black as his rage takes over.

"That's if you see me at all. 'At the end, you probably won't hear anything. Everything just goes black.'" I point a finger at his forehead with a winning smile.

"Listen, cunt, I'm giving you fair warning because it's no fun for me when it's too easy."

"Don't worry, little man. Nothing about this will be easy for you." I turn to leave. "See you soon, Trev, but you won't see me."

"Don't walk away from me, bitch," he barks loud enough to draw attention. The bartender's watching as Trevor reaches for me and I pull away. "Get back here," he hisses, grabbing the back of my coat.

I intended to keep going, determined not to turn around, but I can't stand the thought of him following, even with Zack and the others close. I considered carrying a weapon, but I'm unskilled so having one gives an him the edge and I'm defenseless. I turn, taking a step back at the same time. Trevor's an arm's length away and the closest tables are watching. How do I get away? He's speaking and I move on instinct, grabbing his face with both hands.

"I know it was you, Fredo. You broke my heart," I say too loud, planting a big wet, smacking kiss on his lips, still holding his face. "This time you picked the wrong people to fuck with," I whisper, shoving him back as I smash the beer bottle on the bar. Pivoting out of reach, I stride away, praying my trembling spaghetti legs don't give out during my victory strut.

"Hey," the bartender shouts and I sense Trevor stop, but don't look back. "Hey, buddy. You're not going anywhere." Trevor's fingers snatch at my coat, but the bartender's screaming about the broken glass, and security is headed over. The bartender asks if I'm okay, but I march out the door. One last glance shows Trevor at the bar being accosted, and I bolt as though my life depends on it. And it could because who knows where Owen is.

In the Jeep I'm dizzy, then realize it's from holding my breath and force myself to breathe. *What next?* My mind races without focus. There was a plan but damned if I remember it. *Get out of here, don't sit here.* The phone rings, breaking the trance.

"Great job, baby. You handled him perfectly, and they got the glass. Are you okay?" Relief crashes through me at the sound of Zack's voice, but I'm incapable of a response. "Talk to me."

"Being near Trevor felt revolting. I was desperate to get away from him."

"You're safe. Drive around back, remember?"

Oh, right. "On my way." The steering wheel's wet with blood. I must have cut my hand on the bottle, but there's no pain so it can't be deep. Turning onto the access road behind the mall, I see Zack next to the surveillance van and stop. I hop out and he wraps me in a long hug before steering me over to ride shotgun.

"Debriefing at my place. I'll drive, so you can relax." I nod dumbly, registering the concern in his eyes. "Are you okay?" Offering what I hope is a reassuring smile, I squeeze his hand. "You're bleeding."

I finally find my voice. "It's fine. Drive. Go. Get out of here. I'm second-guessing everything now." My inner voice keeps repeating "It's over" until he pulls into the driveway.

"Awesome job, you killed it," he says, pulling me close. My tension dissipates as I sink into Zack and I don't want to move, but everyone's arriving.

Sonny's confused by the crowd, but is soon basking in attention from friendly strangers. Ryan gives me a high-five before introducing Lucas and Dawn. Daniel walks in with an older, gray-haired man and introduces FBI Supervisory Special Agent Sam Truman.

"You're one tough customer, Cady Blackwell," Sam booms, extending a hand. "Plenty of trained agents crack under the pressure of being face-to-face with a known killer. You did good." The deep, booming voice is a contrast to his grandfatherly looks.

"Sam's a former Texas Ranger, so if Sam says you're tough, we're talking titanium." Daniel smiles, throwing an arm over my shoulders. "The glass is in custody and Sam will get it processed." The FBI has to run the DNA sample and match it to at least one of the crime scenes before arresting anyone.

I sigh, collapsing into Zack's chair. My hands are still shaking and I need to lean on him, literally.

"Well done, Cady. But Fredo? That was too much." Ryan guffaws.

"Trevor was getting mad, and I thought making a scene might get him to back off for the moment. My mind went blank as I started to panic, but my brain's full of stupid quotes."

Ryan's tearing up, he's laughing so hard. "Imagine what went through the dumb fucker's head when you kissed him," he hoots and everyone laughs.

"Acting crazy is always a good power move," Lucas agrees. "That freaks people out, even genuine psychos. The look on his face was priceless, pure shock."

"I wish I could've seen his stupid fucking face," Zack laments.

Dawn can't stop laughing. "As soon as you grabbed his face, I said, 'I knew it was you, Fredo,' and we cracked up."

"You're all talk and small dick complex is the best burn I've heard in a long time." Ryan laughs. "What was the one line from, about everything going black?"

"That's Bobby Baccalieri talking to Tony Soprano," I explain, laughing despite my frazzled nerves. Ryan's hasn't stopped laughing, and Zack wraps me in a big bear hug.

"Better wife her immediately," Ryan warns with a wink. "Or I'll beat you to it."

"Those were the first things to pop into my head," I admit. "I didn't know what to say."

"You were awesome, baby. But the stuff he said is really disturbing. It seems like he's watching us. What does he know?" Zack asks Sam.

"He's probably bluffing, but we'll err on the side of caution. There's no evidence these two are B and E guys. Amateurs usually leave a trail, but anything's possible until we dig deeper. A team will sweep tomorrow and the results are immediate."

Daniel's quiet and looks serious despite tonight's success.

"So, the threat against Sonny," I begin. "Clearly they're not watching me right now because Sonny's been here at Zack's since Friday. Is Lindsay safe?"

Daniel flinches at the mention of her name. "Trevor and Owen are both here, but Sam has someone with her, just in case."

"I'm sorry, but she'll understand. She can call me if she wants to talk. We'll bond over these douchebags." Daniel offers a weak smile, but it doesn't reach his eyes.

"The DNA results will be back in a few days," Sam promises, readying to take his leave. "Outstanding work, young lady. Call me when you need a job, okay?"

"Hey, I'm winging this, but luckily it worked out." I shake my head.

"Even better, that means you're a natural. Come see me once we wrap these bastards up," Sam booms, and I can't help but smile.

"Get some rest, pal. Who the hell knows what's going to happen tomorrow," Daniel says. "I've got to get going, too. I'll walk out with you, Sam."

There's no way we could've pulled this off without Ryan, Lucas, and Dawn. Zack offers them pizza and beer, but they've got to get back to their own lives and promise we'll do it another time.

Everyone reminds us to be careful, then they're gone. Zack and I sit in silence for a few minutes, then he pulls me close. The adrenaline rush has passed and I'm falling asleep on his shoulder when his laughter moves me.

"Ryan went nuts for the Michael Corleone thing. Said I better be good to you or he'll steal you, and Dawn says you're a natural for undercover work. Ever considered the police academy?"

"Hard no there," I scoff. "Keep me away from the public, Strozzi. You should know that out by now."

Zack brushes the hair out of my face. "This has been a hell of a day. You must be beat."

"Let's finish going through the files."

"Those can wait until the morning."

"In the morning, we're going to the gym and the range and I assume you have work."

"I asked for a few days off after working so many nights and being on call for five weekends in a row. I wonder if Kyle has his damn baby yet." He yawns.

"Freaking Kyle." I yawn back. "Not sure how long I'll last, but let's do what we can. If I pass out reading, leave me here."

"First, let's clean up your hand and make sure there's no glass in there." Not necessary, the cut is shallow and doesn't hurt, but he insists. "What did you say on the phone earlier? Did you call me 'West coast'?"

Oh boy. Those words just came out without thinking. Not sure how to explain without blurting out I love you. "That's from a song. I was being goofy." I shrug.

I can't meet the weight of his gaze. "So glad the date's over. You're safe and the next time you see Trevor will be at his trial."

Chapter 13

Zack

Cady doesn't answer at first, then says, "Damn, I have to run home to move the weed before the FBI sweeps the place. There's kind of lots so I can take it to Abby's," she mutters, wide awake now.

"Are you kidding? Bring it here and we'll make good use of it, starting now."

Cady's chatting on the short drive to her place, but she becomes shy when we arrive, looking sideways at the bedside drawer. "There's no reason they'd go through my stuff, right?"

"Got a bunch of sex toys, huh?" The weight of her death glare's palpable as I peer into the drawer. "I'm taking these," I snatch a pair of handcuffs. She's pouting as I fall onto the bed, pulling her on top of me. "Don't be so uptight. I love that most of these are smaller than my dick, by the way, but there sure are a lot," I trail off as she beats me savagely with a pillow.

"No tentacles though, right?"

"Please get the bong and stuff out of the closet," she huffs impatiently.

"Sure, but I'm keeping these." I kiss her cheek, rattling the handcuffs in my pocket. The "and stuff" in the closet is a metric shit ton of paraphernalia. I dump it all in a duffle bag, eager to get home. I'm beat and Cady must be exhausted, and I want her in my arms.

She's lost in thought as we hop into the truck. "I want the research job," she says. "This is a phenomenal opportunity. Besides, ever since I started doing what I *want* instead of what I think I'm *supposed* to do, my life has improved by leaps and bounds."

"What do you mean?"

The explanation is surprising because I can't imagine her shying away from anything. The Cady I know isn't timid or indecisive. "Getting Sonny was the best thing I've ever done, even though everyone said don't get a dog.

"Contacting Daniel was one of the best decisions I've ever made. Getting involved in the investigation and everything else, like meeting you guys and helping stop a serial killer, it's amazing. Doing what I want is working out, so I'm sticking with it. Those were the best choices, even if everything pointed in the other direction." I know Cady has anxiety and hides it well, but I didn't truly understand how hard that must be until now.

"I've never had much confidence and always second-guess myself. For a long time, I was convinced my judgment was awful so I never followed my instincts. But the real reason why things go wrong is because I ignore my gut. It took years to figure it out but now that I know, things are so different and so much better.

"Sounds like something good came out of all this. Well, besides the obvious." I kiss her cheek. "My life was boring and much lonelier than I wanted to admit before you came along."

"Mine, too. I'm always happy, but I've never been content before. This is right, and the research job is the right choice too."

"You'll do great and we don't have to work together." There's so much more I want to say, but worry it's too much, too soon, and I don't want to scare her.

Back at my place, she insists on working because it's still early. I found a case eerily similar to Grace's, then two similar to Charleston, but I can't find the one file, so Cady dashes to my office.

"Find it?" I call out, wondering what's taking so long, then she returns with the wrong folder, and my stomach drops.

"What's this?" Her stare burns through me. *Shit*. This is the last thing I expected, and it's not good.

"You had to know we'd run you."

Her face is a picture of barely controlled fury and a sick feeling washes over me. "You thought I was working for the killer?"

"A stranger showing up out of nowhere asking about the case is really weird. I had to entertain the possibility, but dismissed it right away."

"Were you ever going to tell me?"

"Honestly, I forgot because it's not important."

"Not important? These are private things. You talked to my neighbors and my landlord. There's financial stuff too. How is this stuff even relevant?"

"That's how you investigate people. This is what I do at work. I'm sorry I don't see it the same way because I do this every day. It's routine. I'm not sure what else to say."

"Routine to you, but not for the people whose privacy you violate. I wouldn't've liked it, but would've understood if you'd been honest. Hiding it is a different story."

"Forgetting isn't the same as hiding. Are you honestly shocked? You had to know we'd check you out."

"No. Truly, it never occurred to me you'd pry into every aspect of my life without my permission. Worse, nothing here says you ruled out my involvement or decided it's safe to trust me."

"Of course, I trust you."

"Do you, though? This doesn't say that anywhere." She makes a show of flipping through the pages.

"Come on, you know I trust you." This is frustrating. "No question."

"This says 'Can't rule out connections, need to go deeper.' Was meeting me part of the investigation all along?"

"What?" I can't believe what I'm hearing.

"That's what you wrote here."

"Yes. I needed to find out more, but that's not how I get information. I don't lie to do my job."

"How's this any different from what Trevor did?"

"It's completely different. I didn't do it to hurt or trick you. I had to do this. I ran Daniel before I started helping him. He understood."

"And you told him."

"I would've remembered eventually. This is a formality. I had to. The whole thing only took a few hours. Ask Dan and Ryan."

"So I was the only one in the dark? What the hell, Zack?"

"That was before—when we were strangers."

"Or the easiest way to find your killer was to stick with me."

Why is she so pissed? I run my hands through my hair, frustrated. "I never thought you were involved, but I still had to check."

"Excuse me? You didn't suspect I was a murderer, only that I was helping one? Guess I played right into it by falling all over you and sleeping with you."

This keeps getting worse, and I have no idea how to fix it. "No, you don't understand. Let me explain."

"What's there to explain? You shouldn't have this information. You got it all behind my back."

"I'm so sorry, believe me."

"Believe you? How can I ever? I don't know what to believe anymore. For once, I thought I made a good decision. I thought we were good together.

"We *are* good together. We're perfect together. I was wrong to say it didn't matter and should've told you, but I didn't intentionally hide anything. You're angry and you have every right to be, but I'd never hurt you." Crossing the distance between us, I reach for her hand, but she pulls back from my touch as if it burns. "Let me explain."

"Explain where you got the idea I'm a manipulative whore using you to tank Daniel's investigation? No, thanks." If only she'd yell and swear, throw a lamp or something, I could handle that, but not this. Cady looks sick and won't let me touch her.

I will do anything to make it right. I wrap my arms around her. "Please, Cady."

"No," she whispers, pushing away. "I thought I was falling in love with you. I hate myself for being so stupid," she says with finality.

Every plea I make falls on deaf ears as she calls Sonny and walks out the door. This was my biggest fear, but after a few weeks of us being in a good place, I stopped expecting to fuck this up and make her hate me.

Guess I gave myself too much credit.

***

I've tried to reach Cady all night, but I'm shut out completely. She needs time to process everything, then we can talk, I tell myself, doubting every word. Last night, she was so happy, telling me how she has this new confidence and figured out how to fix her problems. Did my fucking stupidity destroy her new outlook? I'm at a complete loss here. Should I leave her alone as instructed or does staying away look like I don't care? Do I keep trying to talk to her, or give her space? I have no fucking clue what to do or where to begin.

Daniel calls with news at the exact moment when I decide things can't possibly get worse. The prints from the glass match a partial found at one of the crime scenes. Trevor was cleared at the time because he was a cable installer who'd been in the house a few days before the murder. He had no record, wasn't in the system, and had an alibi, plus the police already had a suspect, so nobody looked closer. That was the murder after Grace's, one of Brandon's convictions. Sam's team is working to facilitate DNA testing in every single case. Ultimately, DNA won't only tie Trevor to multiple murders, but it may even link him to more crimes than we expected. The feds are awaiting a search warrant for his loft and are ready to start surveillance.

"We're finally going to get them," Daniel says enthusiastically. "Let me talk to Cady."

"Cady's not here, you'll have to call her." Daniel's shocked she'd go off alone, so I explain.

"Get her back to your place, man. We have no idea where Trevor and Owen are right now."

I suggest he could more easily talk her into going to his place. She won't take my calls or respond to my texts and I can't show up, forcing myself on her when she wants to be left alone. She knows the risks and she's an adult. If I ignore her wishes like I know better than her that would be the kiss of death to this relationship.

He promises to call me if she turns up and the sick feeling in my stomach grows. I've broken her confidence when she was starting to believe in herself.

I was the one who'd told her, "You're a badass, woman. Start giving yourself credit here. What it's going to take for you to acknowledge it? You're the one who threw a wrench into his plans."

She'd smiled, and began to believe it, and now I'd destroyed it.

***

Cady

Nothing describes the depths of my low this morning. His betrayal hurts. Insulted and sick with regret, I don't want to face this yet, but

I can't focus on anything else. I only want to sleep and forget. The worst part is, Zack did this to me, but the thing I want most is to have his arms around me. Part of me hates myself for wanting to give him another chance, but another part says I'm overreacting. I should've realized they'd do a background check and he may have legit forgotten. There's been a lot going on lately and we were still sort of strangers—we slept together and then Zack blew me off—when I approached Daniel. Is this truly righteous anger, or am I so used to being disappointed I'm making excuses to end it on my own terms before he can destroy my heart?

I'm furious and hurt, but I love him and I'm not willing to throw us away. Am I going to give that up because he did one stupid thing?

It's too raw to discuss with anyone. I beg off from a dinner later with my family, telling them I'm under the weather, and technically it's true. Since I don't have a job anymore, I could stay in bed for a few days or a week pretending I have the flu but don't want to be here when Sam's team sweeps for bugs.

There's no way I can fall back asleep, despite my utter exhaustion, so I take Sonny to doggy daycare and head to the gym for a few hours. With any luck, a workout will knock me out. The gym's quiet this early, so I have the run of the place. All of my nervous energy powers a two-hour workout, then it's time for a swim.

The empty pool is inviting and I'm always thrilled to have it to myself, but as I touch the door to enter, I notice movement out of the corner of my eye. The pool area's glass-enclosed and appears empty, but something in the corner of my vision draws my eyes to the far corner. What I see turns my blood to ice. It's Owen, tucked away in a blind corner of the pool room. I hustle back to the locker room to throw on my clothes over my swimsuit, rushing out the door in flip-flops. If he notices or follows, he'll be sorry because I'm driving straight to the police station. There's no sign of Owen as I back out, and I don't take my eyes off the gym entrance until necessary. I call Etna PD and Chief Gruber isn't available, but Sargent Baron calls minutes later. She asks where I am and instructs me to take a specific route to meet her at the station, at the same time dispatching a nearby patrol car to follow me, and make sure there's no sign of a tail.

Sargent Baron assumes Gary Babinski is stalking me, so when I see her, I have to explain the entire story with Trevor and Owen, giving contact information for Daniel and Sam so she knows I'm not crazy.

She's not thrilled my amateur detecting is causing her department more work, but she also doesn't act as though I'm a complete nut when I tell her these are the Shaler murder suspects so I must gain some credibility by association with the FBI. She offers to follow me home to make sure nobody else does and wait while I pack a bag to leave. I'm not sure where to go. It's probably best to stay and let them try to get me. I'd be more comfortable talking to Sam first, but I get his voicemail again so I call Daniel. I explain everything and suggest myself as bait because it could work, but Daniel's completely against it.

"Call Zack now and do whatever he says, this second. Call me when you're safe."

"No. I'm fine here. Nobody followed me home."

"That you know of. Call Zack. This is his job and he'll protect you. He'd kill me if anything happens to you." Now I'm sure there's no way things can get worse, but then Daniel tells me the FBI swept my house when I went to the gym. "There were cameras in the living room, bathroom, and bedroom. From the time stamps, they started rolling the same day you found the back door unlocked."

"So they watched everything I did at home for weeks? Are you freaking kidding me?"

"Yeah, they did. I'm so sorry."

"Video only or audio too?"

"Sound too. There was a feed, so most likely they're aware the cameras are disabled or even watched them get taken out. There's, uh, something else," he stammers. "Sunday night, Owen was in your house. He hid in one of the bedroom closets for a few hours before giving up and leaving. Good thing you were at Zack's." I'm stunned silent. A prickly fear spreads through my chest, turning the edges of my vision black and fuzzy. Daniel's still talking, but I'm not listening anymore. "Cady? Are you okay?"

"Those fuckers saw me in my *bathroom*." I shudder. *They could've been watching while we had sex. Oh my god, oh my god, oh my god.* "The night Trevor wanted phone sex? I kept thinking it was infinitely worse since I was naked, even though he couldn't see me, but he could."

"I can't even imagine how you must feel. Call Zack right now, you'll be safe there."

"Yeah, no," I say in a flat, controlled voice, and it takes every ounce of self-control to not implode. My emotions are all over the place.

"I get it, you're mad, but this could be life or death. Don't be stubborn to the point of getting yourself killed. There are no other options here. You can't stay home."

Daniel isn't happy, but he can't make me go to Zack's, or at least that's what I thought until the doorbell rings. My heart skips, but murderers wouldn't let me know they're there. I peek out the bedroom to see Ryan. My phone dings with a text.

Ryan: Copernicus. Let me in.

"You're as much of a smart-ass as your buddy, I see," I tell him.

"Pack a bag, Blackwell. Let's hit the road," he says with a smile, getting comfortable on the couch. The smile vanishes and his feet are back on the floor in a flash as Sonny comes charging downstairs. Ryan relaxes somewhat when those huge paws stop at my side, but his carefree manner vanishes. I'm not going anywhere, but Ryan won't take no for an answer.

"I don't know what he did, but he wants you to be safe. We'll go to his place and he'll stay at mine, at least until the FBI has those assholes in custody."

That's not happening for various reasons and I list each one in careful detail.

"Jesus H. Christ, you're stubborn." Ryan sighs, annoyed. We go back and forth, but he counters every point, which is infuriating. Nobody bests me in a debate. This guy's annoying. He threatens to use chloroform. He's sick of arguing and isn't leaving alone.

"Do you understand the danger here? This is serious enough for Zack to leave his house so you can stay there while I watch out for you. This is no joke. It's not better safe than sorry, it's 'Do this if you want to live.'"

I don't appreciate threats, but they're professionals, so I relent. It doesn't take long to pack a bag and grab Sonny's stuff, so I'm back at Zack's minutes later, but I won't acknowledge his attempts to reach me. Instead, he bothers me in the online game I'm playing. I accept the invitation and blow him up when the match starts. Killing teammates is frowned upon, but he deserves it. If only there were a way to turn off my brain and force my mind to stop racing. Even weed and movies don't help. Halfway through *Scream*, I'm dozing when a lightbulb goes off inside my mind.

"If the video had sound, he knew everything, but he came anyway. Why?" I muse aloud.

Ryan's clueless, so I explain. "The cameras were in place whenever Daniel and Zack came over, plus they heard all my calls. We discussed the meeting, the ER visit, and the murders in Charleston. Trevor didn't willingly come and let us get DNA so there's no way the cameras could've had sound," I explain.

Ryan gets Zack and Walt on the phone to brainstorm with us, then offers a theory. Lots of things can interfere with the equipment's function and certain types have known quirks or failures. Sometimes it's set-up wrong or cheap equipment. "Sound problems happen more in commercial settings than residential," Ryan adds. "The biggest culprits are fans and ventilation systems, equipment running, water noise, those types of things. The average home doesn't have enough noise, so you only have to differentiate the voices from the background noise: TVs, dogs barking, kids screaming. You know, everyday noises."

"Heavy construction nearby or really noisy neighbors can ruin recordings," Walt chimes in, "but there's not enough ambient noise in the average home, so problems are usually from equipment malfunction or improper set ups."

"Ambient noise, like music?" I muse.

"That might be the answer," Zack says slowly, then explains my habit of blaring my music. The guys concur, it's possible.

"Even music at a quiet volume is enough to prevent recording if the microphone is farther from the targets than from the music source. At a moderate volume, the distance may not even matter unless it's high-end surveillance equipment, which this probably isn't," Ryan says.

"The volume has never been less than moderate in my personal experience," Zack offers.

Walt laughs. "He probably thought you were messing with him because of the music when it was good-old fashioned luck."

"Score one for the good guys."

Zack texts as I dash off a fast email to Sam, copying Daniel to keep him in the loop.

Loud music and a dirty weekend in bed saved your life ♥

Of course, I'm relieved, but the elation is short-lived. There's nothing to do and I can't sleep. I'm miserable. My mind's fuzzy with stress, worry, and exhaustion, so concentration's a pipe dream. The case files sit untouched and I lack the bandwidth to even edit a finished story. There's nowhere else I particularly want to be right now either, so everything sucks. Smoking, watching movies, and aching for sleep is all I can do here.

"Trevor and Owen are the criminals, but I'm the prisoner. This blows." Ryan's sympathetic but doesn't have any useful suggestions for ending my misery. He's game to watch movies and plays video games here and there, but he isn't the best company and I'm lonely.

I don't fully understand what's happening and I hate this. I can't be in hiding forever. When will they arrest the Maines brothers so I can be free again? Nobody has answers, but I ask everyone who will listen and leave messages for those who won't.

This is ridiculous. Everyone thinks I'm at Zack's for fun, but after Ryan goes to bed, I call Abby in tears and she's sympathetic, but thinks I'm over-reacting. Of course, they ran me and so what if he forgot to mention it? He was probably uncomfortable and worried you'd hate him she reasons, which was a valid fear considering current events.

"What about my self-respect? How is this any different from the stalker and Trevor?"

"Omigod, Cady. Those aren't the same things. Of course, you're angry, but don't take out every pent-up frustration on Zack. That's his job, and you didn't really know each other yet, or at least, he didn't know you knew each other yet. What was he supposed to do, let Daniel walk into a potential trap?"

"Whose side are you on? How can I forgive him?"

"Girl, I'm on your side because I know what Zack means to you. Holding a grudge hurts you as much if not more than it hurts him. Don't go nuclear and end things. Calm down first. Take time to think everything through. Let him explain."

I'd love to ask Steph or Lana, but haven't shared the entire story with them yet, so they're not up to speed. Besides, the reality is so insane, they'd need time to process everything and I need quick answers.

"How could he do this?"

"Everyone makes mistakes, and this one is pretty minor. Give him a break. It's more of a misunderstanding than an offense."

"So I'm supposed to wave this off and trade my self-respect for a hot boyfriend?"

"Giving someone you love a second chance isn't being a doormat. If he's not worth it, then I guess he's not as important to you as I thought."

The outrage felt so righteous before, but now I don't know.

Zack keeps leaving messages on my voicemail, which is considerate since he knows I don't want to talk, but he still hopes I'm willing to listen. Hearing his voice makes me want to call him, but that feels weak. Crap. Am I screwed up enough to run away from happiness to avoid the possibility of heartbreak? I expected Abby to agree with me. Her dissent threw me into a tailspin, and I'm more confused than ever.

I made it five whole years without shedding a tear until things got bad these past few weeks, and it keeps getting worse.

Now I've cried a river since I left Zack and still can't stop.

Chapter 14

Zack

Days later and Cady's still ignoring me, but I try to stay calm and give her space. The longer this drags on, the more I want to fight for her, even if that means fighting *with* her. Doing nothing feels like giving up and letting go, but cornering her is wrong too. Ryan's a good friend. The night he came here to help with the surveillance detail, he asked if I was banging her yet or trying to. I told him to have some respect since she's going to be my wife someday. When I asked for help, he agreed without hesitation or a single question knowing I'd never ask if it wasn't important. When he asks me for the third time if I want to talk, I manage a half-assed recap because at this point, I need advice.

Ryan says, "She's overwhelmed and frustrated. After working that shit job, being stalked and threatened for months because of it, the assholes tossed her out. Doing undercover work on a fucking serial killer for the FBI is a ton of pressure for actual agents. The stress on someone with no training has to be huge. She cracked, man. Give her some time to pull herself together."

That's what I've been doing, and it doesn't feel right anymore. The waiting is torture. Ryan starts texting me updates and they're hilarious.

Ryan: Who's Noah? This dude wants her to go dancing, but a word of advice: don't *ever* suggest dancing because her response was savage. Betting you two either get married or murder each other, you're so much alike.

Abby warned her days ago their friends are looking for ballroom dance partners and Cady scoffed, suggesting if Noah and Mikey want to learn to dance, they should dance with each other.

Ryan: Who's Christian? They talked forever then she said she loves him too, but he's dead to her now.

Her cousin moved to Cleveland a few years ago, and that's how she says goodbye before hanging up with Christian every time.

Ryan: She's frighteningly accurate kicking the heavy bag. If the bag was a person, she's hitting the nuts 100% of the time. Apologize way harder to protect your nuts.

Ryan: Been wondering how can anyone smoke so much weed and still be so hyper, but saw her make breakfast and holy fuck does maple syrup ooze out when she cuts herself?

Ryan: Watched Con Air twice. Fucking Con Air. TWICE. What the actual fuck?

That's one of Cady's favorite movies, but apparently Ryan isn't a fan.

Ryan: Took a nap and woke up to Varsity Blues. You owe me fucking big time for this.

Ryan: Vampire movie marathon: Fright Night, Lost Boys, and now Dusk Til Dawn. I'm dying here, bro. Fix things with her.

Ryan: BTW, Fright Night was the Colin Ferrell one & I'm pretty sure she swooned, must have a thing for you swarthy fuckers.

Me: Bitch please, you've always been jealous of this face.

Ryan: A dozen movies in less than 72 hours, dying over here.

Ryan: And she knows every line of Natural Born Killers, so now I'm afraid of her.

The updates and color commentary help pass the time, but my patience wears thin. She's isolating herself from the world, and for all I know, she could stay that way forever. She's hurt and angry, and stubborn as hell. She could ignore me forever. She's used to being unhappy and disappointed, so she may have expected this. For all I know, she's already in recovery mode and I'm another asshole on the list of people who broke her heart.

Ryan: Does she EVER turn off the music? I can't even hear myself think.

The last one breaks my heart because Cady said music was a way to avoid being alone with her thoughts. I call the one person I can open up to besides Cady. I'll wake her, but this is urgent and she'll understand.

"Hey, big brother," Sarah yawns. "Let me guess. Someone's husband came home, and you had to jump out a window. Now you need a ride back to your truck and an extra pair of pants?"

"That happened once five years ago, and I had pants." My sister loves to tease me, but she's better with relationships than I could ever dream of being and gives the best advice. Sarah knows Daniel's work and Brandon's case, even the basics on Trevor, but I've never mentioned Cady, so I start at the beginning.

"This sounds serious. How long have you been together and when was I blackballed from the details of your social life?"

"A month or so. It's new, but nothing has ever been more important."

Sarah has lots of questions but seems torn even after hearing the answers.

"Normally I'd say give her space, but the entire world's blowing up around her and this could be the tipping point. If she walked out on Monday night and is still ignoring you Friday, that's not good."

"Yeah, I get that. Am I a complete asshole to go over there when she doesn't want to talk? Should I leave her alone like she said or go to prove I'll fight for her? For us."

"You know her better than anyone. What does she need the most? To wallow in self-pity for a while or to know you care? How will each of those things help or hurt at this point?"

At first, I struggle to respond, but then the pain pours out. She hasn't acknowledged me for days and might not be willing to give me another chance. No doubt she's hurting and while I may not be the best person to lean on. She's keeping so many secrets there's no question she feels alone. Cady's suffering with no support, and it's all my fault.

"The whole thing sucks and I'm sorry for you both."

"I don't matter, the important thing is for Cady to be okay."

"Guess you're super into this girl, huh?"

"I love her and will never forgive myself if I can't fix this." The call goes silent. "Sarah? Are you still there?"

"*Wow*. This is completely out of left field and you're the last person who, well, never mind. Do what's best for her, whatever you think she needs and the rest is up to her. What have you got to lose?"

"Everything. But that's my problem, not hers."

***

Cady

Zack leaves another DM, possibly the hundredth.

Why don't you want to believe me? Why are you so determined to think the worst of me?

Because maybe this breakdown has nothing to do with you and I'm actually mad at myself for always getting hurt thanks to my own stupid decisions. I should've known better, should've kept walking, never should've let this happen. But I don't respond, unsure if that's even the correct answer.

Ryan gags, pretending to die of disgust as I enjoy Frosted Flakes with chocolate milk, then makes multiple jokes as if the amount of sugar in my coffee is any of his concern.

This little exercise has been going on for less than seventy-two hours, but I've had all the Ryan I can take. Zack's kitchen is full of disgusting vegetables and whole grains and I've run out of snacks. Ryan offers to go to the store, but insists I stay put here. The grocery store's hardly a risk for violent confrontation, so he must want to get away from me for an hour.

Whatever, I'm grateful to be alone and even his weird cryptic text doesn't bother me.

Ryan: Hope you can forgive me but had to do it.

He's probably buying something gross to be a smartass, think kale instead of the tub of pre-made cookie dough on the list, but nothing really matters anyway except sleep, since that's the only time I'm not obsessing over how much life sucks.

Time to turn up the music loud, but not enough for the neighbors to call in a noise complaint and try to relax enough to sleep. Ryan took the guest room so I've been sleeping—more accurately living on the couch—this entire week. Lying in Zack's bed alone is an extreme form of torture. His pillows smell of his aftershave and him. I'm not in great shape here.

Sonny curls up close, offering the only comfort I've felt for days. There's no light at the end of this tunnel. Everything is fucked up: Zack is gone. Trevor and Owen are free while I'm a prisoner. Broke and jobless, I can't even job hunt because I'm in hiding. There's no going home, visiting anyone or even running errands. I hate everything.

Somewhere between dozing and despair, the tears come and don't stop this time.

***

I know someone's in the room immediately. I freeze and my blood ices over, my whole body on alert. The first thing I notice is Sonny's gone. *Did someone hurt him? Where's Ryan?*

"Don't worry, it's me." Zack's voice is a balm on my frayed nerves, soothing my tormented soul even as I remind myself to breathe.

The music's not off, but it's much quieter than before. Why does my chest hurt? Because I'm still holding my breath. *What do I say to him?*

"I need to know you're okay, then if you want, I'll go." He's sitting in the chair next to the bed, but I can't get my eyes to open. "Give me five minutes and if you still hate me, I'll walk out the door and be out of your life forever, I swear."

Hate him? If only. Hate would be easy because then none of this would matter, but I love this idiot. Love is what makes this complicated, painful and fragile. Then tell him and fix this.

He moves to the bed but I'm frozen, torn between throwing myself at him and telling him to leave.

"Cady," he begins, but the tears overwhelm me again.

I put my head in his lap, wrap my arms around his waist and break down. *I love you, so why can't I say the words out loud and end both of our suffering?*

The spoken word isn't my thing. Maybe it's the anxiety or I'm seriously not eloquent, but there's a block in my brain preventing me from expressing myself in emotional situations.

Zack's arms around my shoulders make things all right. "Cady, I'd give everything to go back to the diner and tell you every detail. I don't even know why I didn't, except I wasn't focusing on work or the case, I was caught up in you. That's no excuse, but it's true. I'm crazy about you, but I don't know how to do this."

"I care about you, Zack. A lot. But I'm sick of getting hurt. This feels awful, burying myself in everyone else's mistakes. I won't keep doing it."

"What are you saying?"

"I don't know what to say, everything sucks."

The pain in his eyes pierces my soul. Obviously I didn't give the expected response. "Yes, this sucks in every possible way, but we'll get through it."

That's easy for him to say. I sit up and face him, sniffling. "Sure, you will, as long as I keep accepting apologies and giving out more chances, but what about me? How many times do I have to get crushed before saying enough is enough?"

"Oh, come on, you spend so much time beating yourself up and assume the worst of everyone else. Jesus Christ. I thought I was bad, but you don't trust anyone. Not your best friends, not your family, not even yourself. I don't stand a chance with you."

"Not true. I gave you so many chances, but you keep hurting me. Don't pretend I'm wrong for trying to protect myself from next time." Jumping up, I look for the phone to shut off the music. The last thing I need is a soundtrack to my heart shattering, but I can't find it.

"I didn't mean to fuck anything up. I'd never hurt you. Please understand I'm a fucking clueless idiot, and don't know any better."

"Fine, it was an accident, you're so sorry, no hard feelings. But you need to realize, Zack, my life is so fucked up, and giving anyone the power to make life harder or more complicated is the last thing I need right now. I need to figure things out and..."

I trail off, shocked, as he spins me to face him.

"I know *exactly* what you need," he growls, pinning me to the dresser. Standing nose-to-nose, his frustration is palpable, radiating off him in waves. Anger flashes in his eyes but there's fear, too. "I know what you like and what you want and I'm going to be the one who gives it all to you." His lips brush mine. "Tell me you don't want me and I'll leave right now. Swear to god, I'll never bother you again. But I love you, and I don't want to imagine my life without you so you need to understand that before you decide. Fuck. I'm crazy in love with you and it's making me stupid."

Now I can say it too. My cowardly ego needed to hear it first. "You love me?" *Or not.*

Zack stares, not moving, and my heart clenches. *Did he not mean it? Why is he mute?* Sharp tendrils of panic grip me when he laughs. *Is he insane?*

"I love you and it feels so good to say it out loud. In English. For weeks I've been...never mind. Look, if you don't care, I have to live with it, but if you do, we're not leaving this spot until we get past this."

Everything crashes through my mind in an instant: *I love this man. He feels so right in my arms. I've missed him more than I ever imagined possible, and I never want to let go of him.* Nothing will come out of my stupid mouth, but I'm trying to say "I love you" because I love him so much. Collapsing against him, the tears start again and he crushes me to his chest.

"Yes, I should've told you. I should've known it matters and I'm so sorry. I love you, Cady. Please give me a chance to show you. Let me take care of you. I won't always get it right, but I'll always make it up to you, whatever it takes. Please don't walk away."

Seeing the pain in his eyes, I finally find my voice. "I love you. I'm not going anywhere."

***

Zack

Cady doesn't hate me and nothing else matters. Actually, she loves me, and that matters more than anything else ever has. We talk for hours before falling asleep and we're okay. I only wanted to kiss her cheek and go back to sleep, but there's a twinge of guilt when her eyes pop open.

"You're my prince, Strozzi," she says with a yawn, but I'm confused. "Your kiss woke me up, Prince Charming."

"I love the way your mind works." Laying my head on her, I feel relaxed. Finally.

Cady plays with my hair. "Did you sleep?"

"Off and on. Sonny enjoyed sitting out back for a while, but he's zonked out now." Her smile makes me smile. "What?"

"I love looking at you. It makes my heart beat faster. I could stare into your eyes forever." *Too much, woman.* I bury my face in her shirt then realize it's my shirt, which makes me insanely happy, giddy even. "Don't be shy, cowboy."

I kiss her forehead and nose. "Baby, you're light and love, and everything good I need."

"Missed you, Strozzi." Her skin's damp with tears against my cheek. There's nothing I wouldn't do to make things better, but I have no immediate fix for her problems.

She's crying and angry at the world, mainly at Trevor and Owen, and especially the FBI. Why aren't those fuckers locked up by now?

***

"Five whole years?" I'm beyond shocked.

"I haven't cried since my grandpa died. There aren't too many things I care about enough to get upset over. Most things are, whatever, just deal with it. Then suddenly work sucks and I could go to prison and I lost thousands of dollars almost buying a house and I have a stalker and murderers want phone sex."

"Of course, you're upset," I assure her. "It would be pretty weird if you weren't."

"I need to get my aggression out."

"You never got to go to kickboxing, huh? Seems like a good fit for you."

"I want to blow stuff up, but kickboxing's probably more affordable."

"Explosions are awesome, we can do both."

Cady's face lights up. "You're the best thing that's ever happened to me, Strozzi."

"I missed you so much and I love you, *mia stellina*." By now I've said it countless times, but it's never enough. I want to say it a million more and show her in every way possible.

***

The waiting's hard, but it's easier together and we never run out of things to discuss. After explaining fly-fishing and places I want to photograph and seeing the salmon run in Alaska, she shares her very original dream of faking her death to assume a new identity as a small-town sheriff's deputy out west, which is so very Cady. We discuss favorite concerts, racing, best vacation destinations and the greatest books ever written. This is crazy because it feels like I've known Cady forever, but I'm still learning so much about her. There's a volcano in Indonesia that spews blue lava and haunted castles in Eastern Europe and countless other places she plans to visit, but her true love is road trips. The next plan in her playbook is a trip to Memphis because she loves art deco buildings, and wants to enjoy a drink at the Peabody Hotel bar while watching the famous ducks.

"Let's drive to Memphis, baby."

"Sure, but fair warning, I stop for everything: the biggest ball of yarn and the oldest tree on the highway and the world's smallest teapot. I read every sign and stop on the spot where George Washington's second cousin's sister-in-law hung laundry during the Revolutionary War, or whatever. Literally, every last thing. We'll have so much fun."

I've never seen anyone so passionate about road trips, but I want to throw her in the truck this minute and go anywhere to make her smile. I share my plan for the ultimate cross-country trip, taking thirty west and running the Pacific Coast Highway south, then heading back east on forty.

"Let's do it, that route sounds awesome. I've never been out west, not even Vegas."

"No camping, no forests, and you've stayed entirely east of the Mississippi?"

"Technically, I drove across a bridge in Memphis to Arkansas solely to cross the river; but Chicago's the farthest west I've visited."

"Yeah, you need to get out into the world, baby."

"I'll go anywhere with you, cowboy."

We get on the subject of her dream of being a stunt car driver while making popcorn.

"I've noticed you drive fast and speed into the corners."

"I've never explained how I cornered you." She describes gunning it into the complex driveway to give me the slip, then following sans headlights after I passed.

"Keep going, I've never been so turned on in my life, woman," I admit, pinning her against the refrigerator.

"Cars are my thing, Strozzi. Last year I almost bought a '68 Camaro Z28 but got hung up on a '71 Hemi Challenger and I couldn't decide, of course."

"Oh yeah, baby. Tell me more."

"Sometimes I pretend to be busy so everyone leaves me alone to watch Mecum or Barrett Jackson."

"You're a dream come true in every way," I tell her with a kiss. "What's the sports car road trip again?"

"Drive a Maserati *GranTurismo* through the Rockies and Cascades. Put that bad boy through its paces in the Snake River Canyon, then fly through the Badlands on the way home."

"So fucking hot. I want to hear every detail. What else do you enjoy, what are your passions, tell me," I order in between kisses. "Tell me everything."

"You know the important stuff. If my friends didn't drag me out, I'd spend my life smoking and writing. I love college football, *American Dad* and 90s movies and can relate any situation in life to a scene from S*crubs*. My heroes include Teddy Roosevelt, Dr. Elliot Reed, and Ron Swanson. The most important things in life are to take lots of road trips, have cool vehicles and eat steak often. Cake is a food group, metal is life, those are the most crucial points."

"Let's do it, baby."

"Sure, but isn't it weird to announce it?"

"Is that the only thing on your mind, Blackwell? Let's drive fast cars on crazy mountain roads and buy muscle cars at auctions and visit the Black Hills and everything else. I want to make all your dreams come true, every single one."

"What are *your* dreams, cowboy? Tell me."

"You know this stuff. I want to spend all my time on the things I like doing - hiking, camping, fishing, photography— and you. You know I like to travel and love cars and football and books. There's other stuff, but right now, I'm preoccupied with the idea of you on the hood of my Maserati, naked, begging me to drop the camera because you need me right now."

Her lips on my neck are making me crazy. "Ooh, let's do your thing. Wait, are there two cars or are we sharing? If there's only one, it's mine, but you can drive it too because it turns me on to watch a sexy guy shifting a manual."

"In my dreams, I just give you whatever you want because all I want is you."

She rests her forehead on mine with a smile. "That's the sweetest thing anyone has ever said to me. I love you, Strozzi."

"I love you more, but whatever," I tease. "Let's start with a vacation. I don't care where we go, as long as we're alone and nothing can interrupt us."

"Vacation sounds good to me. We deserve time to unwind after this." She leans over to kiss my nose.

"What about the research job?" I ask. Still on, she assures me, so we'll go see Walt and Janice soon.

"Let's hit the gym tomorrow, then the range," I suggest.

Cady shakes her head. "No, I won't learn anything at the gym. I can only focus on your awesome body."

"You can't possibly get turned on there."

"What does that even mean?"

"This isn't a fancy gym full of hot trainers and people who could be models, it's a boxing gym, completely bare bones. The place is perfect for me, but not impressive in the least."

"Ooh, boxing," she says in a breathy voice. "The idea of you boxing turns me on. Besides, I've skipped the gym all week and can't afford to skip anymore," she insists, pushing me down onto the couch and climbing onto my lap.

I peel the tee-shirt off and there's nothing underneath. *Jackpot*. "No, your body's perfect," I mumble, my mouth busy.

"Not for self-preservation. I'm thrilled you like it—"

"I love every inch of your body," I correct her without taking my lips off of her.

"Well, I love that you love it, but I can't defend myself so there's room for improvement."

"Don't worry, we'll toughen you up," I promise in between kisses.

"Did you know your body releases dopamine during sex, which motivates you and gives you energy for other stuff? Science," she says with a flourish.

"Let's test that, for science," I agree.

Chapter 15

Zack

We've spent the weekend trying to relax and recoup, but there's still work to do. Cady's summarizing the latest findings and something's nagging at me. "What? Got something?"

"Think so," I mutter, rifling through notes. "This. There was a case in Seattle with two victims similar to Charleston. Add the one from Illinois, too. Another thing, if Trevor's the one with self-control, the cases with multiple victims may be when he loses his grip on Owen now and then. When in Rome, right?"

Cady considers this and runs with it. "Owen's raping and Trevor keeps the kills separate and different so there's no connection. Sometimes Owen gets carried away and Trevor has to clean up the mess and figures why not join in the fun? Then Trevor cleans up the crime scene to protect them both."

"Makes sense. The cases with two victims are always beatings with strangulation, no knife with the double homicides, but the single kills are always a knife. The crimes are different enough from the rapes and the other murders in different jurisdictions, but the commonalities are remarkable."

"Outstanding work, Strozzi." Cady writes up the theory with supporting examples before getting back into the files. "Why did the local police link the Shaler murder to the rapes in the first place? That's important." One minute she's working diligently and the next, snoring and half-falling off the couch. Attempts to wake her are futile, so I carry her upstairs, where she wakes up long enough to claim she's only resting her eyes.

"Go to sleep." The bedroom's chilly, so I pull her closer. Going to bed used to be something I did without thinking but falling asleep with Cady is an experience. There's something special about knowing she wants to be here with me.

"Did I grab my gym bag? No, and I only have boots here and those are useless to work out. Will Sam send the DNA report soon? Oh, I didn't tell you the other things—"

The rest is unintelligible. "Baby, go to sleep, I can't even understand you."

"Have to call Abby, so she knows I'm okay." Her attempt to get up is so feeble that one arm lying casually across her body is enough to prevent rising.

"Give up already, Blackwell. Abby called when you fell asleep, so I texted her to not worry and you'll call in the morning. She suggested it was the killer trying to throw off suspicion, so I gave her the safe word. Get some sleep."

"You're the best. What time are we heading to the gym?" With a sigh, I flip her over and start giving her a back massage.

"Please let this shut her up and put her to sleep," I mutter to myself. Despite trying to reply, only a yawn comes out, then she finally passes out. It can't be easy being Cady right now, but she handles things like a champ. She never feels sorry for herself or complains. She deserves all the security and happiness in the world and I'm going to spend the rest of my life making sure she has those and so much more.

***

"I'll give you anything in the world, woman, fuck, you're the best," I choke, meaning every word. There's no better way to wake up. I'm trying not to pull her hair too hard, fully aware I'm completely out of my mind at the moment. "I'll buy you a Maserati *today*, just keep my cock in your filthy mouth," I growl.

The kitchen door opens, then I hear a voice. "Oh, shit."

"Dad? *What the fuck?*"

"Sorry." The voice fades as the door slams. Cady appears to be praying for the earth to swallow her as I jump up and into my jeans. Sonny growls low and mean as he scurries downstairs.

"I'm so sorry, baby," I toss my shirt for her to slip on as I head out. There's a curt discussion in the backyard, heated on my end and apologetic on his, but there's no excuse. I'm back in a few minutes,

172

apologizing profusely. "Dad came through the back, assuming I'd be at work. He didn't bother to call or even look in the driveway. Don't worry, he didn't see you."

"And you played it off, right? So, he doesn't know it was me?" Cady nods, willing this to be true, I imagine.

"No, my parents know I'm seeing you." That's clearly the wrong answer.

"So? Let them think this was some stranger. Pretend you dragged some rando home from the bar last night."

"Well, I *might* have said if Cady dumps me because of this, I'll fucking kill him so, no."

"You realize I can never meet your family now, right?"

"It wasn't the whole family, only dad. Surely my parents are aware I'm no longer a virgin at twenty-five."

"Having that general awareness and *seeing* me suck your dick are totally different," she snaps. "Why do these things always happen to me?"

"This has happened more than once?"

"Not this specifically."

"Something similar?"

"No, but embarrassing stuff in general. Life is an endless series of humiliating events," she sighs.

***

The gym's definitely bare-bones, but Cady doesn't mind. Joe, the owner, rolls his eyes in shock. "You brought a woman here? Are you trying to get her to stop talking to you?"

"My girl needs to learn self-defense, Joe. She asked to come here." Shaking his head in disgust, Joe turns back to the crossword on the desk. I throw in a mouth guard and grab headgear, tossing Cady gloves.

"Where's my gear?" She motions to her head and face.

"I'm not going to hit you," I say in disbelief. "Throw a punch. Give me your best shot, baby. Come on, I can take it."

"That's what she said. Ok, sorry, I'll be serious." She stares for way too long, never moving a muscle. "I'm not hesitating. I have no idea how to throw a punch."

"Not shocking. Watch me," I say, demonstrating. "Try it." She throws what has to be the most pathetic punch ever, and I'm worried. "Really, babe?"

"Did you think this was going to be easy?"

"Right. Keep throwing punches, your form will improve naturally. It certainly can't get worse." But the harder she tries, the more discouraged I get. "Hey, pretend you're hitting Trevor," I suggest. "It'll be easy because he's got such a stupid, punch-able face." Cady only gets in a few decent hits, but her blocks aren't the worst and it's a vast improvement. "I think that's enough for today, agreed?" She nods, too winded to respond. "Mind if I hit the speed bags for a few?"

Cady finds a bench and pulls out her phone, but whenever I look up, she's staring. "Wow, I feel completely objectified." I quip, grinning like a fool as I lean down for a kiss.

"Take it outside, lover boy." Joe barks as he passes. "This ain't the drive-in."

"Ooh, I've always wanted to make out at the drive-in, can we?"

"Sure, baby, we'll go in my time machine."

"What? Drive-ins are still a thing, what's wrong with you?

"No, they're not. I haven't seen a drive-in since I was six."

Cady throws up her hands in disgust. "There's one twenty minutes away, smart-ass."

"Seriously? I had no idea, but I'd love to make out at the drive-in. Now let's hit the showers. I'll make sure it's free." She's horrified at the suggestion, even though they're immaculate. Besides, she reasons, Joe will ban us both, which is probably true.

"The water bill's going to be astronomical with you around."

"Stop getting me all sweaty then, I don't usually need multiple showers before lunch."

"Touché," I say with my most devilish grin.

*****

Cady

"This sound system's excellent. How did I fail to notice so many speakers after being here for weeks? What else are you holding out on me, Strozzi?" I ask with fake indignation.

"I'll tell you everything, but first there's an important disclaimer. This can go extremely loud, but please never turn it up past fifty percent, for the sake of my neighbors." I try to look offended but can't pull it off. "Most of the neighbors are elderly, so I'm afraid you plus my system equals neighbor having a heart attack." He's apologetic, so I can't help but laugh.

"You're right to worry, I'd have caused trouble without a warning," I admit.

"Use it anytime. You probably can't wait to go home once they get Trevor and Owen, but I hope you'll still be spending time here."

"I'll be here all the time. Sure, I miss my place, but I love it here, too. And Sonny is thrilled to have another yard to sniff and different squirrels to hate." Kissing him while we're laughing is my new favorite thing.

"I understand you have to go home, but maybe we can revisit the subject after things get back to normal. If you want to," he adds quickly. He's wrapping my hair around his fist absentmindedly, with a sly grin on his face. "Then we could start every day the way we did this morning," he mumbles, moving his lips across my collarbone.

"Are you asking me to move in, Strozzi?"

He meets my gaze and the heat in his eyes almost stops my heart. "Well, yeah. Having you here is awesome but I'm not trying to rush you."

"No, it's fine. My lease is up in a few months anyway."

"Really? So, you'll consider coming back?"

I nod. "It's fun playing house with you and I'd certainly enjoy *that* with my coffee every morning."

"Love you, Cady. Have to say it again." We've probably said it a hundred times since the first time, but it'll never be enough.

"Love you, too," I murmur into a kiss. "Were you awake the other night when I whispered in your ear?" I'm suspicious.

"No, but wish I was. I've wanted to say it but was afraid it was too soon. After you called me 'west coast' though, I figured it was safe to tell you. I've heard you play that song."

"The words just came out. I didn't even remember saying it until you asked, but it's true. You're my west coast, honey," I admit, laying my hand on his cheek. The smile on my face feels enormous.

"There's nothing in the world I'd rather be than the one you love the most," he murmurs.

"I knew the first time we kissed it should be you and me, Zack."

"Crazy, huh? I've never been kissed like that." There were so many close calls, like the time I nearly asked him out in Daniel's parking lot and he almost kissed me the same night but thought I'd slap him. This took a ridiculously long time. He wanted to make a move the night there was a prowler, but thought it would be wrong since his job was to protect me. I explain how I went to bed but couldn't fall asleep. I knew he was perfect for me, but my entire life was so screwy, I didn't trust myself. "I talked myself out of it, but I wanted to walk back into the living room and take my clothes off without saying a word to see your reaction."

"That would have been super fucking hot, woman," he says in an awed voice.

"I was afraid of embarrassing myself. There were times I was flirting and nothing, so I wasn't sure if you weren't interested but maybe you didn't realize. I'm not great at it."

"Honestly, you're not, I thought you hated me. I wanted to rip the towel off of you when you walked into the kitchen that morning, but I wanted you to like me and didn't want to be just a good time."

"I'm not usually shy, but I liked you so much. Rejection rarely bothers me, but I was sure with you it would've crushed me."

He kisses my forehead. "I fell in love with you so fast but was afraid of scaring you away. I've been saying it different ways in Italian."

"I wondered what you were saying but was too distracted by all the hot sex to ask. Are you fluent?"

"Nah, I only know enough to keep your panties wet, *il mio amore*," he grins.

"Well, it works, Strozzi."

"You make me so happy."

"I've never been happier." I snuggle into him, feeling his heartbeat against my cheek. "But we have so much fun, I worry it can't last, it's too easy."

"I can't promise it'll always be easy, but I promise it'll always be us. Everything else is whatever, we'll handle things and make it work."

"That's right, we kick ass together so we can deal with anything."

"Damn right, woman. We're alive and we're together. What else matters?"

"Nothing else matters." *Zack loves me. This is everything.*

***

The butterflies in my stomach are friendly as I prepare for my upcoming interview at Shields.

"Do you have any idea how many times I've heard the same stupid interview questions since Dunn's went under? Every time is worse than before, and I never know how to answer. 'Where do you see yourself in five years, Cadence?'

My five-year plan isn't exactly something I can share with potential employers since it focuses on vacations, concerts and kind bud, not work. Now it's even worse because who knows where I'll be in five weeks, maybe a safe house because a damn serial killer's after me. Dead? Your guess is as good as mine. 'What's your biggest strength, Cadence?' One time, I confused a murderer with movie quotes, so the FBI could steal his highball glass for a DNA sample. How does that skill fit into the corporate culture?"

"This has all been a colossal pain in the ass, yet highly entertaining because you have such a way with words. There's no question you'll enjoy working at Shields, but we've to get you into real self-defense classes right away though."

"How can you give up on me so quick?"

"We'll still practice, but you need professional help. Let's keep boxing, though, so I can watch your boobs while you bob and weave," he says magnanimously.

A visit to the range reveals I'm a half-decent shot, not an expert, but not terrible. After firing a bunch of weapons, Zack's new Ruger 9mm seems like the best fit. The automatic is small and lightweight, so it isn't completely obvious when I wear it in a holster. The girls and I had plans to watch the Pens game tonight at the Middle Road Inn, but Zack convinced me to go elsewhere since Trevor knows I frequent it. Of course, he's right, but I'm so mad to have to keep changing my life. I'm carrying the gun since I have a permit now but praying I don't have to use it. Back from the range, we're getting to work when Daniel calls with tremendous news that changes everything.

"There's a preliminary match between Trevor's sample and the hospital blood sample from Charleston. The DNA didn't get any direct hits in CODIS, but there's a familial match. Trevor has a male relative currently incarcerated."

"Ugh, I was hoping the Maines family blood line dies out with these two, but I guess not. What's next?" I ask.

"Search warrant for the inmate's family tree to identify their relationship. This could also help determine where he's been in his travels. For example, if he visited the prisoner or lived with him at one time."

"Knowing where Trevor's been could tie him to additional cases that aren't even on our list," Zack explains.

"Plus, they're working on extracting DNA samples from the bite marks, but testing will take a few days," Dan adds.

This may break the case wide open. We're now at a crossroads where we need to place Trevor at the crime scenes via a timeline, plus find a DNA match to proceed. Hopefully, we'll know a lot more in the next twenty-four hours, but since this isn't an official case, the testing can get bumped down on the priority list. Sam promised a name and details on the convict so Daniel will keep us posted.

There's excitement in the air as I lean over for a high-five. "We kick so much ass, Strozzi."

"Hell, yeah we do. It's so hard to believe this is finally happening. For years, everyone's made Daniel out to be a nut. Now someone's finally paying attention." Zack pulls me onto his lap for a long kiss. "Time to decide where to go for a relaxing trip, since this is wrapping up."

"Yes. Let's go somewhere we can do lots of nothing. You work too much, and don't get enough sleep," I declare, playing with his hair. "I want to see you have fun."

"Anywhere where we're together is perfect." Zack's phone rings and I jump up, seeing his mom's name. "Talk to your mom, I've got to meet my girls," I tell him with a peck on the cheek. I stop to give Sonny a lecture about being nice while I'm gone. "I'm proud you've been such a good boy, but *keep* being good when I'm gone, okay? *Don't* scare him. He likes us both and we're keeping him." Blowing Zack a kiss, I head to the door, but he jogs over.

"Be careful, baby. See you soon," he says with a fast kiss. "Sorry, Mom. Cady's leaving, had to say goodbye."

Chapter 16

Cady

Abby, Lana, and Steph are all bursting with excitement when I arrive, but they're alone.

"Where are Jamie and Randy?"

"We need a proper girls' night out, so we uninvited them. Now, I need to hear every single detail about you and Zack," Steph singsongs his name. "Start talking."

"Let's order snacks and ---"

"Cady, you're killing me. I need specifics," Abby fusses. I bring Steph and Lana up to speed on everything after the meeting with Trevor because there's no hiding this anymore. Right now, the sole focus is on my love life though and they expect every detail, so I leave nothing out.

"So, he came home Friday? Are you still bickering?" Lana asks.

"No, it's freaking phenomenal. He's gorgeous and perfect and everything I didn't even know I needed before he came into my life. I want to wake up next to him every day and kiss him goodnight every night. I'm so in love."

"I knew it." Steph breathes. "I'm so glad you guys made up."

"Me, too. I love him and I love everything about him. I want to look at his magnificent face and touch his smoking hot body forever. Zack loves cars and road trips and music and art. He has at least as many books as I do, maybe more, and he's the sweetest, plus he's some kind of magical sex ninja, I can't even explain it. Honestly, there are no words."

"So, you guys have been, well, you know."

"Constantly, and it's freaking amazing every single time. Strozzi's magic."

"So, it's huge?" Abby asks because she would.

Well, yeah but I don't kiss and tell. "No, it's not about that --"

"So, it's small?"

"No, it's perfect. He's so good at everything. There's no other way to describe it. *Magic.*"

"This is a stunning turn of events," Lana says, eyeing me over her drink.

"True. A few weeks ago, you were lusting after this guy but determined to avoid him, now you're madly in love," Steph adds.

"I've never felt this way about anyone, but I love him, completely."

The third period's starting before we even notice the game because there's so much to cover. We've moved on to how screwed Allen Brothers is when I get a flurry of texts from Daniel, all good news: Sam got the search warrant so they're tracking the familial connection and suspect it's his father. The lab successfully extracted biological matter from one of the bite marks and should process the sample tomorrow so things will start happening fast. Abby's reading over my shoulder and lets out a low whistle.

"Cady, this is all so insane. Two months ago, you were a bored office drone, now you're helping the FBI catch a serial killer. How did this happen?" Lana demands.

"This started when I emailed Daniel, but you're right, it's crazy."

With so much to share, I almost forgot to mention the job offer. We ponder the mysteries of my new life and plan a karaoke night to celebrate my new gig as the Pens shut out some random expansion team. Abby has a job interview early in the morning and we're lucky to even get Lana out on a weeknight so we say goodbye when the buzzer sounds. I wait until they're all safely on their way to make sure nobody follows and watch my mirrors as I drive. Sonny's sleeping at Zack's feet and my love is radiating so much nervous energy, he's practically vibrating.

"Did you see the texts? This is finally happening. I just talked to Dan. Trevor's dad is a level three sex offender who committed crimes against children. Sam is sending the details."

"This must be unreal for you guys after chasing a phantom for years. Things are moving so fast now it's hard to keep up with the developments."

"He said any minute and I can't stop checking for it."

***

Zack

Even though it's getting late, we're too wired to sleep and waiting impatiently for Sam's report on the familial DNA match. Trevor and Owen Maines are the sons of Julie and Stuart Wayne Maines of Inglewood, California. Stuart's a nasty drunk who can't hold a job and spent most of his time terrorizing Julie, when not turning her out for drinking money. Stuart went to prison for fondling a ten-year-old neighbor when the boys were five and four but made parole after only sixteen months. In the short time Stuart was away, Julie got herself and her kids a decent place to live in a better part of town but sadly took him back.

She lost her job soon after because of the beatings, many of which resulted in injuries serious enough for her to miss work. When she disappeared a few years later, everyone assumed he'd killed her, but her body was never found. The few people who knew her insisted she loved her boys fiercely and would never have left them alone with Stuart. The boys were treated for frequent injuries but he preferred little girls so they were ostensibly spared the sexual abuse he inflicted on many others.

"Jesus Christ, he's a complete monster. Those two had no chance to be normal."

Cady disagrees. "No matter how much they got beat, I guaran-fucking-tee they know better than to rape and murder people. Otherwise, they would have gotten caught right away. If someone's clever enough to cover their tracks, then they understand right from wrong."

"I don't disagree completely, but kids can't grow up normal in that environment. There's no way."

"Millions of people grow up with drunken, abusive parents but don't become serial killers."

"Sure, but the odds have to be worse when daddy makes mommy turn tricks in front of you and then kills her."

"Well, okay, hard to disagree there," she concedes. "Listen to this: in the weeks preceding her disappearance, neighbors had called the police on the couple on eight separate occasions. The last few calls differed from prior calls because now they were fighting.

Neighbors reported on three of the occasions Julie was screaming at Stuart, telling him to go suck dicks for money if he can't hold a job because she won't do it anymore. Think about that. The prior calls were for Stuart beating Julie, but now she's talking back and fighting back. How much do you want to bet he cut her throat?"

"Holy shit, you're probably right. So they share their father's hatred of women, which explains the way he talked to you the other night."

"And the drunken phone calls." Cady's shaking, so I pull her closer, tucking her into my side.

Sam's report includes photos, and the first one knocks me speechless. "Look at this," Julie Maines is the spitting image of the Shaler victim. "Is this motive right here?"

"Whoa. Did daddy make them hate mommy so much, they kill women who resemble her?"

"Or they're mad at mommy for leaving them. There are so many possibilities, all of them are extremely disturbing."

***

Once we stop working for the night, I can't wipe the stupid grin off my face. "No matter how many times I say I love you, it will never be enough."

"I love you too, cowboy. And now you have to meet my family. I was going to do this in small bits but let's just throw you into the fire."

"Sounds scary. Is there anything I should know? Is your dad one of those psychos who'll make a big production of cleaning his guns while I visit?"

Cady laughs, assuring me they're great but sarcastic as hell. "Not going to lie, this will be an adjustment if you didn't grow up being roasted non-stop every day of your life, but they're fun." Then she drops a bomb: her family knows she's seeing me but has no clue she's hiding here or that Trevor's a murderer or anything about her work with the feds. She's not sure how to tell them because her parents won't approve of the new job. This is shocking. She talks to her mom daily, so it's hard to fathom how she's kept so much to herself. It's difficult, she admits. Lily and Evan know she's here, but they think we're just knocking boots a lot.

"Your secrets are safe with me, but won't you feel better if you level with them?"

"Sure, I'll feel better but they won't so I've got to figure out how to do this."

"I can't wait to meet your family and," I pause, "my mom's dying to meet you."

"To see the whore corrupting her darling son, no doubt. How can I ever look your parents in the eye?"

"No, baby, my mom's not like that. She's been asking for weeks, even before the, uh, incident. I only said I'm seeing someone, but somehow she could tell it's serious. Last night she said, don't punish me because your father's too stupid to knock. I married him, but I didn't raise him."

"Kind of hard to argue with the logic," she concedes.

"Right? She wants us to come for dinner tomorrow, Ryan and Daniel, too. It's casual, no pressure." I pull her into a hug, resting my chin on her head. "She'll love you as much as I do. Don't stress over this."

"Now I'm going to have nightmares of being naked at dinner," she frets and I take another pillow to the head for laughing.

**

Cady

Sonny and I enjoy a long walk around Zack's neighborhood, and it's exhilarating to be outside without looking over my shoulder for a change. Daniel reports Trevor and Owen are definitely at the Strip District loft. They're arrogant little pricks to stay, because they have to know they're suspects, but they haven't left. I'm not thrilled they're close by, but it's better than not knowing their whereabouts. Today, I'm heading into the office with Zack to meet Janice and Walt, excited to give this a shot. Then I'll visit my parents and finally let them in on the happenings in my life. I was brave enough to run home this morning for a professional outfit to wear today. Sonny came along for the trip, and I was nervous at first, but soon anger overtook the fear. I don't appreciate being chased out of my house. Being at Zack's is fun but I resent that we're doing this out of necessity and not by choice. There's a close call on the stairs since

I'm clumsy in heels, but catch myself in time. I hear a low whistle and turn to see him grinning.

"Your ass looks so good in that little skirt. I need to rip it off with my teeth."

"Behave yourself, Strozzi. Every other interview-worthy outfit I own needs ironing, and I'll be super pissed if I have to iron," I give him a look, so he knows I'm not joking.

"There's no reason to dress up or be nervous."

"Are you implying the interview's merely a formality, since I'm sleeping with their best investigator?"

"I wasn't aware you even knew Frank Halligan, especially not in the biblical sense," he teases. "You've got Daniel, a respected client, Ryan, a valued employee, and a damn FBI agent for references, woman. Trust me, they want you."

Maybe it's only a formality but I still can't relax. It's a short drive to the office, but I drain a second enormous cup of coffee on the way and get even antsier. Zack tries his best to put me at ease but can't understand why I'm nervous. Walt's on a call, so I meet Janice first. She's genuine and speaks as though I already work here. I wasn't sure what to expect, but she couldn't be friendlier and her bubbly personality is instantly likable. They met at Parris Island as recruits over forty years ago, then Walt stayed in the Marines while Janice joined the FBI. They've traveled the world working to keep us safe from terrorists and various other bad guys. Janice was on the FBI's hostage rescue team and they're both totally badass, so working with them is an exciting prospect.

She asks if I'm sure I want to work with Zack. Working together doesn't make marriage easier, she admits. It will be difficult, she warns, as it's not always possible to leave your personal life at home or to leave work at the office. Janice wonders if we're ready for that. The idea is intimidating since this is so new, but I probably wouldn't do this without him, either. I have little experience and would feel like a liability for anyone else, but we're so in sync and work so well together, I have no reservations. Besides, he's fantastic at his job, so working together is a great opportunity to learn. If we drive each other crazy, then I have to go because he was here first.

"There's no middle ground. You'll know immediately if this is going to work or not. You'll either love or hate working together from day one." She takes me to Walt's office with a third cup of coffee I shouldn't be drinking and he starts with small talk, assuring me he prefers to keep interviews informal. Walt asks what interests me about the field considering my lack of experience and wants to hear about my role in Daniel's case in my own words. He's impressed that an FBI agent, in the BAU no less, is one of my references. This is going well, so I'm finally relaxing when it all changes.

"Tell me where you see yourself in five years?" Walt asks, sternly.

I start to answer, then reconsider. "Did he tell you to ask about my biggest strengths and how they fit into the corporate culture too? He's such a smart-ass."

Walt laughs, deep and hearty. "I like you, Cady, and I trust Zack. He's one of my best investigators and an excellent judge of character. If he says you'll be a good fit here, then you will. Let's talk about training and the terms of employment." One hour and tons of paperwork later, I'm officially an employee of the Shields Group. A bunch of people gather to welcome me, including Ryan, and one sober-faced little balding guy comes over to extend a hand.

"Nice to meet you, Cady. I've heard a lot about you. Name's Freaking Kyle," he says with a completely straight face and we all crack up. Kyle's wife did have the baby, and he jokes they almost named him Zack since covering Kyle's night shift took such a toll on Strozzi's social life.

There's just enough time to go see Mom and Dad before I have to be at Gary Babinski's hearing. My parents aren't thrilled about my new job, but they're reserving judgment. Maybe they'll be more excited after this case is closed and I can add 'helped the FBI stop a serial killer' to my resume, but probably not. I'm super excited for them to meet Zack, so we make plans for Sunday dinner. We're going to karaoke on Saturday night with Steph, Nina, and the gang, so it's nice to get some semblance of normal life back after all the craziness of the last few months.

Minutes after leaving Mom and Dad's, I receive a call from an investigator at the department of labor and industry, informing me Allen Brothers owes a bunch of us lots of back pay for working long hours as salaried workers. They're also in a lot of trouble with the IRS, and I have nothing to worry about in either case. Best of all, he's quite interested in the packages I sent to Daniel because if any of those documents have changed or gone missing, Pete and Bob could face criminal charges.

I get an update from Daniel right before walking into the magistrate's office. The lab hasn't matched Trevor's DNA to any of the crime scenes yet, but they've only tested the sample against a fraction of cases, so we're hopeful. No new rapes or murders have happened since Charleston, so the Maines brothers are lying low. I'm still worried they could get to me, but having Zack glued to my side is no hardship and the FBI has them under surveillance, so the risk is low.

Knowing I start a new job on Monday reduces my stress greatly and Shields pays better than Allen Brothers, which sweetens the deal. After much deliberation, I asked the Magistrate to show Gary Babinski mercy. Sure, he's an ass, but I pity him, and to be fair, I met the love of my life and got an awesome new job, partly due to Gary, so this wasn't the worst thing to happen. The judge is surprised but agrees to consider the request. Babinski is contrite and appears to be genuinely sorry he had the wrong person, if not genuinely sorry for doing bad things. The guy's screwed up his entire life in a few months and has so much to fix, I don't want to add to the burden. Gary and his parents were extremely grateful for my plea for leniency.

***

Life's going extremely well, except I'm meeting Zack's family tonight so I'm a nervous wreck and can't sit still on the drive to dinner. He stops in the driveway, turning to me as we approach the door.

"Please relax, baby," he begs, pulling me into a hug. "They're going to love you as much as I do, I promise."

The anticipation's probably far worse than the reality, so I give him a fast kiss and power walk to the door. Ryan's already here and Daniel's pulling in as we enter. Zack's parents, Linda and Ray, are so welcoming and his younger sister's awesome, too. Everyone's friendly and funny, so they put me at ease right away. Daniel's positively giddy because Lindsay's coming to visit soon. He can't stop grinning. Seeing him so exuberant makes my heart happy.

Things are chill until dessert when Ryan describes a fancy golf trip he planned as a birthday gift to his dad.

"When my birthday rolled around a few weeks ago, I was excited," Ray mentions casually. "Considering everything I've done for my kids, I was pumped to hear he's handing out fancy sports cars for favors," he nods at Zack. "But I only got Pirates tickets."

"Jesus Christ, Dad." Zack throws up his hands. Ryan tries to disguise his laughter as a cough and Sarah drops her fork. Even Daniel's trying to hide a grin.

"Ohmigod, Zack. Did you tell everybody?" I hiss, livid.

"Not exactly, but yeah, kind of." He's glaring at his father.

Ryan turns to Daniel. "Hey, we've got a man in trouble over here. Better call for help. Copernicus."

"Ray, I told you not to tease the kids," Linda admonishes, but everyone's laughing now. After dinner, Linda pulls me aside to say she couldn't wait to meet me. "I knew he was in love the first time he mentioned you, even before he admitted it. After Ray made such an ass of himself, I was afraid you'd avoid us forever, so I'm thrilled to meet you."

I can't help but laugh because a tremendous weight has been lifted from me and I'm having a great time. Linda asks me to join her and Sarah for lunch soon, and I happily accept.

The drive home is much more relaxed. "Dinner wasn't uncomfortable at all, you were right. But I see those smart-ass tendencies run in the Strozzi family. You clearly get that from your dad."

"Only the men have the sarcasm gene in my family, but our kids are in big trouble, getting it from both gene pools," he smirks.

Chapter 17

Zack

Weeks later, Cady remains here with me as the FBI— excruciatingly slow—builds a case against the Maines brothers. Although they're under surveillance, they're still free. These things are complicated and I understand they've to get it right, but it's frustrating the arrests are taking so damn long. Trevor's DNA from the bar glass is matched to five crime scenes so far, although the mere presence of his genetic material isn't proof of guilt. Sometimes it's conclusive, for example, if there's a match to a semen sample in a rape kit, but presence at a crime scene doesn't mean the guy's a killer, even though we know he's the killer.

Owen's DNA has been matched in nine of the rape cases, which is far more conclusive. Normally, he'd have been arrested after one match, but this is a special situation because they can't chance scaring off Trevor. Sam has complicated explanations for the bureaucracy, but I sum it up as paperwork matters more to the feds than preventing future rapes and murders.

The one bright spot in this waiting game is the feds contracted Shields to trace the Maines brothers' movements over the last few years. Cady and I have been doing this for months, but now we get paid for it, plus it allows her to ease into her new job.

Working together has been seamless so far, and she gets only positive feedback in the office. Everyone enjoys working with her and agrees she's a natural for this work. Most importantly, she loves it and can't wait for the next case, and I've never seen her happier. Ryan asks is it weird to have been living together for most of our relationship and the answer should be a resounding yes, but it's not. If one of my friends told me they were going to move in with a woman they've only known for a few weeks, I'd stage an intervention because that can't possibly be a good idea, but it feels right for us. Our circumstances are weird, but I wouldn't change a thing. Having Cady here is phenomenal.

My parents are right, when you know you just *know*. Besides, if you're lucky enough to find someone who's perfect for you, nothing matters except holding onto them. If she wants to renew her lease, fine. There's no reason to rush through life, we don't have to move in together tomorrow, because we have all the time in the world. Unfortunately, the Maines brothers are still free men, but that should change soon.

Over the last few weeks, we've been able to trace them around the country, primarily through the Pacific Northwest, the Midwest, and the rust belt. There's compelling circumstantial evidence to link them to nineteen murders and twenty-six rapes. The sex crimes will be tougher to prove because not every case has physical evidence, but hopefully, they'll tie Owen to the murders as well, ensuring he's locked up for a long time. Considering the hospital break-in and how seamlessly they got into Cady's house to plant cameras, I started looking into other police reports near the known crime scenes. We think they robbed small businesses to fund their travels.

I finally found a skimpy job history, discovering they briefly worked installing cable television. The company also offered internet service and cheap security systems, which explains their ability to avoid surveillance cameras at the crime scenes. I suspect they used the router information to hack the feeds so they'd know when the victims were home alone but we still have to prove it. The FBI got this information out to dozens of local law enforcement offices, and now hundreds of investigators across the country are working to connect them to additional crimes.

Tonight, we had plans with Sarah to meet my friends for drinks after another dinner at my parents' house, but the weather turned ugly, so we left her behind and headed home instead. It's a good thing too because what started as a gentle spring snow is turning into an icy mess of sleet, making the world treacherous. Even Sonny isn't interested in being outside in this mess.

"Being stuck in the house for the entire weekend with terrible weather might be fun," Cady grins, dropping onto my lap, wrapping her legs around my waist.

"Let's stay in bed all weekend, no matter what the weather does," I suggest. "Last time we did that was the best weekend ever." I love watching her eyes close as my hands work under her sweater.

"What's in your pocket?"

Dammit, I want to unload this without her noticing, which will be tricky now since I forgot it was in my pocket. It can't fall out when I take off my pants. "Nothing, baby, I'm just happy to see you." Cady makes a face, but the lights go out before she can retort. "The ice must be pulling down lines, so I better light a fire. I don't want to freeze before the power comes back." Cady goes to the kitchen for candles as I light the fireplace, but one glance outside and I snap to attention.

"Take Sonny to the bedroom, lock the door, call 911. Remember the code to the gun safe? Take one of the tactical shotguns and don't open the door for anyone but me." Cady's speechless. "Everyone else has power except the Dunhams, and we're on the same line from the pole. It's probably the ice, but better safe than sorry."

"What? No, you come with me."

"Go. Lock the door behind you."

"No, you come with me. Let them try to get us."

"Lock yourself in while I --" but she's not moving, so I humor her and follow. Cady calls 911 to report a break in, and I call Ryan for reinforcement. I'm strapped because I've been carrying as long as they're still out there and wasn't home long enough to get comfortable. Grabbing a couple of flashlights and two tactical shotguns, I load them in a flash, pushing one into her hand. "Stay here."

"No, *you* stay here," she insists. "*Are you crazy*? No confronting anyone. Let them come to us and we'll ambush them. Is the alarm armed?" There's a noise from downstairs that may be a footstep, making the hair on my arms stand. Cady stiffens and Sonny growls, low and deep, so they heard it, too.

"No, and don't fight me on this," I whisper. Ambushing them might work, or they may riddle the room with bullets through the door and kill us both. Intercepting them is probably safer because it gives me the element of surprise. Hopefully. Sonny pads to the bedroom doorway, still growling and hackles up, but I block him in with a knee and hand her a shotgun. "They'll be in the house soon if they're not already. Lock the door and don't leave this room."

"No. Wait for the police--"

"Lock the door," I order, slipping into the darkness of the hallway. Cady tries to grab my shirt, but I sidestep.

"Zack." She whisper-shouts, but I don't answer, determined not to make a sound. Surprising them is my best chance to keep them away from her until help arrives.

***

Cady

Grabbing Sonny's collar, I hurry him into the bathroom, shutting the door and hoping he'll be safe in there because I can't have these assholes hurting my dog. The house is quiet when I stop to listen, filled with an ominous silence. Even the ambient noise is gone without the furnace blowing or Sonny panting. The absence of sound is mocking as I pray for sirens and strain my ears for any sign of Zack, to no avail. I'm frozen, then remember I should lock the door before calling 911 again. This time I'll ask for Etna. They're only a few miles away and if Chief Gruber or Sargent Baron is on, or even Officer Spencer, I know they'll be the cavalry we so desperately need right now. After only a few minutes without heat, it's already freezing in here. Distracted by the chill, my brain doesn't fully register the creaking floorboards until the door flies open, then there's a knife at my throat.

"Hi, bitch, remember me? We're going to have fun tonight." The knife is freaking huge and as cold as the ice outside.

"What the fuck, Trevor? The cops are coming, they'll be in here any minute." I scream so Zack can hear, hoping to scare Trevor and praying the ruckus reaches the neighbors so they call 911, too. How the hell did they slip the FBI surveillance? There's no time to wonder, as a series of loud crashes tells me that Owen's engaging Zack downstairs. Trevor's the smaller of the two, so maybe I stand a chance. Zack's bigger than Owen and in much better shape, so should easily outmatch him. There's a thundering blast downstairs, and I scream for Zack, but I get no response.

"We'll be long gone before the pigs show up. You know what they say, when seconds count, the po-po are only minutes away," he laughs, lowering the knife to grab for my shotgun with both hands.

Knowing he'll outlast me if this goes on long enough, I shove it behind me and snatch the lamp from the nightstand. Raising it overhead, I swing with both hands directly at his skull. There's contact, but he pivots just enough to avoid the full impact. Trevor's hands drop for a split second, so I point the shotgun, but he grabs it with two hands, easily twisting it toward the window.

Turning, I kick out with every ounce of strength I can muster, thankfully connecting with his ribs. The blow knocks the air out of him and he falls to one knee as I raise the shotgun, determined to smash it over his head because he's too close for me to point and shoot. A deafening crash and voices from downstairs grab my attention and in that millisecond of hesitation, Trevor is twisting the gun from my grasp. With one hand still on the gun, mostly for show, I scream his name and ram my knee into his face when he looks my way.

Trevor falls back and one of his hands slips off the gun, but there's movement in the doorway as Owen steps out of the shadows to grab my arms. Sonny's raging at the bathroom door and I pray it doesn't give. *How did I not lock the bedroom door? Fuck.* Panic sets in as I wonder what Owen's done to Zack and I'm screaming. *Please let the neighbors hear this and call the police.*

"Shut this bitch the fuck up, man," Owen barks and Trevor pummels me in the head with the heavy lamp. I see stars and my legs give out, but I don't black out. Suspended only by Owen's grip on my arms, I refuse to stop screaming, trying to kick back at him.

"Shut the fuck up," Owen screams. He starts raining punches on my face and head. Trevor's laughing like this is the most fun he's ever had. Owen rips my shirt off and tries to gag me with it while Trevor pulls out zip ties. *Why aren't the police here yet? What did he do to Zack?* Trevor's talking, but it's tough to make out what he's saying with the ringing in my ears.

Trevor hopes Zack's still alive to watch this, but Owen only shrugs noncommittally. Sonny is slamming into the wood repeatedly and I worry he'll break through the door to sure death. Are there sirens yet? Maybe I can't hear them because of the high-pitched keening in my ears. An explosion behind me gets everyone's attention. Owen drops, howling like a banshee, and I realize it was a shotgun blast. Someone grabs the back of my pants, flinging me into the hallway. I don't know where Trevor is, but relief washes over me knowing that Zack is safe. The air's thick with the telltale odor of Federal ammunition but now the coppery scent of blood hits me. Zack must have hit Owen.

There are two more blasts in quick succession as Owen howls and Trevor screeches with rage. Struggling to my feet, dizzy and having trouble balancing, I realize if I can grab the pistol from Zack's waist, and we empty both guns into the room, we'll hit them. Reaching for the pistol on his back, my hand finds only air. Zack's gone and there's a crash in front of me as they fight over a gun.

"Cady, shoot him," Zack screams, not knowing they've taken my gun. I scramble on the floor, clawing desperately to find one or get to the safe when there's another explosion and Zack screams. By the time my hands close on a shotgun and I fumble with the flashlight, Trevor's closing in on me. Grabbing my wrist, he pulls to extend my arm, then uses the weight of the heavy lamp to smash my forearm.

By a stroke of pure luck, I manage to squeeze the trigger as the bone snaps. Stars swim before my eyes, and the edges of my vision turn black. Everything moves in slow motion and my broken arm hangs limply at my side, burning as though on fire. Zack is nowhere to be seen and I can't fire blindly into the darkness for fear of hitting him if I'm even capable of firing again. The smell of blood is overpowering and I pray it's not his. Owen's slumped in the corner, so we neutralized one threat. Trevor holds his shoulder, screeching madly, still advancing, and I squeeze off another shot with my left hand. Sirens and feet pounding finally break through my shock, but the only thing that matters is Zack, crumpled at the foot of the bed. There's so much blood. It's everywhere and on everything. Trevor is slouched under the window, screaming, and Owen's still on the ground when the police rush into the room.

Screaming for help at the top of my lungs, I have no idea what's going on. I'm hysterical, putting all my weight on the hole in Zack's side, but it's too little to stop the gushing flow. Ryan materializes at my side and tries to pull me away, but I fight him.

"Cady, let the medics work. Give them room," Ryan orders, as his oldest friend bleeds to death on the floor in front of us.

"No. No, no, no, no, no," I'm incapable of forming any other words as he grabs me around the waist, dragging me downstairs.

"Is Sarah here?" Ryan shouts through my stupor and I manage to shake my head. "Did she leave with you guys after dinner?"

"No, just us," I choke, collapsing onto the icy ground. Out here, the storm has stopped and there's not a cloud in the sky. It's a bed of stars. *How can the worst moment of my life be so pretty?* Lights are flashing everywhere and so many people, but nothing registers. I'm still talking, yelling even, and I have no clue what I'm saying anymore. The last thing I remember is Ryan's voice as he wraps his jacket around me.

"I'm so sorry, Cady," he sobs, pulling me to his chest. Then everything goes black.

Chapter 18

Cady

Daniel's dozing in a chair next to the bed when my eyes open and I start to ask why I'm in the hospital. Searing pain rips through my head, stopping me dead. Closing my eyes against the pain helps for a few seconds, but then it all comes back. I open my mouth, but a strangled gasp is all that comes out.

Daniel's eyes fly open. "Zack's in surgery. He made it, but he has a head injury in addition to the gunshot wound."

"Will he be okay?"

"Nobody knows much yet. Zack's family is here and yours too, but the doctors said you had to be awake before having any visitors. Nobody was paying attention though, so I slipped in here." There are so many things I should ask, but I only care about Zack. Owen must have knocked him out, but he came to and rushed upstairs to save me, I tell Daniel.

"Cady, he's a fighter. Don't worry. Keeping you safe was his biggest concern." Daniel's right, but I don't care what Zack thought was right in the heat of the moment. The only thing that matters is for Zack to be okay. The blast of the gunshot and his guttural scream play in my head as my heart shatters into a thousand pieces.

A nurse comes in and begins to scold Daniel for sneaking in, but stops, taking pity on us instead. "He's still in surgery and it'll be a few more hours, honey," she says softly. "Once I get your vitals, your family will be allowed to visit. Right now, you get Tylenol for the pain, but there will be something stronger once the doctor checks you out. You took some bad blows to the head and have a moderate concussion, but no internal bleeding."

None of that matters because the pain is in my heart. Physically, my body feels dead, blank, totally numb. The nurse says I'm in shock and will be thankful for the pain medication, but I doubt it. He has the best trauma surgeon on staff, she promises, but my tears won't stop.

This is Allegheny General Hospital, a level one trauma center, only minutes from Zack's house. He's getting the best care possible, but sometimes that's not enough. Some injuries are just too grave. *Jesus Christ, there was so much blood. How could anyone survive?* Steph, Abby, and my family are here, but that's a story for another time. Suffice to say, mom and dad aren't pleased with the mess I got me into this time. They're relieved I'm safe and worried for Zack, but there's going to be fallout. This is not how our families were supposed to meet, but Trevor and Owen changed everything. It takes far too long to convince everyone to leave, but eventually, they go. Evan sneaks back with a fountain of Coca-Cola and a few slices of Angelo's pizza but I can't force anything down. All I can do is count the seconds as the hours tick away. I don't want to talk; I don't want to listen; I need to be alone.

Ryan stops by with my phone and a milkshake for my sweet tooth. There's nothing new yet, but he's waiting with Zack's family and promises an update as soon as the surgery's over. Daniel disappears for a few hours, then returns and we continue to wait in silence. Despite my absolute exhaustion, I'm determined to stay awake and refuse narcotic pain medicine. My head's cloudy enough, I don't need anything making it even fuzzier. There's also a small but tenacious part of my brain which frets that I may not wake up if I sleep. When my eyes do close, I only see Zack, pale and still. The movie plays behind my eyelids and the soundtrack is his strangled breathing. With every choking gasp, my heart shatters again. It's even more detailed when I finally doze off and I wake in a panic. At some point I passed out and open my eyes to a dark sky. Daniel's gently shaking me awake by my good arm. My battered body burns and even his soft, careful touch sends bolts of searing pain through my head and broken arm.

"Zack's out of surgery but still critical. He coded twice, but they saved him. And he lost a significant amount of blood, multiple pints, but the surgeon said making it through the surgery is the toughest part. I'm going back to the ICU, but I'll be back."

Zack is alive. There's a surge of blessed relief, but so much guilt, too. Yes, he's alive, but no thanks to me and the realization makes me dissolve into sobs once again. Daniel looks stricken, and my heart is heavy with guilt. He should be with Zack's family, not here to comfort me and I want to tell him, but my head hurts so much. The words are mixed up, so I wave and he understands. Stopping at the door, he turns back with tears in his eyes. "Cady, Linda came to check on you while you were sleeping. She cares. Nobody blames you."

Another unquantifiable length of time passes, then Ryan comes in, much worse for the wear, pale with dark circles under his eyes. I look at him hopefully but only get a sad shake of his head in response. "There's nothing new to report, but you should have this." He hands me Zack's phone. The pain in my head makes it so hard to think clearly, and even harder to express thoughts. "There's a playlist on here called Cady. Songs that remind him of you. Figured you need it right now."

I nod and the tears start again without warning when he places it in my hand. Ryan pats my back, trying to comfort me, but he's crying too. We sit this way for a long time until he gives me a hug and leaves without another word.

Eventually, I stop crying because my body runs out of tears. For a long time, I just stare at the phone, not sure I want to see what's inside, but curiosity eventually wins. Zack would call it *eclectic,* but the schizoid nature of the playlist makes me laugh at first, then cry even harder. I'll never forget the memories we made with these songs. *Fade Into You* was playing the first time we kissed on the beach and solely by chance after we left Daniel's house the night he took the picture of the city lights on the river for me. *California Stars* was playing when he said he wanted to take care of me. *Sweetness* was playing when he said he was crazy in love with me, and I'll never, ever forget the feeling.

There are a bunch of the songs from the first night we met and entire albums from the weekend when we stayed in bed for two entire days. There's the song that played when we saw a shooting star, the one from the night we had coffee at the diner, the only song we've ever danced to, and so many more. It seems impossible for so much to have happened in such a short time, and it shouldn't be possible to lose him so soon.

There's another playlist titled 'Memphis road trip' and one called 'camp', then I see one titled 'proposal' and a wave of nausea hits me. Nothing else matters except for Zack to get better. How long do I have to wait and wonder? If only I could sleep until he wakes up and shows us he's okay. This is so unfair. We did the hard work of identifying the bad guys, handing them to the FBI on a silver platter, yet somehow they dropped the ball. The FBI let them get to us, and it may cost Zack his life. I'm filled with rage, which makes my head hurt even more. When Daniel returns, he's not alone. There's a youngish, stone-faced guy with him. The new guy is wearing an expensive but rumpled suit, and the gravity of his expression makes my heart sink.

"Cady, meet Special Agent Ben Greene, Sam's partner," Daniel begins. "He needs to ask you a few questions." I have countless questions for Greene, but when I open my mouth, something else comes out entirely.

"I don't care what happens to Trevor and Owen. Zack is my only concern and I have to see him." Greene looks perturbed, but not surprised, and mutters something I can't hear before leaving the room. It's hours before he returns. I expect an update on Zack, but instead, he speaks quietly again and Daniel nods. Greene steps back out and returns with a wheelchair.

"I'll take you to see him, but you have to leave when I say it's time," he says, and relief floods through me. The stabbing pain in my head brings waves of nausea when I move, and my legs buckle as I try to stand. Daniel's right there, holding me. The tears fall again and I can't use my words, but I give him what I hope is a look of gratitude and he nods in understanding. I'm not sure what's worse, the dizziness or the ringing in my ears, which has gotten louder, but standing's out of the question so I settle into the wheelchair.

This is the longest hallway in the world, and it feels like we take two steps back with every step forward until I finally see signs for the trauma ICU. Bracing myself, my chest tightens and my hands tremble as I wonder what I'm going to see in that room. At least the tears have stopped for the moment.

Linda steps out into the hall to hug Daniel and although she's crying silently, her voice is strong and clear.

"Ray and Sarah went for coffee, but I can't leave him. How are you holding up, Danny?" she asks, squeezing him tight. Daniel buries his head in her shoulder and I hear muffled apologies through his wracking sobs. Suddenly, I remember he lost his parents when he was still a kid, and I'm glad there's a mom here to comfort him. Heaven knows I'm too self-involved for him to lean on, and Lindsay's still trying to find a flight.

"Agent Greene brought Cady to see him," he explains. Daniel steps back and she notices me for the first time. Linda manages a sad smile and moves toward me without letting go of his hand.

She leans down to embrace me in a soft hug, and I dissolve into tears at once. "Zack will be fine," she assures me. "He's strong, and he's a fighter. He wants to live, so he will," she says simply. Daniel puts his arms around her as she begins to cry in earnest, and Greene pushes me forward.

"Just a few minutes," he warns. Then he steps back and closes the curtain behind me.

Zack's barely recognizable and looks dead. He's unmoving, face pale and drawn, and a sharp stab of panic pierces my gut before I finally notice the rise and fall of his chest. There are so many tubes and monitors and lines, I'm afraid to touch him, but I have to feel him. There's even an IV in his thigh, so I lay my hands gently on his other leg.

"Zack, I'm so sorry. I should have told you he took my gun. All I care about is you. I don't care what happens to those bastards or to anyone else. I love you so much. Please be okay and get better. Nothing will ever be okay again without you." There's so much more to say, but my head hurts terribly and it's far too fuzzy to articulate my jumbled thoughts. Slumping onto his bed, my forehead touches his leg and my fingers find his hand. "I know you know I'm here and that I love you. Please wake up, for me, for your family." Then the tears come again, but he doesn't stir. His eyes stay closed, the monitors sigh and beep, and my heart keeps breaking.

Agent Greene's back. "I'm sorry, Miss Blackwell, but I have to take you back to your room now," he says in a voice far gentler than I was expecting. "You said you don't care, but you both need to know Owen Maines is dead and Trevor Maines is in federal custody for the rest of his natural life, thanks to you. A lot of people are going to live now, who would have died, if not for you two. You guys did good." Something grazes my head as it remains resting against his leg. I'm almost positive a finger on Zack's hand moved to touch me and it gives me hope. *Please don't let it be my imagination.*

The next couple of days are a blur because I sleep as much as possible. Everything is fuzzy, but I don't care what's going on around me, anyway. Part of me is still scared I won't wake up, but constant nausea and relentless searing pain in my head are so distressing, I welcome sleep despite the fear. When the doctors decide my arm needs surgery, it's honestly a relief to be knocked out for a while. Tons of visitors come and go, but Zack consumes my thoughts every waking moment. If only I hadn't let Trevor take my gun, or if only I'd told Zack he did. If only, if only, if only. These intrusive thoughts play in my head constantly and nothing changes.

Lindsay arrives from Tacoma and I'm so happy Daniel has someone by his side. She's friendly and sweet and they're perfect for each other. A few ICU nurses have taken to popping in when their shifts end to tell me how tough Zack is and how well he's doing, but it's day six and he's still not awake. At long last, I can finally get out of bed safely by myself and park myself in the ICU waiting room for the rest of the day. I've got one more night here, then I'll be staying with my parents until my arm heals. I've gotten to know Zack's parents and sister, although it's still awkward for me. They're so kind to me though, especially his mom. When I tried to apologize, she shut me down, sweetly but firmly.

"My son loves you very much and trusts you with his life. Nothing else matters to me. I hope you two can make it work after everything." Linda's faith is unwavering that he'll sit up at any moment and start talking as though nothing happened. He was lucky in a lot of ways.

The doctor explained it was a non-penetrating liver wound and it hit the edge of the left side of the liver. Injury to the right side or the center mass of the organ is worse. His liver is going to be fine. It was the blood loss that nearly killed him, and he would have bled out if help had taken even a few minutes longer to arrive. Zack lost all the blood in his body three times over and coded twice so there's significant potential for complications when he wakes up. Zack's surgeon asked to speak to me, Linda says as she and Sarah step out, leaving me alone in the private waiting room as a tall, thin man in scrubs enters. Icy tendrils of dread squeeze my heart because terrible things happen in these rooms.

"Cady? I'm Jack Morrison," he begins. "Zack woke up briefly as we were rushing him into surgery. He was unconscious but I was talking to him, which I do with every patient, conscious or not. It shocked me when he responded, though. So much so, I thought I imagined it at first."

"Of course, it was a very brief exchange because he lost consciousness again." The tears come and Dr. Morrison puts a hand on my good arm. "But Zack's tough, one of the strongest patients I've ever had. He's beat the odds more than once already, and I believe he'll keep beating them. I've never had so much hope for a patient with such grave injuries." The intercom blares his name and I mumble my thanks through the tears as he stands to leave. Morrison pauses as he strides to the door, turning back to meet my eyes. "I'm not in the business of giving people false hope. Sometimes you just know." He flashes a small smile, as though we share a secret, then he's gone, but his words give me the only comfort I've had since the moment the gun went off in Trevor's hand.

My own surgeon threatens to discharge me if I don't stay in bed, so I abandon my ICU post and try to sleep because I should probably listen to her. The thought of going home tomorrow and being so far away from Zack opens a pit of despair deep inside me, but I finally fall asleep. Something disturbs me and even though I don't know the time, there's no question it's late. The lights are low and the hospital's fairly quiet, which only happens after midnight. I don't even know the day of the week anymore, let alone the time. An unfamiliar voice calls my name and I turn away, hoping the vitals can wait. This is the first time I've been warm since arriving here, so I refuse to move, but the voice won't go away. There's a soft tug on my good arm and a hand gently rocks me.

"Cady, it's Sarah. Zack's awake." At first, I thought it was a dream and must've said so because Sarah laughs. "This isn't a dream," she assures me through tears of joy. "He's awake. Come on." Climbing out of bed takes forever, even with her help, but I finally make it. Their parents are with him now and Sarah spoke to him for a few minutes. His first words were 'I'll bet you guys are pretty pissed at me, huh?' then he asked if I was okay.

I must look apprehensive as we approach because she rubs my back reassuringly. "Everyone's glad you're here, Cady. Stop worrying. Zack loves you and he needs you." Sarah gives me the tiniest nudge forward and motions to get Ray's attention. Linda and Ray are crying tears of joy and smiling as they step out. My heart soars· when his eyes meet mine. There are so many things to say and I don't know where to start. I lean over to hug him gently. Zack's arms hold me close as he kisses my head.

"How ya doing, baby?" he asks in a hoarse whisper. Then every thought inside of me tumbles out and I can't stop the words. I tell him how sorry I am and that I didn't want to leave him and how terrifying it was when I thought he was dead. He listens until my words finally stop then he holds me and we cry.

"We're alive and we're together. Does anything else matter?" he asks. I shake my head because it doesn't. Nothing else matters at all.

Chapter 19

Cady

Zack only spent one more day in the ICU but will be stuck in the hospital for another week or two. I hate to leave his side, but he needs to rest, so I try not to be there too much. Janice and Ryan are showing me the ropes. I'm getting acclimated at Shields and doing research to keep busy. My arm needs intense physical therapy and my beat-up head requires lots of rest, so I'm trying to take it easy, even though I'm bored out of my mind. Winter has melted into spring, buoying my spirits despite everything we've been through.

Everyone's worried I have PTSD and a fragile, damaged psyche except for me. I'm angry the Maines brothers were able to get to us, furious I got hurt, and enraged that Zack almost died. But I'm grateful we'll both recover and don't want to dwell on what went wrong. It's time to focus on what went right.

Life needs to get back to normal and the sooner, the better. Therapy seems like a waste of time to me because I think these feelings are normal and need to run their course. Two different therapists agree, so I'm happy to turn a deaf ear to all the unsolicited advice and live my life. If I learned anything these last few months, it's to always do what I believe is best, no matter what anyone else says. I've always done what was expected of me, even when it didn't feel right but I'll never be that girl again. She's dead and gone, and I'm the phoenix who rose from her ashes.

A team of FBI agents came to see us the day after they moved Zack out of the ICU. The feds had lots of questions, which is frustrating because my head's a mess. I can remember most things fine but have difficulty articulating everything I want to say. There are a few blank spaces here and there, but the doctors say I'll be fine.

There's no permanent damage, but it will take time to feel normal again after a severe concussion.

The agents long ago spoke to Daniel, Ryan, and the first responders who saved us that night. Even Trevor's been questioned at length, so they only need to talk to us. Agent Greene came to interview me the day he took me to see Zack but decided it could wait after spending time with me. There's so much to take in, it's overwhelming at first, but we finally have the answers to fill in all the missing blanks. The details make my head spin, but in a totally good way for a change.

The Strip District loft was a house share rental, and though they appeared to be inside, they'd crawled through the ductwork into an empty unit below to reach the maintenance elevator, leaving the building via a service entrance hidden by dumpsters. There was a second apartment in the East End of the city where most of the rapes had happened. Owen knocked Zack out, then came for me because they'd planned to torture us in ways I won't acknowledge. Luckily, Zack wasn't out for long. One of his shots hit Owen in the femoral artery and he bled out before help arrived. *Good riddance, fucker.*

Both of my shots and one of Zack's hit Trevor, but none were mortal wounds, unfortunately. Ideally, I would have loved to have saved taxpayers the expense of his trials and incarceration, but since I wasn't a good enough shot, I'll be spending more time at the range once my arm is fully functional. The debriefing is a shock but it answers a lot of my questions.

"The whole SoCal thing was a complete fabrication because they'd left there for good over six years ago," Ben explains. "A wider search on their prints connected Owen to dozens of strong-arm robberies. Those were nothing sophisticated, just brute force, and while Trevor was involved in a few, the rough stuff was mainly Owen's thing - rapes, robberies, and beatings."

Sam picks up. "So far, they've connected him to most of the Pittsburgh rapes and seventeen other rape cases across the country by DNA, but he's suspected in at least twenty more based on MO, description of the attacker, and where they think Trevor and Owen were at given times."

Turns out, they'd lived a nomadic life since leaving their hometown and funded it completely with robberies and cons. "They both had distinct roles," Ben says. "While Owen was taking by force, Trevor used his boyish good looks and acting skills to prey on lonely older women, living off them, being paid handsomely for companionship, but also stealing money and expensive belongings when the mood struck."

"That's not what I was expecting," Zack mutters. "I don't know *what* I was expecting. None of this makes any fucking sense."

"So Owen was the rapist, but Trevor was the killer? I know Owen killed too, but he wasn't always there, right?" I ask.

"Owen wasn't at many of the murder scenes, but we'd have enough to convict him if he were alive," Ben assures me.

The FBI can tie Trevor to at least thirteen murder scenes with nineteen victims so far, but Sam's confident they'll connect him to others. "The best part is all three of Brandon's convictions have been linked to Trevor," he booms, with a smile as big as Texas. "Brandon will be exonerated, based on the evidence found in Trevor's homes and the DNA testing, and should be released within the week." Daniel hasn't said a word but I already know he plans to take him anywhere in the world he wants to go, or nowhere, whatever Brandon wants.

"Tell me about the evidence against Trevor," Zack looks at Ben and I know what he's thinking. "Maines chronicled everything and didn't try to hide the records. The journals were out in the open since he imagined no one could catch them. Trevor kept extremely detailed journals revealing his urges, plans, cons, and murders which have been extremely helpful for investigators."

Zack was right that Trevor's extremely arrogant. "The journals logged the first time Daniel hit his radar, describing how they decided to stalk him since Daniel was making progress on proving Brandon's innocence." Sam's smile fades away as he lays it out for us. "Everything's there, including specifics on the hack and details of the information mined from it."

"I still have so many questions. Were all the victims random? Did they pick the locations for any specific reason? Are there more cases we didn't find yet? Would they —" I break off as Ben holds up a hand.

"It seemed random at first, but then they started following Daniel. First to the Midwest, then here to Pittsburgh. Until now, they were always careful not to commit any murders at home.

"The local murder only happened because of the female victim's striking resemblance to Julie Maines," Sam explains. Despite knowing how she suffered, and that Stuart probably murdered her, those two monsters hated her, blaming her for Stuart's faults, including his prison sentences for raping small children. If only Julie had been a decent wife and mother, Stuart would've been a great guy instead of a monster who beat and abused everyone around him, they reasoned. Women are useless to them, except as objects to rape, con, and kill. They didn't tell us all that, but they didn't have to because Ben followed through on his promise to give us a copy of the case file, despite it being against protocol. Most of it was horrifying beyond belief, but I needed to see it for myself to put this behind me and Zack did, too.

"You were detailed in the journals, Cady. He explained everything." He glances at Ben and they share a guarded look. It's fleeting and I almost wonder if I imagined it. Was it wishful thinking? No, they're uncomfortable and I say good. They should feel guilty for not acting sooner and I'll do nothing to absolve them. Anger begins to boil inside me but Zack's voice draws my attention back to the room.

"So there was no connection between the threatening calls and these guys, right? That was just a coincidence?"

Ben nods. "Trevor learned you were asking questions, Cady, but not how much Daniel was sharing. You came along just when his access got cut off because they discovered that Daniel got hacked. They needed to find out whether or not you were a threat. He broke in, set up surveillance equipment and found out you were helping Daniel find the real killer, so then they had to do something."

"There's no way they were going to leave you alone after that," Sam admits quietly. He knows damn well this isn't how things should have happened but my need for answers outweighs my urge to tell the FBI exactly what I think of their policies.

"Trevor hit the jackpot right away since Abby came over to watch the game the same night. We were talking and watching hockey, so it was a rare occasion with no music playing. He heard all our weekend plans and only had to go to the Middle Road Inn to intercept me. It couldn't have been easier." Of course, I was only of interest because of meeting Daniel at the bar, so my paranoia did get me into this mess. Zack squeezes my hand like he can tell I'm mentally pummeling myself. "I wasn't their main focus, so what else were they doing?" I wonder.

"He was so confident, but even Trevor was worried after losing control and committing murder right here at home. He was watching Daniel more closely than ever before, not only to see if Daniel recognized him but to access any details from his police sources." Ben pauses and Sam jumps in again.

"Trevor hadn't counted on you being immune to his charms." I guess conning all those wealthy older women must have made him feel irresistible. "Owen was getting impatient this whole thing was dragging out, hence his tantrum at the loft. He wanted to kill you and waiting to do it really pissed him off.

Daniel and Zack feel horrible at this point, blaming themselves for putting me in harm's way, but their guilt is ridiculous. I sought Daniel out and went to him; they didn't bring me into this. Daniel had no idea Trevor was watching and ultimately, they saved me since he had Zack run Trevor, which is how we learned he was a threat. Zack came to warn me at once and kept me safe the whole time. We joke about our plan to have sex all weekend saving my life but it's true. It was a close call and scares the hell out of me, but it's also pretty punk rock that being so hot for each other saved my life. Zack insists I'd have figured it out without them, but I'm not so sure.

Sam was considerate enough to leave the rest unspoken, but we all know their intentions. Zack and Ben share a dark look but I just remind myself to breathe. The FBI never brought it up, but Trevor had a very detailed, angry journal entry after watching us in my bedroom the first night that Zack and I finally hooked up again. Trevor's so full of himself, he thought we were putting on a show to mess with him, so I asked Agent Farrell, one of the female agents and an extremely cool person, to please let him know none of it was for his benefit and we had no idea he could see us. She happily explained to Trevor, in colorful detail, that what he saw is how real men please women - something he's never known and never will. Farrell even showed me a clip of the interrogation, and it was satisfying to watch, especially near the end when the gravity of his position appears to hit him. All along, Trevor thought we were on to him because of the music, believing everything we discussed was misdirection. His narcissism helped us a ton, even though we had no idea until it was over and lady luck was on our side.

Sam asks how the guys met and the answer solves another mystery. Zack always says he owes Daniel but I've never had a chance to ask why.

"Back when I started training as an investigator, I worked an ugly custody dispute. After a heated scene in court, I rushed my client out, leaving behind a briefcase of crucial evidence, all originals. I was sure they were lost forever, but Daniel was in the courtroom waiting for the next case to come to the bench and hopped up a few rows to get a better seat when I left. He found the bag and worked his ass off to safeguard the evidence, identify me, and track me down to return it." Despite being close friends, Zack has always felt beholden to Daniel for saving the case for the client and possibly his career as well. Daniel's a super nice person, so Zack's indebtedness has always made him extremely uncomfortable. After almost dying at the hands of Daniel's killer, Zack's finally convinced they're even, to Daniel's immense relief.

They found surveillance files on future victims in Trevor's apartment, and Ben thinks it's important for us to know who we saved. Even after showing us the files, he's worried we don't get it, and one day he asks to meet us in Zack's hospital room. I'm wondering where Daniel is because Agent Greene should arrive any minute when Lindsay scurries in with a huge grin.

"We have a surprise. Come on in," she calls out into the hall and Sonny trots through the door wearing an illegitimate vest that says "working dog" followed by Daniel wearing an enormous grin. Sonny goes crazy when he sees Zack and goes for a vertical leap straight onto the bed, but I stop him. Instead, he jumps into a chair, tail thumping, and wags over a vase of flowers Lindsay's quick enough to catch. Agent Greene enters with a lovely blond lady a little older than me, maybe early thirties. She has three little boys, a chubby toddler, and two who are school-age.

"I'd like you to meet Gina DeNunzio and her children. We found a file on them which included a plan to jam their security system since Trevor decided working close to home wasn't much of a risk. He saw Gina at the grocery store, and he followed her home and planned to visit them the Friday after you stopped the murderous bastards." Ben leaves the rest unspoken and Gina turns to us with tears in her eyes.

"Thank you all so much, from the bottom of my heart. We had no idea," she trails off, grasping for words. "When I opened my door to the FBI, I was positive someone was playing a joke on us and still can't believe this is real."

***

Zack

I'm thrilled that this adorable family is safe, but I've never been more uncomfortable in my life. What do you say in a situation like this? It feels wrong to take credit since we were trying to help Brandon while keeping Cady safe. I'm no hero and don't want to be treated as one, but rebuffing her appreciation seems wrong. We're all looking around awkwardly for a minute until the little boy calls to Sonny, breaking the silence.

"Hi, puppy. Puppy. Look at me, puppy." The boy dances on the tiny chair, and Sonny's tail is wagging madly as we laugh away the tension.

"Are they allowed to pet him? Sonny's friendly and loves kids," Cady says and the older boys go to Sonny while the mom carries the little one over. The ice is broken and we talk like old friends. A guy in a flannel shirt and work boots enters, and we meet Gina's husband, Brian. He apologizes for being late and says they're having a party in a few weeks and hopes we'll be there.

Sonny's basking in the attention of three kids fawning over him, allowing the adults to be candid. Brian keeps his voice low, but speaks with quiet authority. "Thank you for stopping the motherfuckers who were going to murder my family. We can never repay you, and I can only imagine what it's cost. We'll forever be in your debt." Of course, we protest, but Brian's insistent. "Hey, I build houses. At least promise you'll let me do something, a remodel, a landscape design, anything. Hell, I'll build you a house at cost." Everyone laughs and carries on with the small talk, but he's got my attention because I have big plans. I motion Brian closer to speak to him quietly while Cady's deep in conversation with the others.

"Are you serious with the house thing? No joke?"

"Completely, man," Brian assures me. "Whatever you need, don't hesitate to ask."

"They broke into Cady's place multiple times and had cameras in there, so she wants out. The fuckers tried to kill us in my house and one of them died in my bedroom, so it's already on the market. I can't live there and was going to buy a house, but maybe building's the way to go."

"Truly, I'd love to build you a house, brother. Give me a call when you're ready to start, I'm all yours."

The small talk continues until Gina tells us Greene will give us their contact information and she begins luring the kids away from Sonny. We promise to make an appearance at the party and I hope to see them again soon. Daniel and Lindsay need to get Sonny back to Cady's parents, and soon we're alone. I pull her close and she stretches out next to me with her head on my shoulder.

"What do you think of building a house, *mia stellina*? I was talking to Brian, and he makes it sound doable. I want to and we have to live somewhere. Why not?"

"You should do it. I bet it will be a lot of fun."

"No, I mean building a house together, babe. We talked about you moving in when your lease is up, but I don't have a house anymore." Cady blinks with a deer in the headlights look and my heart sinks. I thought she'd love the idea, but her reaction hardly screams thrilled. "If you don't want to, never mind. Forget it."

"What? No. I love the idea, but I wasn't expecting, well, I was going to ask if you want to stay with me when you get out of here, but I wasn't sure if you'd still want to."

"Why not? I thought that was the plan for this summer, anyway."

"Sure, it was the plan, but you almost died and life doesn't necessarily continue on the same as before after something like this. I thought you changed your mind."

"Are you kidding? I want to pick up exactly where I left off. It was just getting good. I was dating this smoking hot chick and she couldn't keep her hands off of me. We have fun doing other stuff too, but I especially enjoy the naked times."

Cady laughs. "You're such a goober, Strozzi."

"But I'm your goober, if you still want me."

"Of course I still want you, cowboy. Did you hit your head or something?"

"Well, yeah."

"Right, sorry."

"Baby, nothing's changed. We've been through a lot and I don't want to smother you. Whatever you want to do is fine. Level with me."

"I still want to, but you have no idea what you're getting into if we build a house."

"How so?"

"For starters, you have practically no say, because I've already designed my dream house down to the smallest detail and can't imagine permitting even the tiniest deviation. I don't have house-building money. I barely have rent-paying money."

"I've seen the sketches, your dream house is awesome, and I'm okay with using your design. Don't worry about the money. Selling my old house will pay for a lot of the new one." Cady seems hesitant, but I don't care about anything except having her in my life. "Stop stressing about money and enjoy this, please. Promise me."

"Zack, I—"

"Is it easier to say yes if we decide the house is a wedding gift?"

Cady's staring like I've lost my mind. She looks about ready to call a nurse. "What did you say?" she asks slowly.

I pull the box out of my pocket. "I'm afraid I won't be able to get up, if I kneel," I begin.

"Where did you get that?"

"This was my great-grandmother's ring, and they were married for seventy awesome years. She gave it to my grandpa when he wanted to propose because he didn't have money for an engagement ring. He gave it to my grandma and they've made it over fifty years so far, but she stopped wearing it long ago. They didn't have any sons to give it to, so they gave it to my mom for me. My parents hated my ex and never told me about the ring. She never mentioned it until the day she gave it to me."

"Which was when?"

"The night before dinner. Remember mom asking me to help dad move the armoire in the guest room? The whole thing was a ruse. I laughed and told her it's too soon. That I'll scare you away."

"No, you won't." Cady shakes her head with a smile. "But wait, Ryan gave me your phone and the playlist."

"Yeah, I made the playlist when I couldn't sleep one night. I didn't expect to do it so soon, but I knew it was only a matter of time."

"You're so devious, Strozzi. I had no clue. Wait...you already had ideas then your parents come along with this ring out of the blue?"

"Yeah, and I thought it was crazy at first. Mom said I'd have it when I needed it. Besides, she insisted, 'When you know, you know, whether it's three months or three years.' I wondered if it was fate? Is the ring a sign?"

"Your mom is a wise lady."

"She is, which is why I didn't wonder for long. The first thing that popped into my mind was how winging it works great for us. She's right. When you know, you know. I decided before we got home from dinner. Go for broke, right?"

"So, what was the plan?"

"I was thinking of your favorite places and romantic trips we could take but I liked the idea of whipping this puppy out when we were sitting around the fire."

"That would've been perfect."

"Right? That felt like us. I didn't get far with planning; I never even had a chance to put it away. The ring was in my pocket when I got shot and the cops gave it to Ryan." Cady buries her head in my shoulder and I squeeze her tight. "The ring was one of the last things I remember thinking about because I thought I was dying and you'd never know I wanted to spend my life with you. I was so pissed I'd never get to tell you something so important and figured Ryan or my mom would make sure you knew if I didn't make it. Obviously, I wanted to be the one."

"And here you are, telling me now." She sniffles through a teary smile, hugging me within an inch of my life. "We're alive and we're together. Nothing else matters."

"That's right, *il mio amore*."

***

Cady

When he opens the box, the ring is perfect and huge and gorgeous, but I can't take my eyes off him.

"I need you by my side always. You have to marry me, baby."
He doesn't ask, he states it in typical Zack fashion, but it warms my
heart. How totally us.

"I'd love to," I tell him breathlessly.

When he captures my mouth with his, I know for sure everything
is right with the world.

PLAYLIST

All Night Thing – Temple of the Dog

Holy – Pvris (her song)

Room A Thousand Years Wide – Soundgarden

Sail – Awol Nation

Peace of Mind - Boston

DNA – Empire of the Sun

When I'm Gone – 3 Doors Down

Luck – Fuel

The Trip – Still Corners

Tangled Up in Blue – Great White cover

My Ex's Best Friend - Machine Gun Kelly (his song)

Pretty In Pink – Social Distortion cover

The Boys of Summer – The Ataris cover

Knives – Fuel

Imagination – Foster the People

California Stars – Wilco

Wish You Were Here – Pink Floyd

Sweetness – Jimmy Eat World

West Coast – Imagine Dragons

Fade Into You – Mazzy Star (their song)

Won't Back Down (Bring You hell) – Fuel

Anything, Anything – Dramarama

What Is Life – George Harrison

ABOUT THE AUTHOR

Daisy is a prolific reader of mysteries, romance, and true crime. When she runs out of things she's excited to read, she writes her own. She's addicted to music. Her entire life has a soundtrack, as do all of her books. Daisy loves road trips, true crime podcasts, and gangster movies. She lives in Pittsburgh with her husband, son, and the world's derpiest but most lovable dog.

Connect with Daisy:
website: daisyknox.com
facebook: DaisyKnoxauthor
twitter: @DaisyKnoxauthor
instagram: @daisyknox_author
tiktok: @daisyknox_author

www.BOROUGHSPUBLISHINGGROUP.com

If you enjoyed this book, please write a review. Our authors appreciate the feedback, and it helps future readers find books they love. We welcome your comments and invite you to send them to info@boroughspublishinggroup.com.

Follow us on Facebook, Twitter and Instagram, and be sure to sign up for our newsletter for surprises and new releases from your favorite authors.

Are you an aspiring writer? Check out www.boroughspublishinggroup.com/submit and see if we can help you make your dreams come true.

Love podcasts? Enjoy ours at www.boroughspublishinggroup.com/podcast

www.ingramcontent.com/pod-product-compliance
Lightning Source LLC
Chambersburg PA
CBHW031332170626
46807CB00002B/654